MYTH-CHIEF

—

THE MYTH-ADVENTURE BOOKS

Another Fine Myth
Myth Conceptions
Myth Directions
Hit or Myth
Myth-ing Persons
Little Myth Marker
M.Y.T.H. Inc. Link
Myth-Nomers and Im-Pervections
M.Y.T.H. Inc. in Action
Sweet Myth-tery of Life
Myth-Ion Improbable
Something M. Y. T. H. Inc.
Myth-told Tales, with Jody Lynn Nye
Myth Alliances, with Jody Lynn Nye
Myth-taken Identity, with Jody Lynn Nye
Class Dis-Mythed, with Jody Lynn Nye
Myth-Gotten Gains, with Jody Lynn Nye
Myth-Chief, with Jody Lynn Nye
Myth-Fortunes, with Jody Lynn Nye (forthcoming)

MYTH-CHIEF

ROBERT ASPRIN
& JODY LYNN NYE

WILDSIDE
PRESS

MYTH-CHIEF

———

Wildside Press, LLC
www.wildsidepress.com

For more information, contact Wildside Press.

ISBN: 978-0-8095-7277-9

Chapter 1

―――

"You can't go home again."

―Princess Leia Organa

"I still think this is a bad idea," my attractive administrative assistant said, as I reached for the door of the tent.

"You keep saying that, Bunny," I said, pitching my voice low so all the shoppers and merchants passing by us in the streets of the Bazaar at Deva didn't hear me. "We're just saying 'hi' to the old gang. They'd expect us to. If anything, they'd be hurt if we didn't."

"Uh huh. You keep saying *that*." She gave a toss of her short, red hair.

I gave up. I don't know enough women to make sweeping generalities, but I knew Bunny, and once she had her mind set on something, it was next to impossible to talk her out of it. Besides, we had reached our destination.

Standing outside the narrow tent that was the headquarters of M.Y.T.H., Inc., I paused for a moment to let the memories wash over me before ducking into the short entryway. This had been my home for years, my office and base of operations as the Great Skeeve before I retired. Much of my adult life had been tied to this deceptively small abode. It was a lot bigger on the inside than it was on the outside, to quote everyone who had ever stepped inside to do business.

I started to reach for the tent flap that separated the office from the outside world, but hesitated. This wasn't my home anymore. It didn't seem right to just barge inside. Instead, I turned and gave the small gong hanging on the entryway wall a light tap.

"C'mon in," a familiar voice called from within.

I felt more than saw Bunny's wince at the greeting. Back when she ran the office, she insisted that formal decorum be maintained on the premises, particularly in front of prospective clients. Obviously, things had loosened up a bit since our departure. They would probably change back again now.

I pushed my way into the interior.

"It's a raid!" I said, by way of greeting.

A massive mountain of a man rose from behind the reception desk.

"Skeeve!" he roared. "Hey, Nunzio! It's the Boss!"

"Hi, Guido," I said with genuine pleasure. "How's it going?"

Ignoring my outstretched hand, he swept me into a close embrace and thumped my back.

"Gee, it's good to see you," he declared. He held me out at arm's length and gave me a good once-over. I was pretty sure I hadn't changed much on the outside, being a tallish, skinnyish Klahd with blond hair, but the inner changes were there. I hoped my friends would appreciate them. "Look who's here, Cuz."

His cousin Nunzio, a smaller and slighter version of Guido, joined our ranks and started to duplicate Guido's greeting. I fended him off with one hand.

"I'm glad to see you, Nunzio," I said, "but I can only survive one of those bear hug greetings a day."

Bunny stepped forward with her arms outstretched.

"I'll take that hug if he doesn't want it," she said.

"You got it," Nunzio said in his squeaky little voice as he lifted her into the air. Bunny squealed with delight.

"Is Aahz around?" I said.

"No. He's over on Perv visiting the Duchess," Guido said.

"The Duchess?" I said. The Duchess was Aahz's mother. I had met her on my last and only trip to Perv. I had never heard her use her real name, if she had one. "Is anything wrong?"

"I don't know," Guido said. "He didn't say, and I didn't ask. He should be back in a week or so."

"I say, Skeeve! Bloody good to see you again."

"Hi, Chumley," I said to the Troll, who had emerged from the further depths of the office.

As I've mentioned, the headquarters is bigger on the inside than it appears from the outside. A lot bigger. The enormous purple Troll began by extending a hand, in his reticent fashion, but he, too, ended up smashing me in a hug that left me gasping and coughing out strands of purple fur.

"Glad to see you, too," I choked. "Is Tananda around?"

"Right here, Handsome."

I was hit by an energetic bundle of curves and softness that wrapped itself around me and showered me with kisses. This time, I didn't protest. Some overdone greetings are more welcome than others.

Eventually, we got everything sorted out, and the gang settled into various chairs and sofas or perched on desks. Guido insisted on pulling out the most comfortable armchairs for me. I ceded that seat to Bunny and took a wooden-backed chair upholstered with basilisk-leather cushions.

"So how long are you going to be here at the Bazaar?" Guido said. "Do you have time for a meal, or shall we just get straight to the drinkin'?"

"I'm back to stay," I said. "I've given it a lot of thought, and have decided to come out of retirement."

I really don't know what response I was expecting, but what I got wasn't it. There was a long moment of silence while the crew exchanged glances.

"That's great, Skeeve," Guido said at last, but the earlier enthusiasm had left his voice.

"I say, what?" Chumley said. "Happy to hear it, but you know, what?"

"You know, Skeeve, we've changed the operation since the old days," Tananda said carefully.

I held up my hand.

"Hang on, everybody," I said. "Before things get too awkward, I'm not expecting to walk back in here and take over. In fact, I'm planning on opening my own business. Just a small problem solving advisory office. Nothing big or fancy. I just wanted to stop in and say 'hi' and let you know I'm back."

More awkward silence.

"That's swell, Boss . . . I mean, Skeeve," Nunzio said, his high voice squeakier than ever. "Be sure to let us know if there's anything we can do to help out."

"Thanks, Nunzio," I said lamely.

"Speaking of which," Bunny said, rising to her feet, "we've got to get going. We've got to find some space for our office and lodgings."

"That's right," I said, even though I knew as well as she did that we had made no such plans.

I managed to keep smiling as we said our goodbyes, trying desperately not to notice the difference in warmth between our welcome and our farewell.

"Well, that was pleasant," I said as we made our way through the aisles of tents and stalls that made up the Bazaar.

"Actually, it was about what I expected," Bunny said, falling in step beside me. "If anything, it went better than I was afraid it would."

"Really?" I said. "I thought it got a bit chilly in there."

"Let's try this from a different angle," Bunny said. "What did you expect would happen when we dropped in?"

"I don't know," I said. "I thought they would be happy to see me . . . "

" . . . Which they were," Bunny said.

" . . . And I expected them to be glad I was coming out of retirement . . . "

"Why?"

"Why?" I echoed. "Why shouldn't they be glad? They're my friends, and I'm starting a new business."

" . . . Which is potentially in competition with their own operation," Bunny said.

I stopped in my tracks and stared at her.

"What?" I managed at last.

She gave a deep sigh without looking at me.

"Remember when I asked you why you wanted to set up business at the Bazaar?"

"Sure," I said. "And I told you that it was because the Bazaar was where I was best known and had already established contacts."

"Uh huh," Bunny said. "Think about that for a moment."

I did and came up blank.

"I don't get it," I said. "It still makes good sense to me."

"Oh, Skeeve," Bunny said, shaking her head. "Here at the Bazaar, everyone does know about the Great Skeeve. When you retired, you were the hottest act in the dimension. Of course people are going to come to you when you open your own business."

"Isn't that the whole idea?" I said.

"Of course, that's the same pool of clients that are currently going to M.Y.T.H., Inc., isn't it?"

"But . . . that isn't . . . I . . . Oh."

Suddenly everything fell into place, and I was in complete touch with my feelings. Mostly, I felt immensely stupid.

"Two of their biggest clients are the Chamber of Commerce and Don Bruce, both of whom made their original deals directly with you," Bunny said. "How do you think they're going to react when they learn that you're opening your own solo operation?"

Now, in addition to feeling stupid, I was feeling the beginnings of a splitting headache. Sometimes I think being in touch with one's feelings is massively overrated.

"Maybe I should go back and talk this out with them," I said, turning and gazing back toward the tent. "This isn't at all what I intended. If nothing else, there's no way I could take on either the Chamber of Commerce or Don Bruce's jobs by myself—excuse me, with just the two of us." I didn't want to offend my only remaining colleague. My brain felt as if it wanted to force its way out of my eyeballs.

"No. Let it sit for a while," Bunny said. "Like you said, they are your friends. Give it a while to sink in. They don't want you to keep you from going back into business any more than you want to put them out of business. In the meantime, you might put some time into figuring out exactly what kind of work you'll be looking for that isn't in direct conflict with their operation."

I followed her glumly toward the Merchants' Association tent. First things first: we needed a place to set up shop. Then, I needed to think about what exactly I would be doing in it.

Chapter Two

A week later, Bunny opened the box the Deveel messenger had dropped on her desk and squealed with delight.

"Skeeve, the new business cards are here!"

I nodded without looking up from the fifth revision of the proposed lease for the new building that the two of us now occupied. The tent had even less charm than M.Y.T.H., Inc.'s had had when we first moved in, and less than a quarter of the space. The Merchants' Association of the Bazaar at Deva had some idea that since it was me, they were entitled to boost the rent skyward. I was mentally composing the reply I was going to send them, starting with the information that it was still my signature on the first lease, and ending with a reminder that they had not disclosed all the hidden flaws in the first tent I had rented from them, most particularly the back door that opened out into the dimension of Limbo, a fact that would have put us off renting the place if we had known. The argument was pure formality among Deveels, who, among all the dimensional inhabitants I have known, are the most fond of negotiating matters to their own benefit, preferably at the top of their lungs. While we were still in Klah I had thought about changing headquarters to a less potentially haunted location, but after so many years, the old tent was where clients expected to find me. No sense in making people in trouble hunt down another address in the Bazaar. I'd had no idea that it would be necessary for the friends I had left behind that I do so, and promptly.

The Merchants' Association had been happy to take us on a midnight magic-carpet tour of available properties. I had rejected outright an otherwise desirable six-room storefront with a courtyard garden inside for Gleep and Buttercup to play in, mainly because it stood directly beside one of the Bazaar's busiest brothels. Not that I had anything against people in professional horizontal work, but the clients waiting to be interviewed by the major-domo had begun to size up Bunny as new talent. I didn't want any misunderstandings, so I had turned the place down on the spot and dragged Bunny away before she could ask why. Only a moment later, she came to the same conclusion I had, and gave our tour guides a fierce glare. They had the grace to look sheepish, not an easy task for a Deveel, who were born with a greater capacity for gall than maybe anyone but Pervects.

The next two showplaces were, frankly, insults. The property next to the arena selling dragons had fallen vacant, to no one's surprise. It emptied out at the end of every lease, no matter how desperate the tenant. I couldn't even consider it. The noise and the smell alone would have put off clients, let alone the danger of running into some of the merchandise if it ever got loose. And it would have. Deveels had a tendency to cause havoc among people they see as having money they wish to acquire and set up 'accidents,' which they then blame loudly on the moneyed individual, the only remedy for which is a hefty load of cash. It had happened to me enough times to make me wary. I looked over the burn marks on the wall of a stand that faced the dragon lot.

"No," I had said flatly.

One of the Deveels showing us the property sulked openly. I assumed he had a financial interest in the dragon booth and had had visions of gold coins dancing in his brain.

The second one, only a block away, had nothing to redeem it, either. The modest tent faced the wrong way and was invisible from a busy corner not a dozen paces distant.

"Too subtle," Bunny had said. "The Great Skeeve needs a place with more pizzazz. More eyeballs." She had whipped Bytina, her Perfectly Darling Assistant, from her handbag and ordered up a map of the Bazaar. She indicated a few points on the map to the representatives.

"What have you got in these areas?" she asked.

With a sigh, our guides directed the Djinn driving the carpet in an easterly direction, toward the faint fingers of light heralding false dawn.

Location, location, location, as Catchmeier, the real estate Deveel, kept reciting to us, as if repetition made it truer than anything else he said. Just before the sun came up, we landed in front of a tent I wouldn't have looked twice at if I'd been on my own. To my surprise, it lay across a busy passageway from the Golden Crescent Inn, one of my favorite eateries, a reliable spot for private conferences and the workplace of some of my closest friends in the Bazaar who didn't work for me. The rental property lay just exactly at the angle one's glance would fall on as one came around the corner of yet another throughway, one that even at this early hour was full of carts and foot traffic. It had looked promising, even to my increasingly bleary eyes.

"It's got all the comforts of home," Catchmeier said, holding aside the flap of the tent. I peered inside. The décor in the transdimensional building concealed by the magikal portal hadn't been updated in years, maybe not since the spell was laid, but I couldn't see anything basically wrong with it. I got a glance of tired walls painted in faded designer beige, worn wooden floors, and battered lintels in between rooms. "Skylights in the two main rooms. Outhouse out the back. Regular trash pickup. Safe neighborhood—hardly any murders in the last ten years. Well, the last two anyhow. Last two months," he admitted at last. "What do you think?"

Bunny and I looked at one another. "We'll take it," she'd said. The Deveels and the Djinn driver looked relieved.

"Just come with me," Catchmeier had said. "We'll have the paperwork drawn up for you in no time. No trouble."

No trouble. Hah.

I turned over the second to last page, to make sure all the changes we had agreed on were present—this time. A scurry of thin black lines caught my eye. I turned back the page in haste. A clause in very fine print was trying to avoid my eye. I slapped my hand down on it and read through my fingers, shifting them so I could finish without it getting away. Catchmeier had inserted a transitive clause, one that would make me liable for damages for any accidents within a five-hundred yard radius of the building. Not a chance. I growled a little as I reached for my quill pen to scratch it out.

"Skeeve!"

"Huh?" I asked, brought suddenly back to the present, as the curvaceous redhead waved a sheaf of small, colorful pasteboards in my face.

"Lookie, lookie!" Bunny squealed.

Skeeve, it said in gold across the middle of the shiny, wine-colored card, without title or other qualification. *The Right Answer. By Appointment Only.* And at the bottom, in small but unmistakable print: *Fee schedule available upon request.* That last had been Bunny's idea. As she had always had a much better grasp of business than I had, I acceded. The result was a pretty professional-looking card.

"I like it," I said. Bunny's shoulders relaxed. "Why are you so surprised? I trust you."

"I know, Skeeve," she said, giving me a brilliant smile. "But it still surprises me when someone takes my word for something without hesitating. What do you think? I'm so excited!"

I had to admit I was, too. A new beginning, I hoped. One in which I would give myself the chance I had not before.

Every time I thought about the look on my friends' faces when I had said that I was back . . . I had gone away for my own good, for everyone's good, or so I convinced myself. My return had been a spectacular failure through my own thoughtlessness. No, my lack of insight. I would not make that kind of misstep again.

"Do you know what, Bunny?" I asked, looking up from the cards. "I've changed my mind. I don't think I want to do this. Let's just go back to the inn. I think I left something on the stove."

Bunny looked down at me. "After all that discussion—after all our planning . . . " She paused and looked at me. "You're kidding, aren't you? Thanks for giving me a heart attack. You can't possibly be thinking of backing out now. It's the best possible outlet for you. You know that, don't you?"

I did. The two of us had spent long nights talking it over. I was bored and lonely, and I knew she was, too. We needed to get back into the heart of things. I was never going to be a great wizard, but that was never really how I'd made my name. I was a problem-solver—if I confined myself to finding solutions to knotty questions for my clients, it wouldn't cut into my friends' business. I gave Bunny a sheepish grin.

"Well, I have to admit to being a little nervous. What if I make a mistake out of this, too?"

Bunny put an arm over my shoulders and squeezed. "You're not making a mistake. You're going to be using your talents for the betterment of everyone, and that's what you are good at. How could that be a mistake?"

"Maybe all of you overestimate my talents," I grumbled.

"We do not. We know what you are capable of, and what you're not capable of," she added.

Taking one of the cards, I looked at the lines again. "I hope I'm not setting myself up for a fall," I said. "Offering to find exactly the right answer to a client's problem sounds pretty arrogant."

"I wouldn't worry," Bunny said brightly. "If the challenge seems too tough, you'll figure out how to solve it eventually. I trust *you*."

I sighed. It was a heck of a way to come out of my self-imposed retirement.

The impetus had come from a conversation I had had a couple of months before with Big Julie[1], who had once been my opponent on the battlefield, though never my enemy. He had come to be a trusted advisor and good friend.

He had asked me why I left M.Y.T.H., Inc., the highly successful and profitable business I had founded with my former mentor and partner, Aahz. I admitted I thought I wasn't living up to the hype surrounding me. I believed it would be better if I went away for a while. I felt that I had had to get out from my all-enveloping support structure and educate myself so I could live up to the hype that I had enjoyed as Skeeve the Magnificent, Magician to Kings and King of Magicians, Businessman, and Problem-Solver Extraordinaire. The truth was not so glorious: at the time I had departed, I could do very little magik. Most of what I had accomplished, Big Julie pointed out to me, was by thinking—no, more by feeling—out the correct solution to the problem I had been set. He encouraged me to take that talent and run with it.

From the time I had returned to the inn, I had been on fire with the idea of establishing a new business, one in

---

1   Big Julie's advice to Skeeve can be found in *Myth-Told Tales*, a not-to-be missed collection of short adventures that any discerning reader must have.

which I helped people, not necessarily with applications of big-time magik, for, as Big Julie pointed out to me, big-time magicians were a dozen to the silver coin, but with the application of the kind of attention that I had always given problems without really realizing it. It was a natural extension of my instincts. I felt relieved, since I was never going to be a master magician. I had been getting my magikal butt kicked regularly by the equivalent of six-year-old girls. But when it came to finding a solution that just felt right, and did the most good for the most people, that was what I did best.

Oh, I am no altruist: I intended to get paid for my expertise. That was one of the reasons I let Bunny put the line at the bottom of my card. I had found out a long time ago that people don't prize what they don't pay for. If I offered my services for free, I'd be looking for lost firecats and missing spectacles from now until the end of time. I wanted meaty problems, the kind I could really sink my mental teeth into. I loved a challenge. Now was the time to see if I could handle one. And if I didn't, well, I was young. I had time to make a lot more blunders in my lifetime.

I have to admit that it really bothered me that Aahz hadn't been in the Bazaar when I arrived. After all, he had been the one who really taught me about the important things. Not just magik and business, but what's *important*—in spite of what he would say if I told him. I worried for a moment about his mother, the Duchess. I had met her a while back[2] ; she

---

[2]   A complete account can be found in that irreplaceable volume, *Myth-Gotten Gains.*

was a real eccentric, but if Aahz needed any help handling a situation, he knew where to get in touch with all of us.

One of the reasons I had agreed so readily to come out of retirement was Aahz. I missed him. Oh, sure, having a Pervect for a friend wasn't easy. He could be crude, harsh, selfish, greedy, insulting, overbearing, and rude, but he was my best friend. If it hadn't been for him, well, I would still be back in the woods on Klah, trying to eke out a living as—I admit it—one of the most inept thieves ever to cut purse strings. Thanks to him, I'd rediscovered some basic honesty and decency. Though he was tight with a coin and a sharp bargainer who saw no problem with shafting the other guy, I observed that it was easier to leave a little money on the table, because it was a small universe. You never knew when you were going to be allied with the very person whose shirt you were trying to take the previous day.

Without him M.Y.T.H., Inc. would never have been as successful as it was. I should have assumed that once I stepped out of the picture he would take over as president. He was a natural leader. Most of the others had known him long before I came along. I hit myself in the forehead. Why didn't that dawn on me before I blundered into the office and made an idiot of myself?

I wished he had been around. I would have appreciated his input. Maybe he would have been able to smooth out the awkwardness I had caused.

Maybe not. Aahz had never been good at letting anyone else's mistakes go unnoticed. I probably would have been in for a lecture. I deserved one, but I had already given a stern talking to myself.

So, I was on my own.

That was okay, I assured myself. I had to take my own baby steps, right? I vowed not to undercut my friends. I was going to stick to what I planned to do, nothing else.

A roaring noise interrupted my thoughts.

"Look out!" Bunny called. "Get it, Skeeve!"

I ducked just in time. A huge, striped insect the size of my two fists zoomed overhead. In spite of its bulk, it banked like a swallow made a sharp U-turn. I threw a ball of fire at it, but the insect took the full blast of the flame and kept going. Its armored shell would have been the envy of any army in any dimension.

It vanished into a hairline crack in the wall. I ran after it, trying to capture it with a rope of magik. Before I could blink, it was out of reach.

"Gone," I said grimly. Bunny shook her head. I dashed out the rear door of our tent, stepping into the dimension into which our office extended, and examined the walls. No sign of the Humbee, nor a single crack through which it could have escaped. I felt the side of the clapboard house, which was this dimension's face of my building. The walls were only an inch thick, too narrow to conceal the bulky bug. Where had it gone?

One more thing Catchmeier had failed to mention about the new tent was the infestation of Humbees. No one knew where the pesty insects had sprung from, but they were overrunning the Bazaar. Deveel merchants had jumped on the bandwagon already, so to speak, with Humbee repellents, traps, and insecticides. As far as I could tell from questioning friends of mine, none of them worked. Hundreds, if not thousands, of people were trying to find out what dimension they had come from, and who was responsible for importing them to Deva. That person, unsurprisingly, was lying low, fearing the inevitable lynch mob. The beetles were more than a minor nuisance. A blow from a passing Humbee could leave one with a bruise the size of a grapefruit. It had also been discovered that the bees could penetrate solid walls and create a warren the envy of any termite infestation. Because it was common practice to build out into transdimensional locations, the Humbees had no problem spreading to other dimensions.

"Their magik is beyond me," I concluded, returning through the back door.

"Well, there's your first professional question," Bunny joked, as I threw myself back into my chair. "How do they do that?"

Chapter 3

_____

"There are no simple questions."

—Deep Thought

In between dive-bombings, Bunny and I hired a couple of Deveel youths to distribute my cards to places where customers who had unanswerable questions were likely to turn up. Mostly we targeted inns and taverns, but a few stacks went to places like the Merchants' Association office, the Deveel Tourism Board, and Madam Zizzi's See the Future in Living Color emporium.

Once the first cards went out, would-be clients began to pack the street outside the modest little tent. I peered out through the flap at the crowd.

"Well?" Bunny asked. Just behind me, she sat at a modest-looking desk that was actually bolted to the floor with magikal rivets strong enough to withstand even a Troll's charge. I looked again at the gathered mass. My stomach did flip-flops.

"Better than I hoped," I said.

"Remember, most of them won't have a problem that's right for you."

"I know that." I took a deep breath and returned to the inner office, sitting at my desk—a second-hand, heavily gilded number that we had picked up for a small handful of silver

23

coins from a traveling circus from Mexumalita. It had the benefit of looking very impressive while being inexpensive enough to be easily replaced if an overwrought client happened to damage it beyond repair. It, too, was bolted down. I had been in this dimension for a good long time.

With a flick of magik, I caused the outer tent flap to lift, and darkened my office so I could see what was going on without being observed. A group of Deveels crowded in, each trying to be the first in line. Bunny stopped them with an upheld palm and a devastating smile.

"Do you have an appointment?" she asked pertly.

The cluster of red-skinned beings came to a halt and shuffled uncomfortably.

"Uh, no," one of them finally admitted.

"The Great Skeeve sees people by appointment only," she went on. She opened a datebook that she had filled up with names and times. "I have three openings now, then another one in an hour and a half. Would any of you care to make an appointment?"

The Deveels started yelling at once. That didn't alarm me. Deveels usually do business at the top of their lungs. Bunny kept smiling as she jotted their names down. A skinny specimen named Rokra, who had managed to get his name in first, grinned triumphantly at the others as Bunny gestured him toward my door. Three of the others followed him. One of them yanked Rokra back and scrambled to take his place.

"Just a moment!" Bunny said. "Will the rest of you please sit down?"

A free-for-all started, as the four each tried to push past one another.

Time for my secret weapon.

"Gleep!"

My pet dragon shot from the fireproof pad where he had been lying in the corner of Bunny's reception room to interpose himself between the Deveels and my doorway. I smiled to myself. He might still be a baby of his kind, no more than fourteen feet long from nose to tail-tip, but a dragon was a dragon. The Deveels paled to dirty pink and backpedaled. As neatly as a sheepdog, Gleep cut Rokra out of the quartet and herded him in my direction. The rest started to follow, but he whipped his head around on his long neck.

"Hissss!"

A baby dragon's flame is modest in size, but his breath could knock a charging rhinopotomos unconscious. The Deveels halted in their hoofprints.

"Uh, we'll just come back later," the Deveels agreed. They pushed their way out through the throng gathered around Bunny's desk.

Rokra still looked nervous as he walked through the illusionary darkness and emerged in my office.

"Greetings," I said, making my voice echo hollowly off the walls. The Deveel gulped, but he sat down in the thickly-padded leather chair I gestured him into. "Now, what can I do for you?"

It took seconds for Rokra to get over his shock at finding a youthful, blond Klahd behind the massive desk. I waited, poised, eager to give my first new client the benefit of my experience and wisdom. What would he ask me? I could hardly wait. I hoped it was something deep. I had been doing a lot of thinking recently on why there was an 'up' and a 'down.'

The Deveel glanced around as if to make sure the room wasn't bugged. It wasn't; I had swept it again for Shutterbugs and Earwigs just a few moments before.

"You don't have to worry," I said. "Our conference is private. Tell me what kind of problem I can help you solve."

Rokra leaned forward with an oily smile on his face.

"Well, Skeeve, I can tell you're the kind of guy who likes to get right down to business. I need you to help me take out my business partners. We started this . . . er, import business together, and now I think they're planning to freeze me out. So, I want to dispose of them first."

"Murder?" I sputtered. "I don't kill people!"

"Okay, okay, don't think of it as killing them," Rokra said hastily. "Maybe as a surprise departure from this life? Or how about this—dump them off in a dimension without magik. That'd make us both happy. They don't die, but they won't be around any more to bollix up my business. How about it?"

"Sorry," I said coldly, standing up. "I can recommend a couple of Guild assassins I know. Standard rates. You don't need me."

"But they're sneaky!" Rokra insisted. "Look, I heard you're the best. I need the best."

"Sorry," I repeated, a little more firmly. I beckoned, and

Gleep strode into the room, preceded by an almost visible exhalation of sulfur-scented breath. "That's not what I do."

"No one knows what it is you *do* do," Rokra said.

"Maybe so," I agreed, "but what you want is not it. Thanks for dropping in."

Rokra tried holding onto the arms of the chair, but Gleep was good at winkling grub-worms out of stumps on Klah. He wriggled his nose under the Deveel's tail and heaved upward.

Rokra shot out of the chair. "You guys, living on your reputations!" he raged.

That's all I have, I thought, as my dragon escorted him out.

The next would-be client had a proposition. Cardenilla, a tall, willowy Deveel, fluttered red eyelids at me.

"You look like the kind of guy who would understand a girl's problems," she said.

"I'll try," I promised. "What kind of question do you need answered?"

"Well," she began breathily, leaning forward so I got a generous glimpse of cleavage, "all I want is a little peace and quiet. I made a mistake, I admit it. I rented out my roof to a Gargoyle. Whenever I go past him, he dumps water on me. He's a pain in the tail. I want him gone."

"Have you tried talking to him?" I asked. This started to sound intriguing. I had a buddy who was a Gargoyle. The solid-stone guys always struck me as pretty easy-going. I wondered what had set him off. Could Gargoyles go insane? Was he interested in Cardenilla?

"Talk to him? Of course I've talked to him!" the woman said. "Big, ugly oaf. He just says that that's what Gargoyles do. He said he thought I knew. I can't stand it any more. Please, pretty please, Mr. Skeeve. Get that beast off my roof."

"Er . . . " It was tempting. It would give me a chance to get to know a little more about Gargoyles. But, no. "Let me give you a referral, no charge. Try M.Y.T.H., Inc. They're really good at that kind of job. They're right here in the Bazaar. I can give you directions."

Cardenilla waved a hand. "I already talked to them."

"You did? Then, what are you doing here?"

She opened large, outraged eyes at me. "They had the nerve to quote me four gold coins for the job. Four! So, I came to you."

I shook my head. "Well, my price for the job is ten."

"Ten! You're just one Klahd! Why do you cost more than twice what they're asking?"

"You pay for my time and experience," I said severely. There was no way I was going to undercut my friends.

"Well, forget it," the Deveel woman said, rising to her hooves. I could see steam trickling out of her pointed, red ears. "I'm going back to them! You've got some kind of nerve! Ten gold coins, just for throwing one big, fat Gargoyle off one roof!"

She stormed out past Gleep. I sighed. His big blue eyes fixed me with a puzzled look.

"Skeeve . . . okay . . . ?" he asked.

Did I mention that my dragon can talk?

Gleep was far more intelligent than anyone else realized.

Even I hadn't realized he was that smart for a long time. Now we kept the secret between us. Not even Bunny knew. That made him my *real* secret weapon.

"Yes, I'm okay," I said. He lollopped over to me and slimed my face with a swipe of his long tongue. "I miss my friends."

"Still . . . friends," Gleep assured me.

I scratched vigorously behind his ears with both hands, which caused his eyelids to droop happily.

"I know. I just hope they know it."

Chapter 4

"Who cares what people think?"

—George Gallup

The next few days brought dozens of would-be clients. Most wanted me to undertake dangerous adventures, usually the treasure-retrieval type or the disposal of former-friends or business-associates type. Pretty straightforward adventuring. None of them interested me. A few I just turned away, but the profitable-sounding prospects I tried to steer back to my friends. I wasn't going to tread on their territory if there was any way to avoid it.

I sat with my head propped on my palm, trying not to look bored, as my sixth visitor of the day went through his 'simple plan.'

" . . . So all you have to do is go to the Temple of the Six Temptations in Harbold, pry the big yellow stone out of the idol on the center altar, and bring it back to me. Perfectly easy," Oobloo, a hearty Orkta, told me, leaning back at ease, or, rather, sprawling all over my guest chair. The boneless beings had eight limbs and two huge eyes. They slithered, rather than walked, and people were always surprised that invertebrates like that were intelligent.

I cleared my throat.

"There are a lot of other people who undertake that kind

of mission. Not me. You sound like you already have all the details. All you have to do is go ahead and follow the instructions you gave me. It sounds pretty straightforward. You could do it yourself."

"I don't want to do it myself," the Orkta said, his pale green face glowing phosphorescent. "Are you calling me spineless?"

I didn't have a reply that wouldn't sound insulting, so I just summoned my bouncer.

"Gleep!"

"Sorry," I said, looking up blearily at the Indigone. I had spent another long day listening to would-be clients trying to hire me for straightforward magikal enterprises. "What's the question you need answered?"

That took the burly, blue-furred gentleman aback. He thought about it. "How much will it cost me to get you to go and get my grandfather's picture back from my ex-wife before she sells it?"

"That's not really what I do," I explained, for maybe the twentieth time that day. "You know what you need. You don't require my advice. There's no mystery here. You need someone to go and talk your ex into giving up the portrait. Steal it or buy it from her."

"Yeah," the fellow said. "Someone. You. How about it?"

I shook my head. "Not me. I know some great people who can take the job on for a reasonable fee," I said, reaching into my desk for the top card off the stack of M.Y.T.H., Inc. cards I had placed there. "Er, you don't have to tell them I sent you. The . . . er . . . price might go up if you do."

"Gotcha," the fellow said, rising. He took the little pasteboard and stowed it away in a lock of fur. "Whatever. I might just go steal it back myself, since you mention it."

"I'm not suggesting that," I said in alarm.

"Forget it, guy." The fellow leered. "I never heard it from you."

When the flap closed behind him, I could see Bunny grinning at me from the doorway.

"Don't say it," I warned her.

"Not a word," she promised.

I clutched my head.

None of the potential clients were giving me the chance I needed to prove myself! I faced a more complex challenge than I had ever foreseen. Not only was I trying to get my new business going, but I had to keep from cheating my old partners.

"Go get some lunch," Bunny said. "I'll mind the store. Maybe a good prospect will come in while you're gone."

"I'll bring you a sandwich," I promised.

"Hey, Skeeve," Gus the Gargoyle called to me as I entered the Golden Crescent Inn. After the carefully low-key décor of my new office, the inn almost sent my eyeballs into sensory overload. Every surface was brightly colored and shiny, reflecting the magikal light that issued from round white balls scattered around the ceiling. "The usual?"

"Strawberry milkshake," I agreed, leaning on the counter. "And today's special."

"One usual coming up," he said brightly. "And a usual for Bunny when you're done?"

"Right," I said. "Thanks."

I found a seat at a corner table and sat with my back against the wall. From here I had a good view of the restaurant. I harbored no illusion that I was as safe here as I was in my own home or office. Most people liked me, but I knew some who held grudges against me and my friends. I waved a casual hello to faces that I knew. Some looked surprised to see me, but some didn't. Word got around fast.

Gus himself brought my tray. He offered me the milkshake, straw already bent to the angle I favored. I took an appreciative sip.

"No one makes them like you do," I said.

"Thanks, Skeeve," the Gargoyle said, in his gravelly voice. "Hey, it's nice to have you for a neighbor. Glad you're back in town."

"Thanks," I said.

"You got a moment?" he asked.

"For you? Any time. Do you want to sit down?"

"Nah. On duty. Well, listen . . . " Gus looked uncomfortable, his craggy jaw working. "I noticed that you haven't got any of the old gang with you. Except Miss Bunny."

"No," I said cautiously.

"I don't have to know why. Ain't none of my business. I just wanted to know . . . y'know . . . nah."

"What is it, Gus?" I asked.

He looked sheepish, not an easy maneuver for someone with a solid stone face.

"Well, you know, if you are lookin' for some new old help.

I mean, we worked together once, and you thought I did a good job . . . Have any room for me?"

"Well . . . " I knew I was gawking. Gus's mouth turned down, and he backed hastily away from the table.

"I can see you hesitate. Never mind."

"Wait!" I said.

My first thought was that I wanted to open this new business by myself and see how I did before I even considered asking anyone to join me.

My second thought was a lot wiser and a lot more painful to contemplate.

What *was* I trying to prove? *Who* was I trying to prove something to? Myself? I already knew I never got anywhere I wanted to go on my own. Why *shouldn't* I have one of my oldest and best friends around?

"Gee, Gus," I said. "Please come back. Sit down. I was just surprised. I'm not looking for help because I just don't have any jobs yet. I don't even know what I'm going to be doing."

"Really?" Gus looked surprised. "With all the people who've been walking in and out, I thought you had lined up a dozen missions already. I mean, Tanda and the others have been in here every day, watching out the front window."

"They have?" I felt guilty all over again. I guess they were still upset, if they never came in to visit.

"Yeah. They're curious about how you're doing." Gus tilted his head. "What do you want me to tell them?"

I sighed. "Tell them the truth, Gus. I don't lie to them. I . . . I've just been so busy getting set up, I haven't seen much of them. It's my fault."

"Well, Skeeve, I'm sure it'll all be okay. In the meantime—if you meant it . . . "

"I meant it," I assured him. "Once I know what I'm doing, if I can use you, I will."

The big gray face split in a grin. "You're a pal."

I dodged the usual noisome and noisy traffic and crossed the street to my tent. To my surprise, the crowd that had been hanging around for the last few days had dispersed. Completely. I peered up the street. Perhaps Bunny had asked the throng to make a little room for newcomers to enter and make appointments. I poked my head inside.

"There you are," Bunny said. I extended the folded paper bag to her. "Thanks. I need that." She put a straw into her milkshake.

"Where are all the clients?" I asked.

"No clients," she said. "All the curiosity-seekers have gotten a look at the new premises. You've turned down jobs from all the prospects who made appointments. They started talking to one another when you took a break, and they just left."

"Oh," I said. "I didn't anticipate that. So, no one's going to hire me?" I felt my heart drop to my knees.

Bunny reached over and patted my hand. "Just be patient. Let's distribute some more cards and see who turns up."

The next visitor wasn't a potential client, but an old friend. The tent flap yielded to a scaly green hand. I was out of my seat and halfway across the room before I realized that the Pervect entering my office was not Aahz.

"Hi, Pookie," I said, slowing to a walk. My heart took a little longer to return to its normal pace. Behind her was a skinny Klahd female whom I recognized as Spider. The two of them had been working together both as operatives for M.Y.T.H., Inc. and on their own. "Hi, Spider."

Aahz's cousin was a good deal younger than he was, a lot more slender and, if you can believe it of a Pervect, more formidable-looking. She favored clingy jumpsuits, which served to distract opponents and to conceal a surprising amount of weapons, considering how tightly everything hugged her body, an action I was very unlikely to emulate. We shook hands. Spider gave me a shy grin.

"How's it going?" she asked.

"All right so far," I said cautiously.

"You don't have to try and fool us, Skeeve," the Pervect said, showing her four-inch teeth. "Thanks for the referrals, by the way. I just got back from bringing a runaway Nymph home to her family. Guido is out on a job negotiating the return of a family heirloom. The clients said you told them to come to us, but not to tell us you sent them. That wasn't necessary."

"Is everyone still mad at me?" I asked. I didn't mean to sound plaintive, but I guess I did.

"No one's really mad," Spider said. "We were a little surprised, I suppose. It's funny: after all of them wishing for so long that you *would* come back, when you did turn up, they didn't react too well."

"It's my fault," I said. "I guess I should have come in and talked about it before."

Pookie shook her head. "It wouldn't matter how you did it. It was a big change. You just administered it in one single shock. We all knew you'd take over the Bazaar again if you came back. I guess no one had thought about how it would really affect them."

"But I might not have come back here," I said, a little peeved. "I could have set up in some other dimension. Maybe not Klah, but there are other places where my talents would be appreciated."

"Get real," Pookie said without rancour, but without sympathy, either. "The Bazaar is like the crossroads of the world. You might have bought a storefront in Flibber[3] or somewhere with a big, cosmopolitan population, but this is where people go first to find what they're looking for. Everywhere else is second best. We all knew you'd come back here one day."

"It sounds obvious when you say it like that," I said.

"You know it, too. So, we should all have been talking more. It doesn't matter." She shrugged. "There's room for all of us, as long as you don't move in on the old turf. It's ours now, and we need it. If you start showing an interest, we'll all go broke. Guido might as well move M.Y.T.H., Inc. into the Mall in Flibber next to Hamsterama."

"But I have no clients yet."

Spider gave me a big hug, and I felt my spirits rise.

"Don't worry. Once they know the Great Skeeve is back in business, they'll beat a path to your door."

---

3   For a useful travelogue of the delights of Flibber, read *Myth-Taken Identity*, another fine tale.

They turned to go. Pookie looked back at me.

"Just one more thing, Skeeve. Not everyone is completely thrilled about your return. Just a friendly reminder."

"Who?" I asked, alarmed.

She shook her head. "I just heard it from one of my connections. Thought you ought to know. Keep your back covered. That's all."

I set my jaw. "Thanks for the warning."

Bunny's eyes were wide. "I wonder where that rumor came from?"

I gnawed on a knuckle. "I can't pretend I don't have enemies," I said. I had plenty, if I stopped to think about it.

With Pookie's words in mind, I shored up the defenses in our tent. Using the plentiful energy from the force lines overhead, I strung several fine lines of magik that would warn us of intruders. Then, I leaned out the back door of our tent into the fenced-in yard that abutted our office building in the next dimension. The sky was overcast and a light drizzle was falling, but the white beast munching grass at the far end of the enclosure didn't seem bothered by it.

"Buttercup," I called.

The war unicorn came charging toward me and planted his muzzle in my palm. I had thought to put a lump of sugar there as a treat. I stroked his mane.

"Buttercup, I've got a job for you."

His eyes rolled, and his nostrils flared. He understood a fair amount of Klahdish, but I think he read more in my demeanor than in my words. Gleep stuck his nose under my elbow.

"Maybe you can translate for me," I told him. "I need you and Buttercup to patrol the tent to make sure no one breaks in. I don't know who's out to get us, but better safe than sorry. You check things inside, and he'll keep an eye on things back here to make sure no one sneaks up on us. All right?"

"Gleep!" Gleep touched noses with the unicorn. When Buttercup straightened up, he gave a mighty snort, then danced away, making his first circuit of the yard at a gallop. At each corner, he reared up magnificently and let out a yodeling neigh that made the orange-skinned neighbors glance up from their flowerbeds. I thought he looked happier than he had in years. Big Julie was right. He needed to feel needed. Didn't we all?

In spite of Spider's confidence, no one beat a path to my door. Bunny and I distributed piles of my new business cards around the Bazaar, asking merchants to let them sit on the corner of a counter or a table, where potential clients could pick them up. If they did, we never knew about it. The door of the tent remained undisturbed all that afternoon and on into the evening. We finally gave up waiting and swatting at Humbees, and went out for dinner.

"I dunno, Skeeve," the Sen-Sen Ante Kid said. A large, fat man with surprisingly soft hands, he was the best Dragon Poker player in all the dimensions. I owned a half-interest in the club where he played when he visited the Bazaar. The food was decent. The real attraction was the games of chance and, if he was in town, watching the Kid clean up against the local talent. He gestured at the untidy heap of business cards at the end of the green baize-covered counter adjacent to his special table. "People picked up the cards, read 'em, and put 'em down again. I don't think they have a clue what "The Right Answer," means, and they're not gonna pay you to tell them."

"Are we being too mysterious?" I asked.

The Kid considered the question.

"Maybe. Nobody enjoys feeling he doesn't understand somethin'. And answers are what people think they can figure out answers for themselves. They pay for merchandise. They pay for food. They pay for magikal services. You might give them a little better hint what you're offering."

"No," Bunny said thoughtfully. "I think we hit it just right. We don't want to be inundated, and we don't want Skeeve running out to solve simple problems. The people who will respond to our ad will be the ones who really need help enough to swallow their pride and ask."

"That's brilliant," I said, shaking my head. "It's not like I need the money. I want a challenge."

"You'll get it," the Kid said. "Now that I know what you're looking for, I'll talk it up. Meanwhile, do you want to play? Just for fun?" He shuffled the deck at his fingertips. The cards seemed to dance in the air before gathering together again in a smooth rectangle in the Kid's hand.

"No way," I laughed. "That's a question I can answer, no charge."

"You want a piece of advice?" the Kid asked as we turned

to go. "Don't worry too hard about fitting in a niche. Just relax and go with the flow, but keep your eyes open. That's what I do."

"Thanks," I said.

Chapter 5

―――

"You have to put family first."

—Cain

I admit I eyed the Imp with jaundice as he sidled into the room. Imps, with their bright pink skin and small, almost vestigial horns, looked like lesser Deveels. They weren't as smart, as cunning, or as sartorially sophisticated, but they were sneaky and determined. His shiny, houndstooth checked suit was of somewhat better quality than most of the folk I had met from his dimension. That meant he had the wherewithal to pay for my advice.

"So, er, Marmel, what kind of question can I answer for you?" I glanced at his solid tin business card.

"My old dad died last month," he said. Figuring he didn't look woebegone enough, he whipped out a blue and yellow spotted handkerchief and dabbed at his eyes, which teared on cue. Even I could smell the onion he had hidden in the folds of cloth. I coughed, and he put the vegetable back in his pocket. "I've got a sister, see? Her name's Marmilda. Our old mother's gone, too. We're orphans."

"Sorry to hear that," I said. "How can I help?"

"Glad you want to." Marmel grinned affably, his fake tears forgotten. "It's like this: Dad left us both a share in the family business. That's okay. We make wolidgins. Best in all of Imper. Marmilda runs the operation. I'm the head of sales. That's fine."

I nodded, making a mental note to look up 'wolidgins.' "Then, what's the problem?"

"Well, outside of the business and the home—it's not exactly a mansion, but it's big enough for us and our families, see?—there isn't much else. Except for the Hoho Jug."

"The what?"

"That's what the old man always called it. His prized possession. It's worth a bundle. Powerful magik. It's a big pitcher, real fancy looking. You can pour wine out of it forever. It never runs dry."

"Why's it called the Hoho Jug?"

"When you holler down it the echo sounds kind of like 'ho-ho.' "

I shrugged. Imps weren't known for having a lot of imagination. "Why do you need my help with the Hoho Jug?"

"Well, I figure, that since I'm the outside rep for our business, it ought to go to me. Also, I'm the only son. Marmilda, she's the eldest, and she thinks that since she's running the place, and she wants to keep the employees happy, it ought to go to her."

"Who did your father want to have it? What's his will say?"

"No will." Marmel shrugged. "We've looked everywhere. And that's what I don't get, because he was always meticulous about paperwork. But, look, we were both there at Dad's deathbed, and I swear he looked right at me and said I ought to have it."

"Were those his exact words?" I reached for a pencil. This was starting to sound promising.

"Nope. Sounded more like 'uh wah uh uh uv ah.' But that's what it sounded like to me. So, I asked again. I said, 'Dad, who gets the Hoho Jug?' And he pointed."

"At you?" I asked.

"Well." Marmel didn't sound too certain. "Marmilda was sitting next to me. She says he pointed at her. I'm pretty certain he pointed at me. Look, Mr. Skeeve, I need your help. When Dad died, the Hoho Jug disappeared. Dad told us plenty of times that it will only reappear when the rightful heir calls it back. Marmilda said if she gets it she's going to sell it to raise capital. I don't want it out of the family. It's my inheritance. What do you say?"

"Sounds interesting," I said. Figuring out which was the real heir—that sounded like something I could do. It wasn't a guard job, or item retrieval, or any of the other things my friends did so well, so it didn't tread on M.Y.T.H., Inc.'s toes. If there was no clear mandate in the father's words, then maybe I could negotiate an amiable settlement between the siblings. The solution wasn't dependent upon my mediocre magikal skills, and I could do it on my own. "This is worth looking into. You know I can't guarantee that you'll end up with the Hoho Jug as your exclusive property. But I'll help you find out the truth."

Marmel shrugged. "I'll take the chance. My spell or yours?"

"Lead the way," I said. "One minute." I leaned out the curtain and grinned at Bunny. "We've got a client," I told her. "Postpone my other appointments. I'll be back as soon as I can."

"Good for you, Skeeve," she said, beaming. "Break a leg."

BAMF!

I had never spent much time in Imper. After Deva—which was mostly desert, and of that desert, most of it was the Bazaar—Imper seemed cold and damp. A wind full of raindrops slapped me in the face like a wet fish. I sputtered.

"No place like home, huh?" Marmel said, taking a deep breath of rain. He pounded his fists contentedly on his chest. "Welcome to Sirecoose. C'mon, follow me."

Whereas the Bazaar was a warren of tents, wooden buildings, stables, corrals, the occasional sandstone emporium, and an endless maze of curtained stalls, Sirecoose comprised winding, cobblestoned streets lined with three- and four-storey houses and buildings that leaned so far over the throroughfares enough that an Imp could easily have reached out an upper window and handed an object to his neighbor across the street. I spotted plenty of Mom-'n'-Pop stores, where the family clearly lived over the premises. Factories I spotted in the distance. Sparks poured out of the chimneys instead of smoke. Imper relied more heavily than most other dimensions on magik for its manufacturing.

Imps were well known for poor, even frightening, dress sense. I tried not to pay attention as we threaded our way through the noonday crowd. They favored bright colors and wild patterns, the combinations of which made me feel faintly dizzy. A rose-pink woman wearing a brilliant orange moiré dress pushed between us.

Marmel's family business wasn't far from where we had appeared. Trade seemed brisk, as male and female Imps exited the wood and glass building carrying paper-wrapped bundles in their arms. They looked happy.

"So, how many wolidgins do you normally sell in the course of a month?" I asked. I hated to ask what a wolidgin was; it would make me look inexperienced.

"About the usual," Marmel said, ushering me inside the store. Only one customer remained, a stout matron who hmmphed when I accidentally impeded her procession to the exit. She carried her parcel with an air of majesty. I peered around the shop, but nothing stood on display. Whatever wolidgins were, they must be kept in storage until requested.

"Hey, Treesa, my sister around?"

A pert young Imp girl in a bright green and yellow dress smiled politely at her boss.

"No, sir," she said.

"Good," Marmel said with a sigh. "C'mon, Skeeve, I'll show you the old man's room."

"You haven't told your sister that you're employing outside help," I guessed, as we climbed the narrow stairs to the third floor.

"No. She'd blow her top. Here's Dad's room. We've kept it just the way it was when he passed away."

With no disrespect intended to the dear departed, it looked as if Marmel's father had gone out of his way to collect tasteless knickknacks in bulk quantities. Even in the curio shops in the Bazaar I had never seen a matched set of twelve cups shaped like bowling trophies. The stuffed squid on the mantelpiece with "Return to Picturesque Dover" etched on its side in curlicue letters nearly made me gag. No taxidermist should make an animal smile like that. Dirty postcards of naked women from a dozen dimensions had been framed in gold. A couple of them had personalized messages scrawled in the corner.

I whistled. The old boy had gotten around. The bed, a four-poster of green wrought iron, was flanked by pink, white and black end tables that looked as though they had been thrown out of a Trollish bordello for being too gaudy. I could hardly look at the bedclothes. If dear old Dad hadn't had a heart attack from having to look at the crazy rainbow print, then he was either too tough or color blind.

"So, where was he looking when he pointed at you?" I asked.

"Wait a minute!" Marmel exclaimed. "Marmilda is coming! I should have told Treesa not to tell her I was home!"

He grabbed my arm.

BAMF!

I took a deep breath to protest and got a big mouthful of swirling dust. I whooped and coughed. Marmel clapped a hand over my face.

"Shh!" he hissed. "She'll hear us."

It took a moment to recover, but I did so without making any noise. My eyes watered. I forced them to focus on our surroundings. We stood on wide, wooden floor boards. Above us, a weak sunbeam strained itself trying to shine through a filthy skylight in an arched ceiling. We were surrounded by dusty boxes and a lifetime supply of cobwebs.

"Where are we?" I coughed.

"In the attic." He flattened himself on the floor and applied his eye to a crack between two of the boards.

I joined him, finding a convenient knothole in the dust-scented floor.

Marmilda could have been Marmel's twin. On her his stocky figure translated into a buxom, broad-hipped frame. She had the same darting, nervous look.

"He's not up here," she was saying to someone I couldn't see.

"Think he found it?" the other person said in a chesty, gravelly voice.

"No! At least, I hope not." Marmilda chewed on a thumbnail in exactly the same way her brother had.

"Well, he better not. I want it, unnerstand? You better find it by tomorrow, or you're not gonna have to worry about where it is, right?"

The tone chilled me. I had heard it used on a professional basis by the Mob men who had worked for me, though the speaker was neither Guido nor Nunzio. Being on the receiving end would daunt anyone.

"I understand," Marmilda said. Her cool impressed me. Underneath she might be frightened, but she held herself with dignity.

"Good. So long as we understand one another."

Marmel could hardly contain himself until the two left the room below us.

"My sister's in trouble!" he exploded.

"Who was that?"

"I think it's Narwickius."

"Narwickius!" I had heard the name. He came from Titanium. Even Trolls like Chumley spoke of Titans with respect. They were big and tough, all the more formidable because they possessed rapid mental facilities. When they wanted something, they went after it. Few races could stand up to them. Narwickius stood out among Titans; he had a reputation for unscrupulous and violent behavior that stretched all the way to the Bazaar. Luckily, he seldom went there, so I had never crossed paths with him before. "How does he know about the Hoho Jug?"

"He and Dad met a few times at estate sales and curio shops," Marmel said. "He always outbid Dad in auctions. He's been after the Hoho Jug for years. Dad refused to even consider selling. Now I know why Marmilda's been trying so hard to get ahold of it. He might hurt her if she doesn't let him have it! He can't do that to my sister! I'll . . . I'll . . . I don't know what I'll do. Help me, Skeeve. Help Marmilda."

I frowned. "Do you want Narwickius to take the Hoho Jug?"

"No . . . " Marmel said, thoughtfully. "I mean, not if I can help it. But what can I do? He's huge, and he's got big, tough guys working for him. People who turn him down end up walking with crutches, if they can still walk at all. He's got wizards on his payroll, too."

More than ever, I wished that I could go back to the M.Y.T.H., Inc. office and ask for help. But, no, I was on my own. I had to think of a solution that would keep the Hoho Jug in the family, but deal with the problem at hand.

"We'll see if I can help you solve both problems," I said. "First thing, we have to find the jug. Your father hid it before he died. I'm guessing that since neither of you found it, it's somewhere in that room. Let's do a thorough search tonight."

"We can't," Marmel said. "Marmilda will hear us."

"I can take care of that," I said. "No problem."

Chapter 6

_____

"Unexpected company is never a problem."

—Hannibal Lecter

Late that night, we sneaked into the bedroom by means of a trap door in the attic floor.

"Why didn't we use this before?" I asked Marmel, as I let myself down slowly with a levitation spell.

"No time," he said, following me.

I couldn't argue with that. Time is what we had the least of. If I knew Narwickius, he would return with his hoods by sunrise.

I had plenty of force lines near the house to draw from. With my eyes closed, I could see a spiky red line that arced overhead about ten yards to the east, and a wide blue band that snaked beneath the entire street in front of the house. Within a block, I could draw from a thin green line and a faint but powerful gold line as well. Tapping into both of the close lines, I recharged my personal batteries and gathered a good supply of magik for immediate use. I worked up a silence illusion to cover the noise of our search. To make sure no one could surprise us, I also ran thin lines of fiery red force across the top of the stairs, the windows, and the trap door. Not only would those lines inform me of approaching intruders, but they'd also give those same intruders a shock.

I hoped it would throw off their reactions long enough for me to defend us and Marmilda, who was asleep in her room at the end of the corridor.

I found it eerie not being able to hear even my own breathing, but if I couldn't, neither could anyone else. Marmel had tried it out, opening his mouth and yelling. Not a sound emerged. He gave me a big thumbs-up. We wouldn't disturb Marmilda.

Everything within the spell's radius was muffled, so the bedsprings didn't let out a peep when we moved the mattress to look under it. Even pulling the heavy bedstead to one side to look at the floor underneath didn't produce the usual screech and scrape.

The worst part about working in complete silence was that if I didn't have Marmel in my line of sight, I had no way of knowing where he was. While I was leafing through a basket of the old man's correspondence, something bumped into me from behind. I leaped straight into the air and hung there, a ball of force gathered between my hands along with bills and birthday cards. It was only Marmel.

He looked sheepish. His mouth moved. *Sorry.*

I waved an apology in return and holstered my handful of magik. We went back to our search.

The room proved to be full of hidden cubbyholes. Behind pieces of furniture, under drawers, inside books, we found more and more knickknacks. Marmel's father had enough souvenirs to stock a warehouse. I found ewers, pitchers, cups, vases, and urns galore. Each time I unearthed one, I hoped it would be the famed Hoho Jug. No such luck.

I felt around for magikal traces. To protect a precious family heirloom, Marmel's father might have secured its hiding place in every way he could. I let out a silent "A-ha!" as I pulled a tall, gold-plated loving cup full of wine from between the pages of a leatherbound book. The cup was studded with purple gems—appropriate for a never-empty fountain of the fruit of the vine. I waved to get Marmel's attention.

The Imp turned, his eyes full of hope. I held up my find.

His shoulders sank, and he shook his head. He mimed a small object, about the size of a grapefruit. Grumpily, I put the goblet to one side. The scent of the wine tantalized my nose. Though it was difficult, I ignored it. I had a weakness for wine, and I could never let my vigilance down. It was a good thing that I had never come across the Hoho Jug during the low point in my life.

I flipped open the catch on a tiny, carved-ivory music box that was giving off strong magikal vibes. The next thing I knew, sheaves of paper were flying up into my face. I smacked both hands down to try and stem the tide, but the papers fountained upward like a geyser. I batted them aside, trying to get to the opening to block it. My hands were not strong enough. Marmel jumped up to help me. I tried using magik to block the paper inside, but my spell exploded outward in a shower of blue sparks.

Marmel scooped armloads of white rectangles into the corner to get them out of our way, but he was being buried. If we didn't stop the flow, we'd be smothered.

I caught his arm and signed to him. We scrabbled to

the top of the heap and crawled around behind the box. Together, we got ahold of the tiny lid. I used a huge burst of magik to block the flow for just a second. We forced the lid over and slammed it down. I grabbed the catch with a finger of magik power and locked it solidly.

The avalanche of papers ceased. Marmel rolled over on his back, panting. I wiped my forehead and looked around.

Hundreds of folded documents filled more than a quarter of the floor. I unfolded one. It turned out to be a long, skinny map. As I drew my finger from the indicated point A to point B, I saw landmarks and signs as if I were walking along the streets myself. After some thought, I realized it was a Triple-D map of Zoorik, leading from the fabled Bank of the Gnomes to the Pleasure Gardens and the Zeughaus bierundwienerrathskeller, a restaurant that served beer in yard-high glasses.

I tossed it to one side. Marmel and I opened more of the papers, hoping to find the missing will, but only found more Directory of the Diverse Dimensions maps, yet another one of the old man's collections.

I kicked my way through drifts of charts and graphs and started going over the mantelpiece. At least one of the gizmos on display gave off some powerful magik.

Suddenly, I felt a *twang!* Something had set off one of my alarm threads.

I signed to Marmel. The two of us jumped behind the headboard of the bed, and I plunged the room into darkness. Narwickius's thugs hadn't waited for daybreak—they were coming after midnight. Leave it to them to split hairs.

I gathered in another supply of magik from the lines of force to replace what I had expended. In any case, the scads of maps would upset the intruders' footing. Since Marmel could no longer hear or see, it would be up to me to subdue the interlopers.

I waited. My traps told me exactly where the newcomers were. They had opened a window at the rear of the house and were coming up the back stairs. *Patience,* I told myself. My heart began to race. *You've done this a number of times. Unless they outmagik you, it doesn't matter how many of them there are or how big they are.*

Closer now. I couldn't see anything, but a careful outreach of magikal force told me my opponent packed at least some firepower himself. Yes, one wizard was all I sensed. If there were any more bodies behind him, they were set to rely on brute strength. I took a deep breath.

The intruder was a professional. The door opened smoothly, not upsetting the wards I had placed upon it. I readied a handful of power that would stun my opponent long enough for us to tie him up with a souvenir jump rope from the Temple of Shirli in Lahlipop. I put a hand on Marmel's arm to tell him to stay in place.

Then, I leaped.

The intruder ought to have been one pace inside. But nobody interrupted my headlong flight. I slammed into the corner of the door. Red and orange stars danced before my eyes. Shaking my head, I cast around. How had he moved so quickly?

I found out in the next heartbeat. A body dropped down

on me from the ceiling. I thrust the full blast of magik in my hand into its face. Hands closed upon my throat. I grabbed back, mentally gathering more power for a burst of light. My fingers sank into soft flesh that covered steel-like tendons. My attacker let go with one hand, and I felt something thin whip around my neck and tighten. I reeled as my breath cut off. I used magik to try and loosen the cord. It stretched a tiny bit, enough to let me suck in a little air. My room was spinning, but I let loose with a paralyzing blast of magik.

Ker-*POW!*

Instead of leaving my opponent stunned and helpless, the spell backfired and exploded in a brilliant green glow. By its light, I saw a heart-shaped face somewhat distended by partial strangulation, but entirely recognizable.

"Tananda!" I shouted. It didn't matter that I couldn't breathe; my spell dampened the sound anyhow.

She recognized me, too. Her eyes widened just as the green fireball faded. I felt the garotte around my neck release. Gasping, I fell to the floor. With stars dancing across my vision, I undid my darkness spell. The torches on the wall kindled into life once more.

Tananda stood with her hands on her hips, looking down on me. Her mouth was moving.

"Wait," I mouthed. I dispelled the cloud of blue magik that comprised the silence spell with a flick of my fingers.

"What are you doing here?" we both asked at once.

Chapter 7

_____

"Preparation is the key to any successful operation."

—Ethelred the Unready

When she first saw me, Tananda had looked surprised, then delighted—then her brows drew down over her pretty nose.

"I can't believe you're cutting in on one of our jobs!" she said. "A couple of the others said you might do it, but I didn't believe it. I am so disappointed in you. I never thought you'd do anything like that. I thought I knew you."

"What?" I squeaked. I cleared my throat. "Cutting in? Who said that?"

"Somehow, you found out that Marmilda hired us to protect her and the family inheritance," she continued, looking hurt. "Don't you think we can do it? We were all around years before you came on the scene, remember? Or did you just want to show that you could do it better? Just let us know you're taking a case, Skeeve. You don't have to poach." Her eyes brightened as if she was going to cry.

"Poach?" I protested, clambering to my feet. "Wait a minute! I'm not poaching. Marmilda didn't hire me. Her brother did."

Tananda's eyes widened. "Her brother? Marmel?"

"Me," Marmel said, holding up a tentative forefinger

57

from his hiding place behind the headboard. "I just want my inheritance. I didn't know about Narwickius."

"Oh, Skeeve!" Tananda exclaimed. She rushed me like an oncoming dragon and wrapped herself around me. She planted her mouth on mine and gave me such a thorough kiss that it robbed me of breath all over again. "Forgive me. I am so sorry for ever doubting you. I was surprised to see you, and . . . I didn't think. Marmilda came to us with this case only a couple hours ago. She sneaked into the Bazaar after dark. She is very frightened. She said she only has until morning before the problems really start. Then, to find you here made me assume that she decided we just weren't going to be able to do the job and got you in on it, too."

I shook my head. How could she think I would muscle in on their business? But that had to wait. As she said, there wasn't much time.

"You're not the only one on this case, are you?" I asked. "Where's Chumley?"

"Chumley and Guido are both coming before dawn. They sent me ahead to find the Hoho Jug or the missing will. We didn't want to wake Marmel." She grinned, and dimples dented both her cheeks. "I suppose the silence spell was to keep from disturbing Marmilda."

"Right," I said. "I didn't know she had gone for help on her own while we were working in here. I guess the silence cut both ways."

"It happens," Tananda said, then paused.

I took a deep breath. "Well, as long as we're both here, why don't we work together?"

"It's fine with me," she said, "but I'm not the only one who has to agree. I have . . . partners."

"Fine," I said hastily, trying to ignore the pang the word evoked in me. "Then let's make a tentative agreement until the others get here. I figure Marmel and I have looked through maybe a third of the hiding places in this room. I'm concentrating on the ones that give off a magikal aura."

Tananda didn't waste any time. "I'll take that side of the room," she said.

Marmel found Marmilda in the hall and brought her inside. Quickly he told her what had happened.

"I was just doing it to save us both, baby brother," she said.

"I know, big sister," Marmel said, sheepishly. "Me, too."

The two of them helped us by pointing out those hiding places their father used that they knew of, but there were dozens I turned up that surprised them. I found hidey-holes in the backs of paintings, underneath throw rugs, in the false heels of shoes. All of them were chock full of junk.

"I think there's more extradimensional space in here than in our tent," I said to Tananda, then corrected myself. "I mean, your tent."

Tananda stopped pulling stuffed rabbits out of a woolly hat and gave me a wry smile. "Skeeve . . . "

BAMF!

At the blast of outrushing air, I went on guard, magik at the ready.

"Hey, Tanda, any luck?"

I lowered my defenses. The new arrivals, while considerably crowding the minuscule available space in the room, were friends.

"Hi, guys," I said.

"I say, Skeeve!" Chumley exclaimed, then observed we were not alone. "Klahd!" he said, in a coarse voice. "You here?"

In private, the purple Troll was erudite and articulate. In mixed company, that was to say, when some of the people present were not close friends, he reverted to a monosyllabic form of speech he used in his public persona as Big Crunch, a not-too-bright enforcer for hire.

"That's right, er, Big Crunch," I said. "Hiya, Guido."

"Hey dere, Skeeve." Guido held out his hand for a shake. I noticed the bulge in the breast of his big-shouldered, pin-striped suit. He seldom went out without his pocket crossbow, a weapon with which he could pick the eye out of a pinbug at fifty paces. He was ready for business. "Gotta admit, I'm a little surprised to see you here."

"It's a coincidence, Guido," I assured him.

"Uh-huh, and since when do you believe in coincidences?" he asked, narrowing an eye.

"Conference, guys!" Tananda announced, taking both huge males by the arms and dragging them into a corner. "Marmilda and Marmel, could we have privacy for a while, please?"

"Certainly." Marmilda took Marmel by the arm. "Come downstairs. You can help me wash dishes. Let the people do their job. Call us if you need anything." The two Imps retreated from the room.

My former associates huddled. Tananda spoke in a low voice, eliciting muffled exclamations from Chumley and Guido. I couldn't tell if they were upset or not. I waited nervously. What if they didn't want me in on this project? What would I do? I had a client, too. Then, they broke into laughter.

Guido turned to me. "You got the jump on Tanda?" he said, slapping me heartily on the back. I slipped on a pile of multicolored teddy bears and sat down on a heap of shoes. "Dat's more than I ever got."

"Dumb luck," I said modestly, picking myself up. Inside I was slumping with relief.

"No, it wasn't," Tananda said, smiling. "You've gotten a lot better at magik."

"So have you."

"Not me," Tananda said with a chuckle. She held out her hand and displayed a gaudy knuckle-duster with a huge green stone in the center. "I borrowed this ring from Massha. We knew we were going up against Narwickius. Couldn't take the chance that he had left one of his bully-boys on the premises. *You've* improved a lot without having to rely on gadgets."

"Practice," I said modestly. "I'm doing what I can with what I've got."

"Never denigrate yourself, tiger," she said, leaning over and giving me a kiss on the cheek. "It would take most people years to make the progress you have in months."

"Awright, awright, awright," Guido said, holding up his hands. "Enough with the mutual admiration society.

Tananda said youse agreed to a temporary cooperative venture. We ain't got much time until zero hour, so all in favor?"

Chumley put up his hand. "Aye."

Tananda followed suit. "Aye."

"Aye," Guido added, making it three. "Okay, dat's unanimous. I mean, it's just a formality, Boss . . . I mean, Skeeve. We hadda decide in a democratic and fair fashion. That's the way we've been doin' things since you been gone."

"Is everyone upset with me?" I asked. I knew I sounded plaintive, but I couldn't help it.

"No! We thought you were upset with us," Tananda admitted. "You haven't come around once since the time you dropped in. You didn't invite any of us to see your new office."

I hung my head. "It's not much. I thought you wouldn't really want to see it. I felt pretty awkward. I guess I didn't think about what would happen in the future if I came back."

"Neither did we, what?" Chumley said.

"D'you mind?" Guido said. "We can have a real powwow later. We got a high-roller comin' around in about three hours. We gotta work out a plan to deal with him."

"And find the will," I said. "But that can wait until we get rid of the problem. What do you have on Narwickius?"

"Nasty," Chumley said. He plucked a pair of pince-nez glasses from within a tuft of fur on his purple chest and placed them on his nose. He unfurled a scroll and spread it out for me to read. "Pray skip the police blotter. I assure you it is as complete as I could make it."

I whistled as I skimmed the long list of Incidents Precipitated and Alleged Misdeeds.

"I admire your research, Chumley," I said, glancing up. "This guy has caused trouble in over forty dimensions."

"Yeah, he's tough. It's a shame that he hadda pick on a coupla harmless Imps," Guido said.

"How many people does he have working for him?"

"I was able to discern the employment status of over two hundred and fifty different mugs, thieves, grifters, shysters, penny-ante crooks, leg-breakers, and other miscreants who have been used for jobs small and large," Chumley said. "He has a permanent staff of eleven. Two are powerful mages, a Vipe and a Pervert."

"You mean Pervect," I said automatically.

"I say, not this one," Chumley corrected me. "Read subsection three, if you would be so good."

I scanned the details in the paragraph and felt the blood leave my face. "Can you *do* that with a camel?"

"I believe there were at least four witnesses," Chumley said. "The survivors said that the deed was at Narwickius's personal bequest."

"Nasty indeed," I concurred. "Well, what do we know we can use as leverage?"

"Not a lot. Titans move fast and carry a lotta firepower," Guido said. "Not to mention their natural physical shape. You don't wanna get in a clench with one."

"People who move too fast often make mistakes," I said,

scanning the document again. "Do you think we could bluff him?"

"I would greatly favor it to brute strength," Chumley said. "He who throws the first punch has lost the war of wits, what? Yet, I have heard that nothing deters him."

"What he said," opined Guido. "Not that we won't be ready for him. I got a few things with me that could take out a charging whaleosaurus." He patted his side pockets. The 'things' must have been fairly flat, because nothing distended the perfect cut of his pinstriped suit coat.

"We don't know how many of his hooligans he might have with him," Chumley said. "His gang acts as backup, but all decisions I can document were made by him. Most often, his successes have required nothing more than his implication that violence might follow a lack of cooperation. In the ninety percent of the cases where the situation has gone beyond parley, he has acted alone. Seldom have his employees been required to step in. He can inflict considerable damage without outside assistance. He has a reputation as, er, a control freak."

I nodded. "Good. Then, it's essentially a one-on-one situation. We can use that. If I know his reputation without having met him, then he might know mine. I can meet him and try to persuade him he doesn't want to go through me to get to Marmilda and Marmel. If he's heard of the Great Skeeve, he'll have some idea of what I'm capable of. That's not to say that you don't have formidable reputations, too," I said quickly.

"It's all right, handsome," Tananda said with a wink.

"You were the top name on the letterhead. We can make use of that. Just slip into something formidable, and we'll take it from there."

Illusionary disguises are easy for even a beginning wizard. I learned the skill from Aahz, and it served me well for years. All I needed to do was concentrate on the face I wanted to present to the world and superimpose it over my own features. Size wouldn't impress a Titan like Narwickius. As Tananda said, I was looking for a mien that would give the impression of unlimited power. People always said I looked too young to be a great wizard (and they were right), so I went for disguises that made me look at least fifty. In this case, I thought I had better look as though I had been around a lot longer than my opponent. I chose a gaunt, almost skull-like face, seamed with wrinkles. A thin, pointed beard and drooping mustache of steel-gray framed lips that had never smiled or showed mercy. Sharp, dark eyes lurked under deep brow ridges like monsters in a cave. A curved beak of a nose, a widow's peak of silver hair, and pale, bloodless skin completed the image. I considered the whole image for a moment, then transferred it to myself.

"How do I look?" I said, turning to Tananda. Unfortunately, one of the problems with casting an illusion on yourself is that you can't see it. When you look in a mirror, all you see is yourself.

"You'd never get a date," she said with a grin.

I grinned back. "Perfect. Now, we wait."

Chapter 8

"Waiting is the hard part."

—Susan Lucci

With the Imps' help, we set the scene. I arranged myself at the very center of the family showroom in a gaudily gilded, thronelike chair borrowed from the old man's bedroom. When impatient fists pounded the doors, I used a handful of magik to throw it open with a bang. Marmilda and Marmel rushed in to serve me the best wine and food in the house from the finest of their silver-and-chrome dishes. I accepted a goblet from Marmilda, who dipped in a curtsey. I bent my head to take a sip and rolled it around my mouth with an expression of distaste.

Narwickius rushed in and stood glaring at me. Under my eyebrows, I peered at the new arrival. The Titan was a big creature. I had never seen one before, but Aahz had insisted I learn as many of the dimension-traveling races as possible. He stood a good eight feet tall. His shock of silver hair nearly brushed the ceiling. His skin was a pale, metallic blue, and his eyes were charcoal gray. He wore a tunic of thick leather sewn with metal plates and a belt of braided strands that looked like hair. All kinds of hair. Like Klahd, Troll, Kobold, Whelf, and Fairie.

"Well?" he demanded. He glowered at all of us. I felt

rather than saw Guido put his hand inside his coat to touch the butt of his crossbow. Chumley merely crossed his arms.

I deigned to notice the newcomer.

"Ah," I said, delicately placing the wine cup on the Imp woman's outstretched tray. "I believe you are Master Narwickius. I am pleased to see you here at last."

"Dispense with the chatter," the Titan said. "What the Netherhells are you?"

"I am . . . Skeeve the Magnificent," I said, with just the right pause to insure drama. Narwickius let out a loud snort.

"A Klahd? I'm supposed to be impressed by a Klahd in a chair. What do you think, men?" He turned to the hulking brutes behind him. They laughed nastily. With Guido and Chumley behind me and Tananda lurking overhead in the attic, I was not worried about the muscle, but I did sense strong magik coming from the Vipe female at his elbow. Vipes, of sinuous body and narrow, black-eyed face, possessed deadly magikal talents. I didn't like the idea of tangling with one myself, but I was more concerned with the well-being of my host and hostess. Imps had no special protection against poison.

The Vipe was magician number one. I hoped number two wasn't waiting in the wings. I was determined not to let the matter escalate. I rested my elbows on the chair arms and tented my fingers.

"I know why you have come," I said, in my most impressive voice.

"Oh, you do, do you?"

"Little is hidden from Skeeve the Magnificent."

"Such as your impending death?" Narwickus demanded.

"My death is far in the future," I said, nodding as if bored. "I do not fear you. You should fear me. My minions occupy this place, and it is protected by my magik. I have . . . "

"I've got an army out there!" Narwickius roared, interrupting me. "I know about your minions. You've got one Klahd, one Troll and those two pathetic Imps. They cannot stand against my army!"

So he hadn't detected Tananda yet. Her skills as a trained thief and, regrettably, occasional assassin gave her the ability to hide herself. I was concerned that if the Vipe wizardess started probing by magik Tanda might be found. I meant to have Narwickius expend as little energy on us as possible.

"You do not know what powers we wield," I said. "But no matter. Why are you here?"

"I'm here for the Hoho Jug."

"But why do you want such a small thing?" I asked, gently.

"Because it's . . . I don't have to explain myself to you!"

"But I stand between you and your goal."

"Do I have to tear you apart to get what I came for? Move aside! I have no time to waste on you!"

The size of the force he had brought meant we stood little chance of persuading him to go away. Besides, an idea was beginning to form in my mind. I had to hope Guido and Chumley would go along with it.

"I am not here to impede your desire," I said, spreading out my hands.

"Stop wasting my time!" Narwickius bellowed. He blinked. "What? Explain yourself! Hurry up!"

I smiled. This was going to work. His impatience was better than any other weapon I could have used on him.

"Since our time is also valuable, I will be brief," I said. I gestured to Marmel and Marmilda, who huddled together in the corner. "The lady and gentleman here do not know where their father's legacy is. They do not want trouble, and they fear harm. I could enter into battle with you, but it could result in injury to innocents. I might not win, but I doubt that I will lose."

"Well?" Narwickius asked belligerently.

I smiled gently. I had him now.

"I offer you a bargain: if you can find this Hoho Jug, you can have it." I turned to Marmel and Marmilda. "Do you concur?" I had discussed it with them. If the only way to get rid of the threat was to give up their inheritance, they had said they would do it. Marmel had not been happy, but he had gotten a good look at the invading army—he had to see that discretion was the better part of valor. Besides, I saw a chance to get rid of the problem and perhaps still hold on to the Hoho Jug. If it was still there in the old man's room.

Narwickius snorted. That appeared to be his favorite way of expressing himself. "Okay. It's a deal. What's the catch?"

"No catch." I held myself imperiously. "You can look for it until you give up. If you find it, fine. If you don't, then it's not here, and you agree to leave these people alone for good. I will place you under no other geas."

With that, I spread out my hands and caused the room to

go dark for a moment. A brilliant fountain of light surrounded me and poured up to the ceiling in a fountain. It was cheesy magik, but it worked. Aahz always said a little pomp and pageantry went a long way. Narwickius looked dazed and impressed in spite of himself. He recovered quickly.

"What the Netherhells?" Narwickius said. "I agree. Come on, men!"

He pushed past me and up the stairs. In a moment, we heard them rummaging around upstairs. Plenty of swearing floated down the stairs to our ears, along with swishing as they kicked their way through the piles of Triple-D maps. One of the Titan oafs stayed at the foot of the stairs. He faced us, arms crossed on his enormous chest. The Vipe wizardress curled herself onto one of the steps and stared at us with unblinking eyes.

"Now what?" Marmel whispered.

"We wait," I said. I retrieved the wine and took a sip. "Very nice, Marmilda. Usually Imp wines are too sour for my taste. Is this from the Hoho Jug?"

"No," the Imp woman said, frowning. "I ran it through one of our best wolidgins. It translates everything, not just language. The wolidgin translated Imper wine into Klahdish. You're Skeeve the Magnificent, and you don't know that?"

Behind her, my friends were grinning at me over her head.

"I don't know everything," I said, feeling my cheeks redden. "I just figure that I can find out anything, given enough time and resources."

"But what about Narwickius?" Marmel said, casting

a nervous glance at the Vipe wizardess, who eyed us unblinkingly from the foot of the stairs.

"We wait," I repeated.

"How long?"

"As long as it takes." I allowed myself an evil grin. "You might as well make yourselves comfortable. I think it'll be a while."

"I get it," Guido said. "I thought we was headed for one serious throwdown, but this is a more discretionary form of handlin' the problem. If it works."

"It should work," I said. "I hope."

"What is all this junk?" Narwickius bellowed from above. "Just toss that stuff out the window!" We heard a SMACK, as the casement overhead was thrown open, then a noise like falling snow. Outside the door, showers of paper fluttered down into the street. "Cobrita! Get up here!"

The wizardess rose from her perch and slithered upward.

"It will be a while," I said cheerfully. "Anyone for a game of Dragon Poker?"

Chapter 9

___

"Patience is a virtue."

—The Chicago Cubs

My employer didn't find it easy to endure the hours that followed.

"How can you sit and . . . and play?" Marmel said, pacing around us like a dog on a short leash. "How does that help get rid of him?" He tilted his head toward the stairs and the imperious guard who still stood there staring at us.

"It would help if you could just calm down," I said.

"But he could kill us all!"

"He won't," I said. "Not until he gets what he wants. He seems pretty goal oriented. Three disks. Call." I tossed in my bet.

"Elf-high flush," Guido said and spread out his cards. I moaned. With a chuckle he raked in the pot of glass disks, which had been supplied by Marmilda in lieu of coins.

We had all agreed not to play for money. I am not and have never claimed to be a great card player, but I enjoy the camaraderie of the game. In fact, I realized, as I threw in my hand in surrender, that I had missed my friends more than I realized. It was good to be back—only I wasn't back. This détente was temporary. We'd go back to our separate businesses when all this was over.

I felt my heart sink into my belly. If only I had been able

to find Aahz and ask him the best way to reintroduce myself to the business. I hoped the Duchess was all right. She was eccentric with a capital "Eccentric," but she was Aahz's mother, and what hurt him hurt me.

"My deal," Chumley growled, holding out an enormous purple hand for the deck.

"Nah, it's Tuesday. The dealin' reverses itself every seventh hand."

"Wha? Okay." For the sake of our company the Troll pretended to be confused about the rules. The look of puzzlement on his face was so convincing I nearly broke down and explained it to him. I stopped myself before I made a fool of myself again. He was generally the one who reminded us of the subtleties of Dragon Poker during our friendly games. It *had* been too long.

I felt eyes on my cards and looked up. Marmel hovered at my elbow. The Imp wound his hands together nervously.

"Are you all right?" I asked.

"What if he comes down again?" Marmel asked.

"He won't," I assured him. "We made a deal. He's going to look. We'll wait."

"Are you sure?"

"I am sure," I said. "I gave him my word."

"Yeah, he's the great Skeeve, remember?" Guido said. "You gonna bid or just shop?"

"Uh, I'll bid," I said. "Three coins."

"Yeah, Narwickius wouldn't dare do anything," Marmel said. "That's right. You're the most powerful wizard in the world, right?"

"Nah," Guido said. "Crunch, you in?"

"Fold," the Troll growled.

"Raise," Guido said.

"You're bluffing."

"Call me and see," the enforcer said with a grin.

"Yeah," Marmel said again. "I shouldn't have anything to be afraid of. No!" He shouldered up to the Titan at the bottom of the stairs. "You wouldn't have the *guts* to take on the Great Skeeve, would you? Big guy? Tough guy?" He punctuated every word with a poke of his bony pink forefinger. "Huh? Huh?"

The Titan growled low in his throat.

"Marmel?" I called.

"Yeah, Skeeve?"

"Did you hire me to help you find your inheritance, or not?"

"That's exactly why I hired you!" Marmel said.

"Well, then, did you buy the insurance rider against grievous bodily harm? Because I don't remember signing up to fight Titan bodyguards when we discussed the contract."

The Titan grinned down at him, silver-white teeth gleaming.

"Uh, no . . . " Marmel said.

"Then maybe you ought to say 'excuse me' to the nice, big Titan and come over here before you have an accident?"

Marmel didn't need long to assess the situation. The forefinger retracted into his fist, and he backed away three steps. "Sorry, Mr. Titan, sir."

The bodyguard showed his big, square teeth. "No problem, squirt. Boo!"

Marmel jumped. He scurried away from the staircase and cowered in the corner of the room farthest from it. I sighed and shuffled my hand.

"I hope Tananda's all right," I said, staring upward. She had not yet revealed herself, but I knew she was keeping an eye on things.

"She's fine," Guido said. "Watch the cards. Dis is a little trick I picked up on Taro."

He sorted out the Dragon suit from the deck and spread it out on the table. With a wink at me, he waved his hand across them. We waited, as though we were in a séance hoping the ghost of our rich old aunt would communicate the location of her hidden cache of treasure. Suddenly, the deuce, the lowest-value Dragon card, twitched itself out of the pack. Guido pushed it back.

"She says 'bupkis,'" Guido confirmed in a voice too low for the Titan nearest us to hear. "They have failed thus far to find anythin'. Private signal. Works real good. Your deal, Skeeve." He gathered up the cards and handed the deck to me.

I suppose we didn't really need the confirmation. Narwickius would have stopped throwing things out the window if he had been successful. More objects hit the ground while we waited. Chairs, books, knickknacks of every description precipitated from above like an unusually heavy rain. Shattered glass filled the street.

"There go the souvenir shot glasses," I observed, watching them tinkle to the pavement.

The littering had alarmed the residents of Sirecoose, but when a policeman came by to demand it stop, I invited him to go upstairs and reason with the army of Titans on the premises. At the mention of Titans he retreated, never to return.

Marmel had a hard time with the wait, but the rest of us allowed ourselves cautious enjoyment. Marmilda was a terrific hostess. She kept beverages coming, and at mealtimes brought us food she had cooked herself, then carefully translated according to our dimension of origin. She served me a marvelous fish-and-potato pie, just like my mother used to make from troutpikes I caught in the brook on my father's farm.

"I gotta buy me one of dose wolidgins," Guido said, patting his stomach with satisfaction. "When I remember all the places I been where the food ain't really been to my taste, I could just run it in one end of dese and get a steak dinner out the other end."

"We'd make you a very special price," Marmel said, rubbing his hands together. "I mean, what with the advertising value of being able to say the Great Skeeve uses our product. And his friends," he added nervously, as Guido shot him a dirty look. I didn't miss it.

"Good," Chumley said, carefully extracting a long orange tentacle from between two molars and placing it carefully in his dish. "Food good." He grinned at the two Imps, who backed up a pace. I thought by this time they would be used to him, but a Troll of his size can be daunting.

"Get them up here!" a voice roared from above.

"I think I see a break in the case," I said, rising to my feet.

The Titans thundered down the stairs, single-file and made for us. Two of them grabbed me by the shoulders, but I was ready for them.

"*Ahhh!*" They jumped backwards. I grinned. That magikal shocker I had bought in a gag shop worked every time.

"Never lay hands upon the Great Skeeve," I informed them haughtily. Guido and Chumley shook off their grasp, and the three of us made our way upstairs toward the bellowing Narwickius.

"What's the holdup?" Narwickius shouted. He came rushing out of the small bedroom, nearly barreling into me. "Where is the Hoho Jug?"

"I told you, we have no knowledge of its whereabouts," I said calmly. "The owner passed away without informing his children. I have not seen it, nor have my colleagues. I give you my word on that."

"Aaggh!" Narwickius said, clutching at his hair. He had clearly been tearing out handfuls of it in frustration. I could see silver strands liberally scattered over the waist-high mounds of junk that literally filled the room.

The Troll's people had been at work: gone were the Triple-D maps and the souvenir rock collection from Bezoar. The furniture had largely been reduced to boards and rags. As I watched, the Vipe wizardess pointed her poison-green wand at a heap of brightly colored teddy bears. They vanished with a small explosion.

Boom!

"I found another hiding place, great master!" one of the Titans announced, holding up a small, cut-glass box.

I sensed the magik in it. I'd seen its like before.

"No, wait!" I shouted.

Too late. The big, blue oaf flipped open the lid, and hundreds of spring-loaded snakes leaped into the air.

"Aargh!" Narwickius bellowed, batting at them. He lunged for me and grabbed me by the throat.

"Gack!" I choked, as I hung in the air.

"Where . . . is . . . it?" he demanded, shaking me at every syllable.

Guido and Chumley were at my side in a moment, wrestling the Titan back. He dropped me.

"I don't know," I gasped out, massaging life back into my neck. "He hid it here somewhere. That's what I surmise."

"I can't stand it!" the Titan exclaimed. He yanked open what seemed like false drawers in the dismantled headboard, releasing streams of silk scarves, commemorative whiskey bottles (full) and rare birds' eggs (empty), leaving us chest-high in clutter. "Get rid of this trash!"

"Yessss, massster," the Vipe wizardess said. She pointed the wand.

Boom! Boom! Boom!

I staggered as the mass of junk collectibles vanished. Chumley swooped to keep me upright with one massive paw. Narwickius kept pulling down hidden trap doors, flicking open hatches secreted behind decorative wall plaques, and releasing false bricks in the fireplace. Every one of them catapulted a ton of junk out onto the floor.

"Find it for me," the Titan growled. "Then I will leave, maybe even with the rest of you alive!"

"That wasn't our bargain," I said calmly. "You just have to keep looking. If you kill me, it will let loose more magik than you have ever had to deal with in your life. It will follow you no matter what dimension you go to. I will haunt you when you are asleep. I will whisper ugly secrets about you to your girlfriends. I'll tell everyone at the poker table that you have a ten-high nothing in your hand . . . "

"You're bluffing," Narwickius said, though he didn't look at all certain.

"Try me," I said, putting up my chin. "I haven't died since . . . gee, last Wednesday, wasn't it, Guido?"

"Thursday, Boss," the enforcer said, with a glint in his eyes.

The bluff worked. Narwickius spun away. He took out his frustration on the room. He pulled down every shelf and threw it on the heap in the middle of the floor. With a mighty wrench, he ripped the mantelpiece off the wall. The objets d'art went flying in every direction. The stuffed squid hit the floor with a wheezing noise: *hoho*.

Chumley's eyebrows went up, almost hidden in the purple fur of his face. I signed to him to be calm.

"Aaaagh!" Narwickius bellowed. "I can't stand it! Are there any more collections?" he asked the Vipe.

She scanned the room with her wand. "I don't sssee any more, massster."

"Do *they* know of any more?"

The cold, black eyes swiveled toward us, and the end of the wand leveled at my nose.

"No," I said, before the Vipe could discharge magik in my direction. "Neither do my associates. Didn't I give you my word?"

"What does the word of a Klahd mean to me?" Narwickius demanded. "That means the Hoho Jug is out here already!"

"Or she made it vanish," I said, tilting my head toward the wizardess. I didn't want him getting any closer to that squid until I could examine it.

"What?"

"Well, you've been having her destroy everything in your way," I said. "Did you check it all? I bet she blew it up right under your nose."

The Titan's eyes flew wide. "Never!"

"Well, it's understandable," I said. "We're in pretty tight quarters here. You don't want all this stuff underfoot, but I just wonder . . . did you check *all* of those mamushka dolls before you threw them out? I mean, open every one of them down to the baby in the center? Some of them have maybe thirty layers, like onions . . . "

Narwickius tore at his hair. "No! No! Not after all these years!" He spun to confront the Vipe. "Did you do it?"

"I only do what you tell me, massster," she said, fear showing in her eyes for the first time. She gave me a very dirty look. "Those things were ordinary, with no magik to ssspeak of."

"Go find out! Wherever you sent those things, go look!"

"As you wisssh," the Vipe said sulkily.

BAMF!

I grinned. My biggest threat had just been defused.

"Keep looking," I advised him. "I mean, if you're sure that it's still here . . . " I leaned casually on the discarded mantelpiece, and surreptitiously shuffled the squid behind it for safekeeping. I presented the Titan with my most innocent expression, all the while casting an illusion over the squid to make it look like one of the hundreds of costumed teddy bears already on the floor. Without the Vipe, he'd miss the glamour of magik upon it.

But I had planted the seeds of doubt. I had to admit I got a kick out of watching Narwickius turn over the thousand and two artifacts scattered everywhere over and over again. He had pulled out almost all his hair.

Living in the Bazaar for years, I had met some mad collectors, but Narwickius took first prize for obsessiveness. Even someone in search of the last lost Magikal Decoder Ring of Marfus Ayoodi would have given up long ago. Night came and went again. I was hungry, my feet hurt and I was dying to go find the necessary, but I sensed the end was coming soon.

Narwickius called all of his men from the floor below. One at a time the Titans felt around in the safes, caches, and niches. One at a time, they palpated pillows, stuffed toys, and articles of clothing. They shook bottles, emptied boxes, and turned socks inside out.

The sun was setting for the second time when Narwickius flopped down on what was left of the old man's mattress.

"Give up?" I asked pleasantly.

"Curse you," he hissed.

"We had an agreement. We had every reason to believe that your old rival hid the item you wanted so badly somewhere in here. You have given this place the most thorough search you possibly can. Are you willing to concede it's somewhere else?"

"You took it," he gritted.

"If I had, would I have spent the last two days helping you look?" I asked.

"No . . . I . . . you might . . . I don't know!" Narwickius shouted. "You're confusing me."

"Let me help you make the decision, then," I said, moving close enough to place a fatherly hand on his shoulder. "Give up."

"No! I mean . . . I never give up!"

"But you have already searched everything here," I said. "What benefit is there in doing it again and again? You were sure you would recognize your prize right away, weren't you?"

"Of course!"

"Well, everyone knows the great Narwickius's powers of discernment," I went on smoothly. "If you haven't seen it, then it's not here, is it?"

"Well, when you put it like that . . . I suppose . . . "

At my back I could feel Guido and Chumley let out huge sighs of relief. The Titans, with armloads of kewpie dolls in their arms, sounded just as relieved.

"Okay, then it's settled," I said in a brisk tone before

Narwickius could change his mind. "You're finished looking. You promised once you were satisfied you couldn't find it, you'd go. Right? You don't have any more time to waste on one little gizmo, not when there's an estate sale in Warfengang starting in about . . . five hours."

The light went on in the Titan's gray eyes. "What? I know several Fen in Warfengang! Is it Olbius? He was on his last legs when I saw him."

"Sure to be," I said, mentally crossing my fingers behind my back. "I don't recall the name . . . "

"All right!" Narwickius said, shaking off my hand. He rose magnificently and drew his hand up to his chest. "I must get to the viewing before all of the good things are taken. We leave this wretched place, never to return. I, Narwickius, state this to be true."

"Good," I said. "Nice doing business with you."

He gave me a haughty look and waved a hand.

BAMF! All of the Titans vanished.

"Nice work, Skeeve," Guido croaked out.

"Which one is it?" Chumley asked, kicking at the debris on the floor.

I reached around the broken handsome mantelpiece and drew out a rainbow-colored teddy bear.

"This is it," I said. "I hope. Let's go see Marmilda and Marmel."

The Imps were asleep, sitting up on a couch with their arms around one another's necks.

"Sweet family concord, what?" Chumley asked.

I nudged them awake with the toe of my shoe. They leaped up.

"This is all your fault," Marmilda exclaimed. Marmel went on guard.

"I didn't make a deal with a Titan!"

"I didn't have a choice!"

"If you had told me you promised our inheritance to someone else, I might have understood."

"If you hadn't been so greedy, it might have been possible to hold a civil conversation with you!"

"Excuse me," I said, waving a hand between them. The Imp siblings paused. "He's gone."

"What?" They both turned to look at me.

"Narwickius gave up," I explained. "It took a while, but it's over. I don't think he's ever coming back."

Marmilda jumped up and hugged us all. "Oh, thank you! You've all been so wonderful I . . . I just didn't know what to do. You just came in on such short notice, took charge, and you were all so calm. I was terrified! I don't know about Marmel . . ."

"I was terrified, too," the Imp admitted.

" . . . But I just absolutely have to say that everything we ever heard about M.Y.T.H., Inc. is true." The siblings beamed at us.

We all fell into an awkward silence. I was starting to get used to them. Guido cleared his throat.

"Uh, thanks, ma'am. We endeavor to give satisfaction."

"Oh, you have!"

"Narwickius's departure fulfills the terms of our

contract," Tananda said. "I hate to be a hero and run, but we have got some other appointments today."

"Oh, of course," Marmilda said. She gave Marmel an embarrassed glance. "Six gold coins was your fee, I think you said?"

"That's what we discussed," Guido said, "but we couldn't have done it without Mister Skeeve, so you'd better give him half of the dough."

"No!" I protested. Tananda gave me a sharp look that told me 'not in front of the clients!' I subsided.

I turned to Marmilda with a smile. "Internal book-keeping. Actually, if you will give it all to Big Crunch, he'll make sure the money gets back to our accountant and is distributed properly."

"Of course!" the Imp female said, counting coins into the enormous purple palm. "Thank you so much. I am going to tell every one of my customers how wonderful you have been."

"Yeah," Guido grunted. He gave me a sideways glance. "Well, we gotta go. Nice hangin' wit' you, boss."

"The same, Guido," I said, putting out a hand. He gripped it.

Tananda gave me an all-encompassing hug. "Don't be a stranger."

"I won't," I said.

"Bye," Big Crunch, a.k.a. Chumley, said laconically. Tananda went through some magikal gyrations and . . .

BAMF!

"Well," I said to the two puzzled Imps standing in front of

me. "Marmel made a side deal with me. Your father's Hoho Jug is a valuable artifact. Not that he didn't leave you plenty of inheritance . . . "

"Most of which is lying on the sidewalk outside," Marmilda pointed out.

" . . . But this is the only thing you two are really fighting over," I concluded. I brandished my rainbow-colored stuffed bear.

"That?" Marmilda asked, with every evidence of distaste.

I hastily undid my illusion, revealing the terrifying smile of the stuffed squid from Dover.

"That?" she repeated.

"That," I said. "If you're the rightful heir to this piece, it should regain its ordinary appearance if you call it."

"That's easy," Marmel said. He held out a hand. "C'mere, Hoho Jug!"

The squid hung there in my hand.

"Then it's mine," Marmilda said, with a pleased smile. "Hoho Jug!"

The squid didn't change for her, either.

"What is this?" Marmel demanded. "Did you do something to it? It can't belong to neither of us! We're Dad's only heirs!"

A slow smile made its way from one of my ears to the other. "It doesn't belong to *either* of you. I will bet my fee that it belongs to *both* of you. Didn't you tell me you were sitting together when he said he wanted you to have it?"

They looked at one another.

"That only makes sense," Marmilda said.

"No, it doesn't," Marmel whined. "I want it for myself! You'll just try and sell it."

"Selling it could help pull us out of debt."

"It's our heritage!"

"Hey, hey, *hey*!" I shouted over the escalating voices. "Look, if you two are going to fight about it, I'll go find Narwickius and tell him I located it after all. He might buy it, or he might tear your heads off and take it, after all he went through trying to find it. You can decide if you want to keep it in the family or not later on, after I go home. All right?"

"Okay," Marmel said, sulkily. "What do you say, sis?"

"Yes."

"Good." I brandished the squid at the pair of Imps. "Talk to it."

"And that was it?" Bunny asked, as I sat back in my chair with my feet on my desk. "That disgusting squid was the Hoho Jug?"

"Yup," I said, feeling pretty pleased with myself. Gleep sidled up and put his head in my lap, looking for a scratch behind his ears. I scrubbed his scales with my fingernails. "When both of them called it, it morphed back into a ewer. Incidentally, it does echo back 'ho-ho' when you holler into it. One question answered, one fee collected. We're in business."

"What about the others?" she asked. I didn't have to ask who she meant.

"What about them?"

"What did they say?"

I shrugged. "It was a little awkward, but it all worked out."

Chapter 10

"Of *course*, that's in my job description."

—Sweeney Todd

My new office was off and running. I didn't expect to be inundated by old friends and former employees, the latter a happy subset of the first category, but Bunny and Tananda must have spread the word that I was starting out slowly, and I would ask for help if I needed it. Many people who had worked for or with M.Y.T.H., Inc. stopped by to offer support, but no one was pushing. Exactly. Yet. I had a feeling that the dam would burst at some point, and I had to work out precisely where I was going with my new business before I started hiring. I didn't want to hurt anyone's feelings, but I needed to have the right answer for myself, first. In a way, I was my own primary and ongoing client, and I had to report that no progress had been made yet on *my* question.

Bunny started talking about advertising me on the Crystal Ether Network through her PDA, or Perfectly Darling Assistant, a little red disk of a gadget that she called Bytina. What about rewriting my card, or taking out ads, hiring a flying dragon to write my name in the sky?

"It's too soon," I insisted. "One success in a row is not an indicator of a viable business."

But I found myself drumming my fingers on my desk, waiting for something to happen.

I was so relieved that the others weren't upset with me that the fact I wasn't doing much business didn't bother me as much as it might have. I had made peace with my friends, and I was happy about that, but it wasn't going to be smooth sailing yet. I still had to figure out how to describe my new profession so it wouldn't lead to so much confusion.

" . . . But they keep asking me, what do you do with an in-between skill? A talent no one knows how to harness?"

"What?"

I startled out of my daydream. The minute girl in the blue dress on the guest chair twisted a handkerchief between her fingers. She gave me a shy smile, which made her small oval face lovely.

"I'm sorry, I know my voice isn't very loud," the girl said. She was a Pixie, a denizen of Pix. "I mean, my parents think I should just train harder, but I don't want to be a flower-fairy. Flowers make me sneeze. Oh, I know there are spells to counteract that, but I don't . . . I don't *like* flowers," she said with a defiant scowl, as if daring me to contradict her. Her little nose turned pink. "I just could never be as good as my friends. My mother is the foremost rose sculptor in all of Pix. I can't equal her, but she wants me to follow in her footsteps. I just want to make my own way. I just don't know how."

"So," I said slowly, feeling as if I was asking myself, "what is it you do?"

She looked happy, as though no one had ever voiced the question before. She fluttered her tiny hands. From between her fingers, a flash of red appeared. A brilliantly colored bird took shape and took wing. It soared up over my head, then angled off, circling the ceiling of my office.

Gleep's head sprang up from his forepaws, and he bounded after it.

"Gleep, no!" I said, jumping up. I lunged for his collar.

Too late. His jaws snapped shut on the bird. He landed, his blue eyes wide. His tongue snaked out, as though tasting the air. I was aghast. I turned to Flinna.

"Gee, I'm sorry about your pet," I said. "Gleep doesn't usually misbehave like that."

Flinna smiled at me. "It's all right. It wasn't real."

"Wasn't real?" I realized I was echoing her. "What was it?"

"It's a kind of fairy illusion," she explained. "I can do hundreds of them, all completely accurate. They feel real, but you can't keep them. Once you touch them they go pop."

"Really?" I asked. So that was why Gleep was casting around and looking confused. "Wow. That is a special talent."

"But useless," Flinna said, hanging her head. "I don't know how to do anything but flower magik and illusionary birds. I can't make a living at either one. What can I do with, well, what I can do?"

"Let's see if I can find someplace for you," I said, rising and extending my hand. "I know a lot of people here in the Bazaar."

———

The Geek stroked his chin. The wily Deveel and I had been on opposite sides in several deals. As far as I could tell, he still owed me for some shady dealing that nearly killed some students of mine.[4]

"I don't know, Skeeve," he said, watching Flinna put varied and colorful waterfowl in a row, each a masterpiece of magikal art. "I mean, don't get me wrong—they're great ducks, but my new show, "Teal or No Teal," is only in the planning stages. It could be months before I could use the girl."

Flinna looked devastated. "Oh," she said.

"Do you know anyone who is hiring?" I asked, feeling just as dismayed but refusing to show it. "She's willing to travel."

"Hmm," he said and resumed chin-stroking. "Well, you could talk to Hyam. He's got a variety show heading for the provinces. The pay's so-so, but you get expenses and meals."

"We'll try him," I said, rising and offering my hand. "You still owe me, but thanks."

"Hey, glad to help, glad to help," the Geek said. "Don't hurry back, huh?" He leaned out and pinched the plumply pretty Deveel at his reception desk on the cheek. "Marlys, send in my next appointment."

We sat in the second row of the huge, echoing theater. Flinna watched openmouthed as act after act mounted the stage and performed. Illusionists, fire-eaters, high-wire walkers,

---

4   A complete account can be found in that irreplaceable volume, *Myth-Gotten Gains*.

prestidigitators, ventriloquists, and almost all of them doing their tricks without benefit of magik. I was impressed.

"Ya gotta be able to do it either way," the green-skinned Sittacommedian at my side informed me. "We travel to all the dimensions, Klah, Perv, Imper, Kobol. If there's no force lines, you still gotta be entertaining. I don't fancy bein' run out of town on a rail. Had it happen enough times." He extended a forearm, and I could see pucker marks in his green skin. I guessed they had been caused by hot tar and feathers being applied.

"Well, I don't know much about show business," I admitted.

"No kiddin'," Hyam said, stubbing his cigar out on the back of the chair ahead of him. He bent forward to yell at the voluptuous female on the stage. "Honey, either shake it or get out of here! I'm a busy man!" He leaned back. "If you knew anything, you wouldn'a gone to the Geek for advice. He don't know nothin'."

"He seems to be successful," I said.

"Smoke and mirrors," Hyam said. "Just don't invest money with him." He turned to Flinna. "Okay, honey, wow me."

Flinna looked delicate and lost in the huge beam of the spotlight. She hesitated, and I gave her an encouraging gesture. She shot me a quick smile, and raised her hands. I crossed my fingers. Success here would validate her faith in me, and I could use the shot of confidence.

The flower fairy started producing her illusions. I heard murmurs from the other acts sitting in the dark behind us that rose to startled exclamations of pleasure as wrens, robins, jays, finches, canaries and juncos flew from her hands. She moved on to bigger species: owls, falcons, gulls and a huge, brown-winged pelican. The air was full of them. She spread her hands farther apart. I was agog as Flinna made a blue heron, a phoenix, three different eagles, six parrots and an ostrich. We had discussed her grand finale. Mentally, I wished her good luck. Hyam gave a puzzled grunt as she moved over to one side of the stage and opened her arms as far as they would go. A gigantic beak appeared between them. She walked backwards through the spotlight toward the other side of the stage, moving her fingers all the time as the enormous roc took shape. Red feathers the size of her body came into being. As soon as it was finished, the illusory bird sat up and let out a squawk that shook the theater. The other performers behind me burst into applause and cheers. Trembling with shyness, Flinna came downstage and clasped her hands together and waited.

I turned to Hyam, who was trembling, too, but with rage. His face had turned an ugly purple. He glared at Flinna.

"For that, the Geek sent you to me?" he bellowed. "That's all you do? *Bird imitations*?" He stood up and leveled a finger toward the exit. "Geddada here!"

"I don't believe it," I said, trying to cheer her up as we trudged out of the theater. "I think he was just jealous. I have never seen anything like that. And did you hear the others? They loved it."

"They don't matter," Flinna said, miserably. The little

female's wings drooped low. "He hated it. I'll never find a place."

"Oh, yes, you will," I said, giving her a pat on the shoulder. "We just haven't made the right connection yet."

I took her back to my office. I left her petting Gleep and went to talk to Bunny.

"I admit that there probably isn't a lot of call for insubstantial bird images," Bunny said, but she flipped Bytina open and set the little PDA to work. "I'll check the Crystal Ether network for want ads."

Thanks to advances in magik, most of them pioneered by the Kobolds, reading crystal balls was no longer reserved for people with their own talent, or even in magikal dimensions. Crystals and related philosophical devices like Bytina seemed to generate their own auras. As a result, a virtual industry had sprung up to provide readers with something to look at when they weren't predicting the future. Theatrically minded wizards put on plays. People of every race with way too much time on their hands made images of themselves or their pets. Naturally, Deveels and Pervects figured out a way of promoting commerce through the ether. Practical as ever, the Kobolds themselves began to solicit lists of needs and wants, gathered across the dimensions, which one could read as clearly as a scroll on one's own tabletop. It was through these want ads that we read now.

"Wouldst thou see the universe as more beautiful? Become a traveling peddler in Avalon goods and render those you encounter more fair."

"Troll seek pretty girl. Marry and have babies."

"Earn five hundred gold coins every week in your spare time! Send a non-refundable twenty coin deposit for information and a free kit to Evondell, the Bazaar, Deva."

" . . . Here we go," I said, pointing to an image in crabbed green handwriting in one corner of the image.

The ad read, "Ecologically-minded game warden to oversee target range on royal estate. Must love animals. Preserve endangered species for the sake of the royal hunt."

I frowned. "Gee, it sounds like they don't know what they want."

"Don't you know this name?" Bunny asked. "Prince Bosheer of Whelmet."

I frowned. It sounded familiar. Yes, Massha had told me about him. She had borrowed Gleep to do a favor for a friend, who had ended up married to Prince Bosheer.[5]

"Yes, I do," I said. "She said he's a good guy."

"Should we answer this ad?"

"Oh, I don't know," Flinna said timidly.

I gave her an encouraging smile.

"Why not? It's worth a try. He can always say no. We'll check with Massha to see what she thinks."

Massha was enthusiastic about the idea of introducing Flinna to Prince Bosheer.

"He'll think it's a hoot," she promised, so we BAMFed over to Whelmet.

---

5   The exciting details appear in "Myth-ter Right," one of the many fine stories in *Myth-Told Tales*.

The Crown Prince and Princess were a big, hearty couple. I liked them immediately. Gloriannamarjolie had thick blond braids bleached lighter by the sun surrounding a sun-browned face in which twinkled very intelligent blue eyes. Her husband, a Whelf named Bosheer, was big, handsome, and friendly, like most of his kind. The throne room, a huge beamed hall, was hung with as many hunting trophies as royal banners. Weapons of every description and some that defied description decorated the walls.

"Massha has told us so much about you," Gloriannamarjolie said, kindly gesturing to us to sit down. I boosted Flinna into a chair made of the foot of some huge bird, and sat down in an armchair made of immense curving tusks.

"I am honored to meet the Great Skeeve," Bosheer boomed at me. "So where did you say you kept game before?"

"I have never been a gamekeeper," I said.

Bosheer frowned. "Massha sent us a note saying you were coming by. Couldn't understand why you wanted the job. I thought you liked wizarding."

"He retired," Glory murmured to him, closing her hand around his wrist. I noticed that she had two thumbs on each hand, one on either side of the palm.

"That's right. I'm launching a new career," I said proudly.

"Ah. So what about the job appeals to you?" Bosheer asked.

"I like to solve problems for people."

"How does being a game warden solve problems?"

Bosheer looked puzzled. I was beginning to realize that Gloriannamarjolie had married him more for his looks and personality than his brains.

"I answer questions," I said. "Flinna here asked me to help her find a job. I think she'd be ideal for your purposes." I indicated the Pixie.

"Her?" Bosheer asked. His voice was making the little girl recoil. "What does she know about hunting?"

"Nothing . . . sir," the Pixie admitted in an almost inaudible tone.

"Really?"

"Well, I like animals."

"I do, too! Especially birds. They make good sport!"

"Bosheer . . . " Glory said warningly. "Not everyone likes to hear about that. Such as me."

"And that is exactly why we're here," I said, moving into the phase Aahz used to call 'closing the deal.' "In your ad you said you wanted someone who could help conserve species. Flinna does really wonderful illusionary birds."

"Illusions? What do I want with illusions? I like shooting real birds."

The wince from his wife told me that Massha's assessment of her former charge and her new mate had been spot on. Having once been the quarry of the Wild Hunt, Gloriamnamarjolie liked the idea of illusionary birds so the real thing wouldn't be targeted unnecessarily.

"We hardly need to eat songbirds, darling," Glory added pointedly. "A wild boarotamus feeds the entire castle for a week."

"But I like shooting at them," Bosheer said. His handsome lip drooped in a pout.

"And you can, all you want," I said. "The same one several times over, if you like, if Flinna comes to work for you. She can manifest any kind of bird you want. I bet she can make them die really dramatically. In all different ways."

"Oh, yes," the Pixie said, her eyes shining.

"Really?" Bosheer brightened. "I say, that would be fun. Can I see?"

Flinna sat up on her chair and put her tiny hands together. From the shelter of her palms, a pointed beak poked out, followed about a foot later by beady black eyes. The head gave rise to a neck, then a body about the size of a melon with long pointed wings on either side. Two very long legs escaped next, until a blue storkron was walking around the room.

"Terrific! Where is my crossbow?"

A Whelf servant ran to the nearest wall and returned with a loaded weapon. The Prince took it from him and sighted down the quarrel at the bird. It squawked and tried to fly away, but Bosheer tugged the trigger. The quarrel smacked into the storkron, which staggered back and forth melodramatically a few times across the room before it collapsed to the floor and vanished. Bosheer was overjoyed.

"Tally ho!" he caroled. "You're hired, young lady!"

"I miss having Massha around," Princess Glory said. "I got used to having magik around the palace. We would love to have you here, Flinna."

Prince Bosheer strode over and picked the Pixie off the

ground. "Marvelous!" he exclaimed. "Infinite numbers of birds to shoot and not endanger the breeding population? That will be just *jolly*. Could start a new trend! We could have really big shooting parties. We both love parties. We'll do it. Thank you, Master Skeeve."

"Just Skeeve," I said, modestly.

"Thanks," Glory whispered to me.

I collected my fee and left Flinna with her new employers. Everyone was happy. I'd found the best possible outcome.

Not a bad start, I thought, wandering out of the castle. Between Flinna and Marmel, I had been successful twice. Two for two. A few gold coins in the kitty. Whistling, I BAMFed out of Whelfdom and back into my own office.

To my surprise, there was someone in the office besides Bunny. The curtain to my private office had been pulled back, and someone was sitting in my desk chair. Someone with green scales and yellow eyes and four-inch pointed teeth.

"Aahz!" I cried.

He scowled at me.

"Where the hell have you been?" he asked.

Chapter 11

"Who needs competition?"

—Ma Bell

As much as I had been looking forward to seeing my old mentor and partner ever since returning to the Bazaar, now that the moment had arrived, I felt strangely uneasy, almost shy.

To my surprise, Aahz seemed to feel almost as awkward as I did. He quickly rose from the chair, offering it to me with a sweep of his hand.

"Sorry," he said. "I just returned and heard you were back. Just dropped by to wish you luck, and Bunny said you were off working yourself, so I thought I'd take a look at your new set-up. Didn't expect to see you so soon."

Like while you were trying out my chair, I thought, then was annoyed at myself for the territoriality of the reaction.

"I didn't think you'd mind," Bunny said, clearly nervous herself.

"No problem," I said, forcing a smile. "Nice of you to stop by, Aahz. It means a lot to me. Really."

"I like what you've done with the place," Aahz said, looking around. "Classy, without being ostentatious."

"Bunny gets the credit for that," I said. "Interior decorating never was my strong suit. Somehow, we never got around to that in my training."

"Too busy running for our lives, eh?" Aahz chuckled. "Those were the days. Do you mind?"

He indicated the pitcher of wine and accompanying goblets we had set out for prospective clients.

"Help yourself. I'd join you, but I've been trying to cut back on the stuff . . . and definitely not during business hours."

"Probably a good policy," Aahz said, pouring a goblet for himself.

"Oh, what the heck," I recanted. "Pour one for me, too. It's not every day my old partner comes to visit."

Policy was well and good, but I didn't want Aahz to think I was avoiding drinking with him. Besides, I *had* just finished an assignment. I lifted the glass and drained it in a toast to my success, and to seeing Aahz again. The wine felt warm going down.

Aahz hesitated slightly, then poured a second glass for me.

"About that visiting thing," he said as he passed me the wine. "Sorry if I haven't been to see you very often. We've been kind of busy lately."

"So I've heard," I said, taking an appreciative sip from the goblet. As with the decorations, Bunny had chosen the wine. I no longer trusted myself to do the liquor shopping. "M.Y.T.H., Inc. is still the hottest ticket at the Bazaar."

"We try," Aahz said with a modest shrug. "It's been tough, though. As you know, we've been a little short handed."

That struck a bit of a nerve, but I decided not to let it bother me.

"That's funny," I said, carefully. "When I first got back

to the Bazaar, I dropped by the old offices to say 'hi,' and they seemed to have everything in hand. If anything, things seemed to be running more smoothly than I ever remember. As a matter of fact, I cut my visit short since it seemed I was more underfoot than anything."

"I heard about that," Aahz said with a grimace. "In fact, it's one of the reasons I stopped by. In hindsight, everyone realizes they gave you a bit of a lame reception. It's just that you caught them flat-footed. I mean, they've stopped by Klah once in a while to see how you were doing, but no one expected to see you back here at the Bazaar. Not permanently, anyway."

"Setting up shop for myself, you mean."

I realized my goblet was empty, which surprised me. Aahz didn't normally pour light. I got up and refilled it. I meant to pour half a glass, but they were small. I hadn't really noticed that before.

"I really didn't mean to throw anyone a curve," I continued. "It's just an idea that Big Julie suggested to me, and I wanted to give it a shot. It wasn't until I saw how awkward the crew was when I stopped by that I realized how it must look. It never occurred to me that I was potentially setting up in competition to M.Y.T.H., Inc.'s operation. That was never my intention."

"Yeah. Well, I don't think you have to worry about that anymore," Aahz said with a smirk. "I've set them straight on that score. There's no way you're competition to us."

Something inside me went a little dark at that last comment. I took a sip of wine to give myself a moment before responding.

"How did you convince them of that?" I asked. "Just out of curiosity."

"Well, first of all, I pointed out that you'd never deliberately do anything to hurt us," Aahz said. I nodded agreement. "Then again, there's the difference in the scope of our operations. I mean, you may be the great Skeeve, but you're still only one person . . . two and a half if you count Bunny."

"Thank you, Aahz," Bunny said, dimpling and giving him a mock curtsey.

"Oh, I don't know," I said, refilling my goblet. "We've been doing all right so far. We've only been in business for a little while, but we've already handled a couple clients' problems for them."

"Good for you," Aahz said, lifting his goblet in a small toast.

"And you're right. We've been careful not to step on M.Y.T.H., Inc.'s toes." I smiled. "We've even managed to send a little business their way. Nothing I couldn't handle, you know, but I'm keeping to the terms of my new operation."

"Oh you have, have you?" Aahz said, setting his goblet down with a click on the chair arm. "Sent us some jobs you weren't interested in, is that it? Too easy for you? Or taking pity on the folks you left behind?"

"Hey, Aahz," Bunny said, stepping forward. "It's no big thing, really."

"I wouldn't say that," Aahz said, staring at me. "Even while he's trying to get his own new business launched, the Great Skeeve is careful to make things as easy as he can for his old crew. No, Bunny. I'd say that *is* a big thing."

"I figured it's the least I can so," I said, staring back at him. "After all, they're my oldest and best friends . . . even when they don't act like it."

"Skeeve . . . " Bunny said, but Aahz rolled right over her.

"Well, maybe they're a little unsure about how to act," he said, "after their 'best friend' walked out on the business and left them to twist in the wind."

"At least I told them up front what I was doing and why," I snarled. "I seem to remember *someone* who walked out on everyone without a word and went back home to Perv. I had to hold things together then!"

Aahz tensed and opened his mouth to speak, then hesitated.

"You're right, Skeeve," he said finally. "I'm in no position to be critical. I will say this much, though: you can forget about walking on eggshells around us. I don't think you would be much competition for us, even if you tried. Especially not at your current level of powers."

"Says the one with no powers at all," I shot back.

The words hung in the air.

"So, this isn't really about the team at all," Aahz said softly, even dangerously. "You're still trying to protect your old partner. Well, I'll tell you something, *kid*, powers or not, I can still perform as well or better than anyone else . . . including you! *Outperform* them, even."

"And exactly how are you measuring performance?" I said through gritted teeth.

"How we have always measured it," he said with a fierce smile. "Who can earn the most?"

"That sounds like a challenge," I said.

"Does it?" Aahz said, innocently. "All right. Have it your way. It's a challenge. The one who takes in the most money will take over the leadership of M.Y.T.H., Inc. The others will go along with whatever I commit them to. What do you say?"

"All right," I said, clapping down my own goblet. A few drops splashed. I thought I had drunk all of the contents, but it was half-full. "Starting tomorrow. The first two clients that come in. You take one, and I'll take the other. We'll toss a coin to see who get the first and who gets the second. Then we'll see who 'performs' the best. I'll show you I belong back in M.Y.T.H., Inc."

"Sounds like a plan," Aahz growled.

"You got that, Bunny?" I asked. "The first two clients tomorrow. Winner take all."

"I got it," she said emotionlessly.

"I'll see you tomorrow," Aahz said, and swept out.

"I really don't believe that," I said, looking after him.

"Frankly, neither do I," Bunny said.

Something in her voice caught my attention.

"C'mon, Bunny," I said. "Did you hear what he said to me?"

"Sure," she said. There was a pitying expression on her face. "He said that he's missed you and wishes you well, to a point where he's gone to bat for you with the old team."

I blinked.

"When did he say that?" I asked.

"Right after you told him how much you've missed him and still need his praise and approval."

I shook my head.

"Now, I know I didn't say that."

She looked at me.

"No. You didn't," she said and walked out.

Chapter 12

——

"I've always believed in 'winner take all.'"

—Genghis Khan

The first client to walk in the door. I sat at my desk, drumming my fingertips. I was still kind of smarting from the confrontation, but more determined than I could ever remember to succeed. So much was at stake: my reputation, my friendship—especially my pride. Gleep lay on the floor with his chin on my lap. He rolled his big blue eyes up toward me. I scratched his ears with my fingertips.

"What if the client doesn't have the kind of problem that can be solved with money?" I asked Bunny, who stood holding up the door frame with her hip. She wrinkled her upturned nose at me.

"Really, Skeeve, how many people would that cover? Most problems have something to do with money in the long run. I'll be fair. If it really is something nonfinancial, I'll wave them off for now. Otherwise, you take what I give you. The same goes for Aahz."

"We'll see to it that he sticks to the terms, what?" Chumley said. He and Nunzio had moved a couple of chairs from the waiting room into my office to keep me company. "Little sister is sitting with Aahz to ensure his compliance. Should be an interesting competition, eh?"

Interesting? I shrugged.

"What about some three-handed Demon Pinochle to pass the time?" Nunzio asked in his high voice.

"Thanks, but I couldn't concentrate," I said.

"Oh, don't fret, Skeeve," Chumley said. "We're all rooting for you, you know."

I brightened. "You want me to win?"

After Aahz had left, I spent a lot of time trying to reconstruct our conversation. It was a muddle. I should have known better than to drink more than one glass of wine—but it had been so easy to fall back into bad habits, like going along with whatever Aahz wanted. I had been very nervous about what the others thought about the contest.

When Aahz showed up at our tent flap this morning, most of my old friends had been with him. They'd agreed who would stay with each of us and offer help or just observe. I realized too late that they all had plenty riding on the outcome of our competition, but was relieved that they didn't seem to mind that the challenge had been offered.

Chumley shook a finger at me.

"I say, I'm not committing to a victor in this contest. You and Aahz made the terms: who wins, wins. My friendship is still yours. I do not mind either way as long as the contest is fairly run and fairly won. If you succeed, I know what to expect after years as your partner. I would not cavil at a return to those days—with some exceptions, of course."

"Of course," I echoed.

"If Aahz wins, then there may be some changes because he has a different way of doing business, but I don't think it is incompatible with our previous customs."

"Maybe not." I sighed. "I guess I never really admitted to myself that I wanted to be in charge again when I came back. I suppose that's because I didn't know where else I would fit in the organization."

"Don't sell yourself short, boss," Nunzio squeaked. Gleep moved his chin from my lap to Nunzio's and made a hopeful noise. The Mob enforcer had a way of scratching the dragon's ears that made him purr like a cat. "You'd do fine. You always called us partners. I mean, then you should have no trouble no matter what happens."

"Yeah," I said. "I guess so."

That pretty much summed up my mental geography lesson. I had to figure out where I really fit, whether I won this bet or not, and if I really meant it when I called everyone my partner.

I heard a murmur from the front room, then Bunny raised her voice.

"Of course, Princess Hermalaya. I'll show you in to Mr. Skeeve's office."

A princess! If that wasn't a big-ticket case, I didn't know what was. I shot to my feet. Chumley followed suit somewhat more slowly for the sake of the furniture and the ceiling, which was a trifle low for someone of his stature.

"Okay, boss," Nunzio said, standing up and straightening his knife-sharp lapels, "it's showtime!"

Bunny held open the carpet, and an elegant creature sashayed into the room. She had long white fur from her muzzle to the black tip of her bushy tail. She unwrapped a silken stole from her slender shoulders and presented me with a long, slim hand.

"Hi, there," she said. "The kindly lady in the office told me you might be able to help?"

"That's what we do here," I said, bowing gallantly over her hand. "May I introduce myself? I'm Skeeve. These are my associates, Nunzio and Big Crunch."

"Well, I'm charmed," the lovely lady said. "I'll just return the favor? I'm Hermalaya, princess of Foxe-Swampburg in the dimension of Reynardo—or I was?"

I raised my eyebrows. "Welcome. Will you sit down and tell us all about it?"

"Well," Hermalaya said breathlessly, sinking into the client chair. "I shoulda known that something was gonna happen after Mama and Daddy died. I'm the firstborn in my family, so of course they put me on the throne. We're the oldest family in Foxe-Swampburg, the first Swamp Foxes to put down roots there? I'm proud of my heritage, and I love my people. One thing Daddy always told me was to trust the folks who know what they're doing? So I did. We got a real smart prime minister and a bunch of other people who ran things for Daddy? I just left everything in their hands. My subjects came to me when they had troubles. I passed them along to the prime minister? 'Cause I don't have a whole lot of experience yet? I learned other things suitable for a princess, of course. I'm a good listener. I'm a pretty darned good cook. I mean, sooner or later I gotta think about ensuring the succession, so I want to get married and have kits? But in the meantime, I'm trying to catch on to what's going on? Except I just didn't have a chance?"

"Why not?" I asked.

Hermalaya acquired an indignant pout.

"Well, because that darned prime minister just up and usurped me last week!"

I frowned. "He threw you off the throne? Why?"

The Swamp Fox princess shook her head in bemusement. "Well, I'm sure I don't know. We had us some hard times in Foxe-Swampburg, that's for sure. We had these nasty bugs? They were just everywhere, and we couldn't get rid of them. They bored holes through everything? I mean, my subjects were just going broke trying to fix things. The cisterns all sprang leaks, and people were running out of clean water? So I told the chancellor of the exchequer to open up the Treasury? I mean, we all woulda been bored full of holes, too, if it wasn't for the old folks protecting us."

"I know what you mean," I said, as a Humbee buzzed over our heads like a swooping vulture. Gleep made a leap for it, and settled down to chew noisily. Hermalaya stared in amazement at the invasion and capture. I cleared my throat. "Uh, please go on."

"Well, not much to tell, except I tried to help my people, because that's what I'm supposed to do? Mommy and Daddy always instilled in us the deepest sense of responsibility toward those who depend upon us."

"Most admirable," Chumley said, then lowered his heavy

brow as Hermalaya turned to stare at him. "Big Crunch mean, 'good foxy!' "

I frowned. "So what do you need from us? We're not an army."

"Well, what do you think?" Hermalaya asked. "My people need me. They can't just have an old prime minister as their leader? You can see what kind of chaos that would lead to. I mean, how can he make unpopular decisions if there's no one for them to love when he's being mean? He's got no one to explain to the people in a friendly way that that's the way it's got to be. Of course," she added reflectively, "I mean unpopular decisions that don't involve bouncin' his lawful monarch out the door? Mister Skeeve, I'd be just as grateful as possible if you would help me get my throne back!"

"Well, ma'am," I said. You know our reputation, or you wouldn't have come to M.Y.T.H., Inc. We'd love to help you, but our assistance doesn't come cheap. Uh, it's awkward, but can you handle our fees?"

Hermalaya looked crestfallen. "Well, that's the trouble, you know. I just don't have any money. I have heard of you all, and one of the things that people told me? Sometimes you come in and help for the sake of helping?"

I winced. Just when I needed to find a way to score a lot of coins from a client, our reputation for occasional altruism came out. But, wait—Bunny promised that she would not send me a client with whom it would be impossible to win the contest I had going with Aahz. If I trusted anyone in the world, it had to be her. For the life of me, at that moment I couldn't see how I could turn this one around.

I sighed, and put my chin on my palm. "Tell me some more. Maybe we can figure something out. Why did it happen?"

"Well," Hermalaya said, "that ol' prime minister—his name's Matfany, by the way—he's been pretty good at explaining things to me most of the time. But when he found out I had the chancellor of the exchequer hand out a lot of our money to those poor people who lost everything to the bugs, he just lost his mind!"

"Literally?" Nunzio asked with interest.

"Not exactly right out of his head," Hermalaya admitted. "But it was a pretty darned mean thing to do. He marched into my rooms one day, and he didn't even look at me. Normally he looks at me. A lot. But that day, he just couldn't. He said that he had just talked to the chancellor. The treasury was empty, and it was all my fault. He said I didn't have a right to hand out the money. That by just giving it out to anybody I was endangering the kingdom? Being broke leaves Foxe-Swampburg vulnerable to anybody who wants to invade it? Or have our creditors come in and claim just every little thing we have. That'd make us—what did he call it?—a client state instead of a free principality? I had gone against everything that my daddy and his ancestors had ever done to keep us from being taken over by enemies or revenuers. Matfany said he wasn't going to let Foxe-Swampburg fall like that? He said that he didn't have a choice? He was gonna have to toss me out of the kingdom for the good of everyone. Now, I thought that I was acting for the good of everyone. I've been their princess all my life, and I have never done a single thing against them, I swear."

"I'm sure you didn't," I said.

"It was just so hurtful, all the things he said. He accused me of sitting around all day eating Cake! Now, look at me," she said, displaying her svelte figure with indignant pride. "Do I look like I do nothing but eat Cake?"

"Cake?" I asked. "What kind of cake?"

"Not cake, Cake."

Even I could hear the capital C in Cake. I guessed it was a local delicacy. "And then what?" I asked.

"Oh, yes, and then he condemned me to death," Hermalaya added.

"He did *what*?" I jumped out of my seat.

Hermalaya waved a hand. "Oh, yes, and he said he didn't have a choice about that, either? For the good of the kingdom I had to go into exile? If I could just return freely any time I felt like it, then anything he tried to do to bring Foxe-Swampburg back into prosperity could just be undone. So I and anyone who was associated with me back in my very own homeland was subject to a death sentence. He sent all of my pages and my ladies-in-waiting home to their mamas. He didn't give me more than an hour to get my bags packed? Then he had a whole troop of guards escort me over the border? They weren't any help at all. I've never seen such discourtesy. I had to hike all the way to the next town before I could get a ride to the archduke who lives next door. He's a nice fellow. He had his royal wizard transport me here. He said you folks were the best at solving problems. So, here I am, all alone in this world."

I pounded my fist into my palm. "Well, we're going to help you."

Hermalaya fluttered her long eyelashes at me. "I'd be so grateful?"

"Seems to me we have three problems," Nunzio said, ticking them off on his fingers. "One: you've got a usurper who took over and has at least some popular support, because royalty's generally carried forward by inertia. It has to take something drastic before the people want to throw them out, so some of 'em aren't gonna want her back. Second: you've got the money angle. Foxe-Swampburg is in the hole. Putting Princess Hermalaya back isn't gonna solve that. You're just changing a finance guy for a figurehead, one who by her own admission has no talent for fundraising. The prime minister is going to be in a better position to pay our fee than she is. The kingdom might need him more than they need her."

"True," I groaned. "Third?"

"Third is lack of interest from anyone to step in and help. Foxe-Swampburg's just a backwater. To be honest, boss, deposed royalty is a dime a silver coin. We've had plenty of tin-pot kings come knocking on the door looking for help. What she needs are powerful allies to lean on Matfany to bring her back. I think the kingdom's creditors would be the best prospects, but I wouldn't sneeze at influential monarchs who have an army at hand, but what's their motivation? You can't get people to listen without a more interesting story of some kind. Something that sets them apart from all the other hereditary office-holders whose constituencies tossed them out. You need an angle that sets her apart."

An angle. I eyed Hermalaya. She was all graceful curves and big sad eyes. Nunzio was right. I'd had my share of former monarchs, oligarchs, and despots come to my new office who wanted me to put them back where they belonged. I had been grateful to say that that wasn't what I did. Nor had I sent them to M.Y.T.H., Inc. By the same token, I would probably have sent Hermalaya away if Bunny had not assigned her to me.

"Tell me about the Cake you're supposed to have been eating," I asked, desperate to change tack. "How is that different from the fluffy stuff with frosting?"

"You're a Klahd," she said, but it wasn't with the usual scorn. "You don't know anything about the Way of Cake. It's a holy ceremony in Reynardo, with many centuries of history behind it. I have been a practitioner since I was a little kit. My mommy had me initiated. Why, I've been serving Cake since I could only handle Cupcakes. The Way has made my life so much better than it would have been. I find peace and fulfillment in the ceremony."

"Really?" I asked. I had the beginning of an idea. If I knew something about the culture, I could formulate a way to help her. "May I . . . experience the Way of Cake?

"If you have any reason to think it will help me to regain my throne," Hermalaya said. She sounded doubtful.

"What do you need, your highness?" Nunzio asked. "We can get almost anything right here in the Bazaar."

"Why, thank you," she said, favoring him with a delightful smile that made me wish I had been the recipient instead. "I'll make you a list. Has anyone got a little old piece of parchment?"

Chapter 13

"Swamp Foxes pride ourselves on existing with just any kind of resources we can turn up, sir," Matfany said. He was a decent-looking specimen. He had the long nose of every Swamp Fox I'd ever run into, which, counting him, was two. His black coat was wavy, except for the pelt on his chest and the tuft between his tall, triangular ears, which were tightly curled, and he had a pair of wire-rimmed glasses perched on his long nose. He had the sardonic look of a stand-up comedian, but the eyes were sincere and very serious. That kind of expression always made me nervous. It usually meant a fanatic of some kind.

"We do with what we've got, or we do without. That is the way of the Swamp Fox, from time immemorial. But we haven't got, sir. That's our problem. I am having to recreate a government out of a sea of neglect, is what I am doing. To put a sadly blunt comment upon it, out of my usually polite way of putting things, you understand? But we are broke as a shattered vase, sir."

I stood up from my chair. "Too bad. We don't take charity cases very often, pal, and we're full up on our quota for the month." Matfany stood up, a bemused look on his face.

"Sir, I don't understand."

"I have to explain 'no' to you?"

"*Aahz!*" Tananda fired off a warning shot. "What did we just finish discussing?"

I knew. I sat back and signaled for him to do the same. I had agreed to take the next case to come through the door and make more money than Skeeve could, no matter what it was. I sighed and poured myself a half-bucket of single malt, drained it, and refilled it.

"All right, tell me all about it."

The sincere eyes fixed on mine, and he hooked a thumb beneath the suspender holding up his trousers, took a deep breath, and began.

"Well, sir, you may have visited Foxe-Swampburg in the past. The thing is that it looks like a pretty nice place, and it is, only I have to tell you that underneath what is a very handsome and appealing exterior are problems that would just curl your hair, sir, if you had hair, that was. No offense intended to people with scales. It's just an expression. Now, I have had the enormous responsibility . . . "

"Of course I could do better than the kid!" I had reasoned, once Tananda and I were alone in my private office. "I just didn't want him to feel bad."

"Not bad after you just tore strips out of him for walking out on us?" Tananda had countered.

"And how did *you* feel when he walked out?" I asked.

"Pretty awful. But I made up with him. You haven't."

I had to admit she was right. The one time he came to find me I'd been pretty glad to see him, but he had a ridiculous job on tap for which wanted my help. I turned him down flat because *he* should have turned it down. And the fact was he came out of it without a bent copper coin. Oh, maybe they gave him the D-hopper which was currently in my right-hand pants pocket, but so what? A Klahd was only asking for trouble getting involved with ten Pervect females.[6] But Skeeve never listened to what I said. And he never came back to find me again.

Hell with it.

I had plenty of other friends, Tananda included. But to have Skeeve waltzing back into the Bazaar after an absence of months and expecting to take over M.Y.T.H., Inc. again like he had never left didn't take into account anyone's past feelings or present positions. We'd all moved on.

Including me.

Except we hadn't. Not really. That's what hurt. We trusted him, and he walked off without looking back. The whole M.Y.T.H., Inc. enterprise was possible mostly because of his . . . I don't want to say leadership; call it glue. He was the glue. Once he was gone we hung together in a kind of loose fashion, mostly because of inertia. We liked each other, but, well, maybe I understated it when I said we liked him. I never knew a Klahd who could engender such loyalty, and all without seeming to know what he was doing.

He said he had his reasons. Maybe our expectations were too high where he was concerned. Not mine. I knew what Klahds were capable of. Skeeve just exceeded those capabilities most of the time. He should have been born a Pervect. Together, we could have taken over dimensions.

---

6   See the whole account in *Myth-Alliances*, available from your more reputable purveyors of fiction.

Nah. The upkeep'd kill you.

" . . . And what do you think, after all that? She says the treasury's not up to her expectations, and what am *I* gonna do about that? What am *I* gonna do? I'm supposed to keep filling it up so she can just empty it again? With what? Our people's got what they've got, sir. And, as I said, what they've got at the moment is nothing. We've got creditors breathing down our necks, and we don't like it. We like to keep ourselves to ourselves, sir. I collect taxes to pay the bills, but when there's no income, there's no taxes, and when there's no taxes, there's no revenue for nothing else."

I made a face. Back to business. I snapped on my asset-counting hat.

"Can you increase exports of anything?" I asked, mentally going down the checklist.

"We don't really export anything, sir," said Matfany.

I raised an eyebrow.

"So how do you make money?"

"I thought you said you'd heard of Foxe-Swampburg? Hospitality, sir. Ours is an economy based upon visitors, especially repeat visitors. We used to get plenty of guests from off-dimension looking for a little getaway, if you understand me?"

I leered at him. "Sure do."

Matfany looked sternly at me. "Sir, we're not Vaygus. I mean, you want to go and empty your pockets while having your eardrums and your eyeballs pounded, that's where you go. If you want a quiet week drowning bait or stumping up hills, lying on a beach, and maybe sucking down some local brew, we're the stop for you. Food's pretty good. People are nice. You can just relax yourself to pieces."

"I've been there," Tananda put in, with a mindblowing smile at Matfany. "It's pretty."

"Don Bruce went fishin' there one time," Guido put in. "We rubbed out about fifty-eight trout. The Don offered Foxe-Swampburg his official seal of approval. We also got some business accomplished during the trip." He gave us a significant look with one eyebrow raised. I could make an educated guess what kind of business had drawn the Mob Boss to an out-of-the-way locale like Foxe-Swampburg. Matfany looked baffled.

I cleared my throat.

"Not my usual kind of vacation, but it has its place. So, what happened to derail Foxe-Swampburg's success story?"

"Pinchflies," he said. "Some empty-headed fool imported a few breeding pairs because their wings make pretty jewelry. Thought they could get an accessories trade going. Could've told you that'd come to no good. If anyone had asked the government, and by that I mean me, for an import license, I would have said no way. Man didn't think things through, you can just tell."

"And what happened?" I asked.

"Well, sir, no one can relax when flies the size of your finger are biting you every other second, now can they? Some species don't care, but most of 'em canceled their reservations in a hurry. We lost about seven years' bookings all in one week. Those darned flies also ate about every leaf and needle on every plant, and burrowed holes in nearly everything except metal. I've got clothes that're so well ventilated I don't need a fan in the summertime, sir."

"Don't draw me a picture," I growled. "And what about the pinchflies? Is that what you need us to do?"

"Oh, we got rid of them pinchflies, sir," Matfany said. "Soon's we figured out that was the big problem, we found a wizard from Shelf who came in and took care of them, no problem. Big fee, though. Took about everything that was left in the treasury. And when that was gone, that girl was still honking on about what was she going to use for clothes-money? The treasury's about empty. That was when I realized that girl was only going to cause more problems than she was gonna solve. I mean, she was the princess and all, but she just isn't the administrator that her daddy was. I tried to get her interested in the day-to-day workings. I'm not sure if she wasn't interested or she didn't have, well, you'll excuse me, the mental furniture to understand what needed to be done. I kinda had to take over the government completely then, because unless I did we weren't gonna have one any more. Now, I like that girl plenty, but she's a nuisance. I didn't think she was that empty-headed, but you tell me! Clothes-money! We've just got to put things back together, or Foxe-Swampburg's pretty well doomed. I've got creditors barking at me day and night. They want satisfaction, and for the sake of the principality, I've got to find it for them."

I exchanged glances with Tananda. This case sounded like a financial dead end, but I had taken the bet.

"You must have some kind of asset we can raise money on," I said. "Something that you might not even see. Let's go and take a look."

Chapter 14

———

"Let them eat cake."

—Sara Lee

"Candles?" I said, comparing my list with the contents of the enormous pile of cloth sacks on the floor.

"Check," said Nunzio.

"Doilies?"

"Check."

"Noisemakers?"

"Check."

I put the list down with a sigh and looked at my client. "That's everything, your highness."

"Well, good," Hermalaya said, pleased. "Now, all of you scoot on out of here while I get ready. I'll let you know when you can come back in. Shoo, shoo!"

That had been our third foray into the Bazaar to shop for the Cake ceremony. Hermalaya wouldn't settle for second best of anything. The elaborate service took a lot of time to prepare. She took over our kitchen, which she immediately declared ill-equipped, and sent me running for supplies to correct the shortcomings. Fortunately, we were not far from Polkey's in the Bazaar, the biggest purveyor of cooking items and implements for six dimensions in any direction. I came back with a load of tiny boxes of sugar novelties, enough pans to cook for a small standing army, and a pile of oddities that looked like miniature torture devices. The princess took them with a shake of her head and disappeared into the kitchen. Nunzio, Chumley, and I shrugged.

"Let's get some lunch, what?" Chumley asked. "We can discuss possibilities over a comestible or two."

"I could murder a strawberry shake," Nunzio said and grinned at my shocked expression. "Not literally, boss. More like threaten it with a straw. What about you, Miss Bunny? Would you like to join us for noonday sustenance?"

Bunny straightened up with surprise. She had been leaning over listening to the other room, where Aahz was meeting with his mystery prospect. I strained to hear, but I couldn't distinguish anything beyond a couple of baritone murmurs. I'd take an educated guess and say his client was a man, but since leaving Klah I had run into several genders and a range of voices as wide as the spectrum of sound. Eavesdropping left me none the wiser.

"What's going on in there, guys?" she asked, aiming a thumb at the kitchen.

"The client's going to do a Reynardan Cake ceremony," I said.

"Really?" Bunny perked up. "Do you mind if I sit in, too?"

"Not at all," I said. "I hope to learn something from it. Maybe give me some ideas."

Bunny nodded. "As long as you don't expect any input

from me, all right? We all agreed we'd help both of you, but one of us has to remain neutral, and I got selected."

"No problem," I said. "Lunch?"

"I'd better stay here in case Aahz has any problems," she said. "Can you bring me back a box of grilled lizard parts with honey-mustard sauce?"

When we returned, my office had been transformed. Ceremonial balloons had been blown up and arranged in bunches upon the walls. An artful scattering of glitter lay across the floor. The furniture had been rearranged so the desk was shoved against the wall underneath a huge, woven tapestry depicting a very happy dragon that didn't have a tail. All the chairs sat in a circle with their backs to one another. And on a low table covered with a brilliantly colored cloth sat the most gorgeous cake I had ever seen. It had to be at least three layers, but it was such a perfect cylinder that I couldn't guess where one left off and the next one began. The violet icing smelled delicious, its perfume combining vanilla, honey, citrus, and a dozen other delightful fragrances I couldn't guess even though I had bought the extracts to make it. Hermalaya had covered it with scrolls and ridges of frosting that, while elaborate, were not in the least overpowering or tacky. She had taken the colored-sugar decorations that we had brought her and changed them so they looked handmade instead of cranked out of a cylinder. The Cake was just . . . perfect.

Beside this marvel of pastry sat a pile of plates that I had picked up at Polney's, and an elaborate silver cake server that must have belonged to Hermalaya.

"Yum!" I went to pick up the server, ready to cut a piece of cake for myself. Hermalaya appeared from our kitchen and met me with a sharp paw to the chest. She had on a full apron and a cloth tied over her ears. Both were handsomely embroidered. She fended me away from the table with a sweet, indulgent expression that nevertheless brooked no nonsense. I backed off.

"Do not touch it. Now, the ceremony begins." She smiled, showing all her sharp teeth, and put a hand on our shoulders. "Welcome," she said.

"Thank you," I said.

"Thank you for inviting us," Bunny said, with a correcting eye on me.

Hermalaya looked surprised. "You know something of the Way of Cake?"

"I read about it in a magazine. There's a similar custom on Klah."

Hermalaya nodded. "Then lead this one in the responses, will you? I will continue."

I was mystified, but I followed Bunny's lead. The vixen princess led us to the small table. She knelt beside it. The billowing apron settled around her slender knees like a ball gown. She gestured to us to join her on the floor. Bunny assumed the correct stance with grace. I found it less easy to fold myself up. The hard floor made me want to squirm, but Hermalaya didn't move a hair in spite of the discomfort, so I could hardly complain.

"Now, as you are the guest of honor, Mister Skeeve, I will ask you how old you are?"

I told her, and she counted out small, colored candles from a small box. The number she placed on top of the Cake did not correspond in any way with the number I had said. She flicked her thumb and forepad together, and a tiny flame appeared between them. She touched the fire to each of the pristine white wicks. Closing her eyes, her hands shielding the flames, she sang a keening song that traveled up and down the scales. Bunny nodded in time with the music. When the princess finished, she opened her eyes and looked at me.

"Blow out the candles," Bunny whispered.

I obeyed, then had to scuttle backwards, as Hermalaya seized the beautiful Cake server from the side of the table. She wielded it like an expert swordswoman might a longer blade.

Flick, flick! Four slender, perfect pieces of Cake had been dealt onto the small plates as slickly as cards. Inside the purple icing the layers were chocolate. My favorite. Hermalaya took another implement, this one with a rounded blade. She picked up a round earthenware pot that had been sitting just out of sight under the edge of the table. It looked humble and ordinary, like a jam jar, but from it she scooped the most luscious-looking ice cream I had ever seen. Somehow with a knife she managed to make perfect hemispheres, one of which she deposited upon the first sloping wedge of Cake. Bunny held her breath, but it didn't slide at all. That seemed to be important. A dollop of whipped cream followed. Then, the princess rubbed her fingers lightly together over the Cake, and a glorious rain of sprinkles descended, seeming to make the otherwise ordinary confection glow. Even I gasped.

Bowing her head, Hermalaya handed me the plate with both hands. I accepted it, and sat wondering how I ate it, while Bunny was given her Cake. Hermalaya then handed us beautifully wrought silver forks, and offered us crystal goblets brimming with white. I followed Bunny's lead, mashing the ice cream and whipped cream into the cake and cutting bites with the side of the fork.

Once we had all been served, Hermalaya wiped the server on an embroidered cloth, returned it to the table, and sat patiently with her paws folded on her knees.

"How's this different from a Klahdish birthday party?" I asked Bunny in a whisper.

"Shh!" my assistant said. "A Cake Master studies for years to get everything exactly right."

I shrugged and ate my cake . . . er, Cake. I had to admit it was the best I had ever eaten, in any dimension. It tasted at least three times as good as it had smelled, and the ice cream reminded me of my own childhood. The glass was full of pure white, sweet, ice-cold milk that made the Cake taste even better.

After we ate, Hermalaya rose gracefully to her feet and held out a hand to me. I rose, feeling awkward and out of place. She led me to a line drawn on the floor in glitter and handed me a long piece of green cloth cut into a long, thin triangle with a long pin attached to the top. She took the cloth from around her ears and made to tie it over my eyes.

"Oh, no," I said. "No, thanks."

"Skeeve!" Bunny admonished me. "It's part of the ceremony!"

"All right," I said. I turned to my hostess. "Sorry."

"It's all right," she assured me in her soft voice. "You're just not an initiate?"

I allowed myself to be spun in a circle five or six times, then I staggered forward, feeling my way toward the embroidered wall hanging. My hand touched cloth, and I plunged the pin into it. I heard snickers come from behind me. I snatched off the blindfold and looked at the wall. The dragon now had a tail on its head. Gleep, crouched underneath my desk out of the way, gave me a sorrowful look.

Each of my friends took their turn in solemn silence. Bunny, with a little more foreknowledge of the culture than the rest of us, did better at all the rituals. I admired her skill so much that I didn't feel bad when Bunny got to the only empty chair ahead of me to win that game. Hermalaya oversaw everything with an austere eye, guiding us with a little magik here and there.

When it was all through, Hermalaya gave me a small box she had wrapped in colored paper. It contained a pinch of the sprinkles that had been on the cake. I felt as if I had been given a treasure chest.

"Thank you," I said.

"Thank you for coming," Hermalaya said, formally, urging us out into Bunny's foyer.

When we came back in again, Hermalaya sat exhausted on the lone chair. Bunny and I started to clear up. There was little in the way of leftovers, but Chumley crammed the remaining half of the Cake in his mouth with every evidence of Trollish enjoyment, and I only wished I had thought of getting to it first. Nunzio carefully took down the dragon tapestry, now well pinned, and I gathered up all the glitter and spilled sprinkles with a handful of magik. The swamp vixen didn't protest at all until I reached for the silver server. She swooped down on that and her ice-cream knife.

"No one touches the tools of a Cake Master," she said apologetically. She cleaned them off and placed them in a small fitted case covered with mother-of-pearl. "I'm sorry to seem discourteous."

"Not at all," I said. "I'm the one ignorant of your customs."

"That was beautiful," Bunny said. "I'm so *moved*. I never saw the real thing."

"Few have," Hermalaya said with a shrug of her narrow shoulders. "There are pale approximations all through the dimensions—you alluded to one yourself. It's a shame, because I think it's so uplifting?"

The mental candle that had been trying to light itself over my head finally burst out in a flare of brilliant flame.

"Would you consider introducing more people to the joys of Cake?" I asked.

"Why, what do you mean?" Hermalaya asked. Bunny raised her eyebrows warily, but let me explain.

"I was really impressed by how skilled you are at the ceremony," I said. "Like Nunzio said, you need to get important people on your side. I think that if you offered to host a high-end experience for honored guests, guests with a lot of influence and money, we might be able to get you home again and refill the treasury. You should be unique with this kind of approach."

"That's true," Nunzio said. "Big gestures are lost on important people. I like this because it's a subtle approach."

"But I couldn't ask people for money," Hermalaya said, looking distressed. "That would be *vulgar*."

I frowned. "You're right. We don't want to lower the tone of the ceremony by making it about money instead."

"Ask offering?" Chumley asked. It was difficult for him to express complex concepts in his persona as Big Crunch, but he was good at conveying what he wanted in a monosyllabic fashion.

"That might do," I said. "It'll be my job to look for the best prospects. I will approach them and tell them your story. If they're sympathetic, I will line up their support on your behalf for a move against Matfany. At worst, I'll go for a loan or a grant of some kind. In exchange, they get to experience the Cake ceremony. I'll . . . have them wrap up the gold like a present. If they enjoy themselves, they can give it to you."

"Well, that's better," Hermalaya agreed.

"I am sure once they've been through the rituals with you, it will change their lives," Bunny said. "They'd have to be dead not to be wowed."

"I'll have to write down some of the details of your experiences to tell them," I added.

"Oh, you don't have to do that," the princess said. "I've got it all written down already? I've kept a diary all of my life—ever since I could write, that is. The last volume is right here in my bag?"

She opened up the dainty clutch and drew out a huge gem-studded tome bound in pure white leather tooled in gold. "It's all here," she said. "Every single one of my thoughts and experiences over that terrible time."

"Read me some of it," I said, reaching out for a line of force and a sheet of parchment. The Bazaar was filled with those streams of magikal power. I gathered a good handful from the curly green line that ran beneath the tent and formed it into an earlike shell. I aimed the opening toward Hermalaya.

"What's that, boss?" Nunzio asked, curiously.

"It's a new spell I worked out recently. It takes down everything a client says on this paper. Later I can invoke it and see exactly what they said and exactly how they said it. I don't want to forget details I might need to solve their questions. You can read it again and again as long as the parchment stays intact."

"Clever," growled Chumley.

"Go ahead," I told the princess. She turned to a page in the middle and began.

Hermalaya had been born in the wrong place. She should have been a dramatist. Her observations of her people were keen, filled with interesting little details. She spared nothing on her tale of the invasion of the insects and how her subjects' lives were changed. I felt my heart go out to her when she told how she listened to them pleading for help, and I wanted to dash out and bring down Matfany when she narrated the events leading up to her expulsion from Foxe-Swampburg.

"Perfect," I said, letting the roll of parchment snap shut.

"But what'll you do with it?" Hermalaya asked.

"Bring it with me and show it to prospective donors," I said. "*The Princess's Diary* is so evocative, it's got to convert people to your cause. It'd be too undignified for you to go out and ask for support, so I will make all the connections and conduct the interviews. I'll offer the ones who promise sympathy—and money—a chance to experience your Cake ceremony. If they bite, they get to meet the princess and have Cake made and served by her own dainty royal hands. I hope our twofold approach will even get some of them to lean on Matfany to give you back your throne. It can't miss."

"Good," Chumley said, grinning. "Work wonders."

"Yeah, boss," Nunzio said. "Nobody could fail to be moved by the poignance of her situation."

"Gleep!" exclaimed my dragon.

"That's really pretty clever," Bunny said, tilting her head.

"If I do have to say so myself," I agreed. "Do you think Aahz will do anything like this?"

Bunny gave me a flat look. "I'm not going to tell you. You know better than that."

I shrugged. "It was worth a try."

Chapter 15

BAMF!

"Welcome to Foxe-Swampburg, gentlemen," Matfany said.

We appeared in the middle of the so-called busiest street in Foxe-Swampburg, which would have been a safety issue almost anywhere else I have ever visited on purpose. I could count on the fingers of one hand the number of dimensions I had visited that were prettier than Foxe-Swampburg. The sky was a rich lapis blue. Flowers as big as my head bloomed in insane neon colors on bright green bushes. Birds twittered in the trees, and the blue-green sea washed up and down a perfect, broad, sandy beach. However, the place was deserted. Practically nobody was out browsing the windows of the shops, or riding the shaggy-pelted donkeys munching feed from nosebags, or rowing in any of the numerous small boats moored along the rocky shore. The second we appeared, a dozen pedal cabs converged upon us from every direction. The drivers shouted and rang handbells to get our attention.

"Hey, madam! Come on! Most comfortable cab in the city!" a red-pelted Swamp Fox shouted. "Cleanest seats!"

"Hey, he spit polishes his cushions," a gray-pelted Fox countered. "It ain't his fault. He just don't know any better, pretty lady. Ride in my cab. I know every beauty spot in the entire city!"

The rest of them yelled sales pitches, full of exaggerations and downright lies. They were like every cabbie I had ever seen, from downtown Perv all the way to the smallest backwater dimension.

Guido got between us and the most aggressive ones, sticking his hand in his breast pocket meaningfully to suggest there would be a penalty for hassling us. I always appreciated his gift for the subtle, but this time it was too subtle. The cabbies were too desperate for a fare to give up in the face of potential deadly retaliation. I turned and snarled at them, showing my Pervect four-inch teeth. The drivers recoiled, but kept coming. They didn't back off until they noticed Matfany. The prime minister gave each a look that was half stern teacher, half policeman. As a deterrent, it worked better than pepper spray. I thought I could hear a couple of the cabbies whimper as they withdrew to their stands. They were more afraid of him than they were of me. That impressed me. He must be a lot tougher than he came across.

"We'll walk, if you don't mind, ma'am," he said, bowing to Tananda. "Truth to tell, the budget won't run to a limousine, and you can see our fair city a whole lot better without rushing around."

"No problem," Tananda said, attaching herself to his right arm. "I've done a little street-walking in my time." Matfany looked shocked. Tananda gave him an outrageous wink. I grinned.

"It ain't the worst place I've ever seen," I said. "But I'm an urbanite myself. This is a trifle away from the bright lights and big city which is my preferred habitat."

"A lot of people say that the first day," Matfany said. "By the end of the week we got most of them asking if they can extend their reservation. Well, we did, before the pinchbugs. This is our main street."

He waved a hand. The once handsome lake shore was lined with rental domiciles of every size, everything from the Gigantico Hotel chain out of Imper down to Pappy Johnstone's Pink Roof Inn. I guessed the latter must be a local establishment. A statue in the parking lot of a Swamp Fox in a straw hat waving its hand seemed to be the company trademark.

Every one of these places had two things in common: their walls were full of little holes as if they had been attacked by a horde of insane carpenters with half-inch drill bits, and every establishment was empty. Not one tourist. The bare trees waved forlornly over swimming pools and lawn chairs, all vacant. Vines grew up and sometimes into abandoned buildings and stands up and down the street.

"Come on," I said. "Let's see what else we can find."

Matfany cleared his throat. "I am afraid, sir, that you are bound to be disappointed."

A few hours later, I had to conclude that Matfany hadn't lied. Apart from food preparation and hand workshops that turned out souvenirs, there was almost no infrastructure in the main city of Foxe-Swampburg. My feet were killing me, and I saw the presidency of M.Y.T.H., Inc. fluttering away like an escaping bird.

"Okay," I said. "What about manufacturing?"

"Don't do much of that," Matfany said. "I've tried to introduce the concept of factories—honest truth is, we don't have a lot of dry, level land to spare for big facilities. We buy off-dimension most times. Tourist money is usually rolling in. Our credit was pretty good on Deva and Flibber and a bunch of other places."

"Natural resources?" I was grasping at straws.

"Not enough to export, sir. Half the time the lamps run on fish oil, and the other half on magik."

"What about location?"

I already knew the answer to that one; it had taken us four jumps to get here. That meant Foxe-Swampburg was useless as a strategic location for refueling, armaments, manufacturing, or just about anything except tourism. Which had dried up.

A pony-drawn cart trotted toward us, the driver drowsing over his reins. He looked up hopefully at the sight of three obvious strangers and steered toward us. Then he noticed Matfany. His eyes went wide with fear and alarm. He turned his wagon all the way around and whipped up the pony. It trotted away with the driver looking back over his shoulder.

"You have more than money problems, pal," I said. "You have a PR problem. Your own people are scared of you."

"I know it," Matfany said with a sigh. "I thought they would be grateful they are now in the hands of someone who would save them from ruin, but they're not."

"Why do you think it is?"

"Well, I had to reintroduce some pretty fierce

punishments," he said. "We had a lot of theft and assault when things started to get tight around here. I didn't want anyone to get the idea that they could just push me around. But only for those felons who deserve it. I don't go around handing out sentences on innocent people. But I don't hold back where it's merited."

"Punishments like what?" I asked.

Matfany sounded hesitant. "Well, imprisonment. Whippings. Death."

I eyed him. "Sounds like a house party on Perv."

"Beg your pardon, sir?"

"I get the picture. Got any ideas?" I asked Tananda and Guido.

"This is your show," Tananda reminded me, not without sympathy. "What can you work with?"

I kicked a stone. It went bounding across the deserted road and knocked into the pillar of a gigantic, white-enameled structure that stuck way out into the very picturesque waterfront. It was one of three similar handsome oceanside structures. Each had what looked like an oversized gazebo at the end, and along the way there were steps leading down to small jetties at water-level and several food booths, all shuttered as if it was the middle of winter instead of a sweltering summer.

"Nice pier," I said.

"Yeah," Matfany said.

"What do you call it?" I asked.

"Oh, well, we call it The Pier." He pointed right, then left. "That one's The Other Pier, and that one's That There Pier."

I raised one scaly eyebrow. "Isn't that a little confusing? Why don't you call it Smith's Pier, or something a little more tourist friendly?"

"Smith didn't build it," Matfany said. "Why would we name it after him when it's not his?"

"There are a lot of places that people didn't build but are still named after them," I said, when the idea struck me like a ton of Imper garlic sausage. "In fact, some of them are willing to put good money into having their name attached to just the right thing. It gives prestige to the donor. Some of them even consider it an honor."

"Yeah, but these are not colleges or libraries," Guido pointed out.

"We got a few of those, too," Matfany pointed out.

"There, you see," I said, warming to my topic. "We could sell naming rights to parts of Foxe-Swampburg. Get the right people involved, and there could be a bundle of money in it." I started to see gold coins piling up before my eyes. I saw a stack of signed contracts. I saw envy on Skeeve's face as I put my feet up on the president's desk. My desk.

"Like who?" Tananda asked, quite reasonably, interrupting my thoughts. I frowned as the bubble popped, but I dragged myself back to the present.

"Well, Deveels, for one. Deveel enterprises like to have their names on things. Once this place gears up again for the tourist season, it's a natural match. What percentage of your souvenirs come from the Bazaar?" I asked Matfany.

"Most of it, except the handmade stuff," he said. "Barco Willie, he makes these trivets out of shells . . . ?"

I brushed Barco Willie aside. "And Imps—they'll do anything to make up for being born Imps. Here they can invest in something tasteful, like a forest or a library."

"Well, I dunno . . . " Matfany said.

"It'll work," I said. "I can't think of any way it could go wrong. What do you say? Do you have to consult anyone before you can rename the local points of interest?"

"Well, there's the Old Folks, but they don't have a say, exactly. It's just common courtesy . . . "

"Good, then it's up to you." I gave Matfany my biggest grin and had the satisfaction of watching him back up nervously. "Trust me. It'll earn you brownie points. When things start to improve for the Swamp Foxes, they'll embrace the prime minister who had their best interests in mind."

Chapter 16

"Put it out on the World Wide Web!"

—Shelob

"Bobbie Jo! Great to see you, kid!" Massha grabbed my arm and dragged me through the enormous double doors. The woman with pale blue fur sitting on the modest but obviously expensive divan looked as if she had a wide fur skirt spread around her feet. "It's been too long."

"Massha, honey!" The woman rose up high, then her body settled in between three sets of arched legs as if it was in a hammock. That big skirt was a set of long legs like those of a spider. I have never been big on spiders. She made toward us with two arms outstretched.

I cringed. "I've never seen a spider that big," I whispered to my former apprentice.

"Hush!" Massha whispered back. "Don't mention spiders. They're Octaroobles. Now, smile!"

The spi—okay, Octarooble—came to air-kiss my former apprentice on each cheek. I felt a little awkward as Massha shoved me forward like a six-year-old ordered to play violin for the guests. The woman, with owl-like eyes and a crest of stiff hairs on the top of her head, regarded me with curiosity. I smiled weakly. Her jaws moved sideways instead of up and down, reminding me far too much of a spider's palps.

"Bobbie Jo, this is Skeeve the Magnificent. Skeeve, this is Robelinda Jocasta, Chief of the Clans of Octaroo."

"A pleasure," I said. She extended a blue-furred hand. I bowed over it, trying to remember I'd met uglier and more fearsome creatures. This was for a good cause, I reminded myself. I was here for Hermalaya. "I am honored to meet someone Massha holds in such esteem." I placed my hand on top of my head, fingers up, as Massha had instructed me.

Chief Robelinda Jocasta sent me flying with a backwards knock of that same hand. "He's a pretty talker, Massha! No wonder you like him."

You'd think I would have no trouble getting in to meet people of high rank or lofty offices, but I had been out of touch for long enough that many of my connections had gone cold. In contrast, Massha, who now held my old job of Court Magician to Queen Hemlock of Possiltum, had plenty of numbers in her little black book and was graciously willing to share them with me.

I had had my share of humility lessons since the end of my self-imposed retirement, and this one was no less grating on what was left of my ego. Massha, specialist in gadget-magik, gaudy dresser, woman of size—make that extreme size—brassy, bold, and awkward, had grown into a difficult job with aplomb and grace. She had expanded her duties to fit her presence, whereas I had spent a lot of time ducking to keep from having to do too much work and putting myself in harm's way. Massha reveled in every detail. She and the queen had become good friends. Massha was brash and prickly, but Hemlock, not exactly a shrinking violet herself, liked her style. She had sent Massha out on a lot of missions of good will on behalf of the kingdom, so when I asked about prospects for me to approach about Hermalaya, Massha had a long list. Possiltum was not one of them. When I asked Hemlock, out of courtesy, she snorted. "Are you crazy?" she had asked me. "I've got my own problems." She had always been notoriously unsympathetic. However, she had allowed me to take Massha with me, or rather her to take me, to meet her friends and drum up support.

"Thanks for meeting with us," I said.

"No problem, kid! And call me Bobbie Jo. After all the stuff Massha's told me about you, I couldn't wait to meet you. What can I do for you?"

"I'm here on behalf of Princess Hermalaya of Foxe-Swampburg," I said.

"Fine old family. I knew her dad, Tinian. We met at a monarchs' conference in Vaygus." Bobbie Jo returned to sit on the divan. The legs settled around her again, making her look only about ten percent as scary. "Could that man cut a rug? Wow! And his lady, Indicia, was a sweetie, too. She and I used to exchange recipes. I was devastated when they died." She patted the seat beside her and beckoned to me. Nervously, I sat down. "So, what's been going on with her?"

If there had ever been a cue, that was it. I unfurled my parchment of Princess's Diary and let the spell play out.

Chief Robelinda sat up as the image of the Swamp Vixen appeared. She listened carefully to the soft voice as Hermalaya read from her diary. When she got to the part about the aftermath of the pinchbug invasion, I saw tears in Bobbie Jo's big, round eyes. By the section in which Matfany threw her out and placed a death sentence on her, the Chief of all the Clans of Octaroo openly sobbed into a silk handkerchief. The image faded, and I rolled the scroll up again.

"Ay!" she exclaimed, blowing her nose on the now sodden silk. "That poor thing! But what can I do for her? I'm not going to invade a neighbor dimension. I could provoke a lot of our hereditary enemies into a preemptive strike. This whole dimension is a powder keg. I can't put Octaroo into an untenable position even for the sake of an old friend's daughter."

"To be honest, I'm looking for several kinds of help. Hermalaya needs to find some leverage to get Matfany out. If we can destabilize him, maybe we can get the people to depose him. Do they owe you any money?"

Bobbie Jo waved at a page, a young Octarooble about ten years old. He came running on eight pale-gray legs and beamed up at her with his sideways mouth. "Go get Hirame, baby." The little one sprinted out of the room like a whole track team.

In a little while, a thin, wizened male with pinched cheeks and a pinched expression entered and bowed deeply over the armload of ledgers held in two of his furry arms. I took a moment to wonder why all government bureaucrats looked alike, no matter what their species. And sounded alike.

"The principality known as Foxe-Swampburg," Hirame intoned, peering at me as if I was an unruly student, "has indeed a long-running item upon our rolls of accounts receivable. An outstanding invoice of fifty gold coins. Running for over three years now. They had been keeping up the interest, but not in some . . . time. Are you here to make payment?"

"No, I'm not," I said cheerfully. "In fact, we're hoping that you'll call in the debt."

"And may I ask why?"

"Oh, we're hoping to overthrow the government."

"I . . . see," Hirame said, but his wrinkled brow said he didn't.

"Why, that's brilliant," Bobbie Jo said, grinning at me. "And reinstate the credit if you manage to get Tinian's daughter back in?"

"Uh, well, if we do get her back on the throne," I said, "we were hoping you might just forgive the debt entirely. The kingdom's in no shape to pay it or the interest. *And,*" I took a deep breath. This was the sticky part, "perhaps you could see your way clear to a loan or a grant of capital, to tide them over until Foxe-Swampburg recovers? She needs to rebuild the treasury, and there's no real prospect of income until we get the tourists coming back. It might be an uphill battle, after the pinchbugs."

"A further loan?" Hirame asked, his round eyes regarding me coldly.

"Something for nothing?" Bobbie Jo asked, her crest rising. "That's just not like Tinian or anyone in his family." The knees started to go up again.

Hastily, I waved away the suggestion. "No, of course we're not asking for an outright gift. Have you ever heard of the

Reynardan Cake ceremony?" I launched into my sales pitch. I could tell that Bobbie Jo was more than interested. Even the disapproving Hiram was agog, though he tried not to show he was listening.

"Of course, you may honor anyone else you like by admitting them to the Cake ceremony," I said, with a nod toward Hirame. The disapproving stare became just a little less glassy. There's nothing that can pry open a wallet, I mused, like the chance to experience something exclusive and mysterious. "The princess would consider it a pleasure to share an intimate part of her culture out of gratitude to those who helped her regain her title."

"Nicely put, Skeeve," Bobbie Jo said with a grin. "It's been a good year. I think we can squeeze out a little something, can't we, Hirame?"

"I do believe it is possible, Chief," Hirame said, straightening up with his crest erect on his head.

"Great!" I exclaimed. "So, may I tell Hermalaya that you would like to have her here soon?"

"Tomorrow wouldn't be soon enough," Bobbie Jo said. "Massha, you've got to stay and see it with me."

"I'd love to," Massha said.

"So, it's settled."

"There's just one condition." I stared at her in alarm. She pointed. "I want a copy of that scroll. I haven't cried that much in ages. That's better than most of the novels in my library."

"I'll ask the princess, but I'm sure it won't be a problem." I said jubilantly. That also gave me an amazing idea for publicizing the princess's situation.

"Great! In that case, we look forward to welcoming her."

She stood up, and I understood that my audience was at an end. No matter. I couldn't wait to get back and tell Hermalaya the good news.

Chapter 17

——

"I promise you'll get the royal treatment."

—Robespierre

The Cake ceremony in Octaroo went off without a single hitch. Hermalaya received free rein over the castle kitchens, and turned out a cake that outdid her previous efforts. The royal purple icing decorations seemed to defy gravity. Bobbie Jo and her fellow clan chiefs were dazzled by the rituals as well as the food.

As a courtesy to her fellow monarch, I was invited to participate in the event. I did better than the locals in Pin-the-tail-on-the-Dragon, but I was far outclassed in Musical Chairs. The seats had to be placed several yards apart so that the Octaroobles weren't able to cover several at once in anticipation of the music ceasing, and I just couldn't keep up. Not that I minded. I was getting used to the spiderlike characteristics of my hosts, but I was just as happy to get out of their way. In an effort to win, they threw hanks of web at one another when their hostess wasn't looking or stretched out those long legs to trip each other. Hermalaya, as always, held herself with extreme dignity.

Neither of us knew for certain whether Bobbie Jo would add a little to the beleaguered Foxe-Swampburg treasury, but we hoped for the best. At my suggestion, Hirame brought in a small box tied with ribbons to be presented to Hermalaya at the conclusion of the ceremony. It would contain whatever gold coins—or none at all—that she chose to donate to Hermalaya. I was aware my contest with Aahz relied on what the nobles contributed, but I just couldn't bring myself to sully the moment with the mention of money. I was just as sure that wouldn't stop Aahz. I had to be me, though. I wouldn't do just what he would do to win.

When they emerged from the ceremonial chamber clutching their tiny boxes filled with magik glitter dust, everybody was in a great mood. They couldn't stop talking about the experience. When Hermalaya completed the last, private elements of ceremony and came out into the main hall, they gave her a round of hoots, the local equivalent of applause.

"Why, thank you all," Hermalaya said, beaming at them. She looked weary but happy.

"I believe that even the Homdom of Benos has never been transported like that," one of the chiefs exclaimed. "Marvelous!"

"I bet he'd love it," Bobbie Jo said. "Here, let me give you a letter of introduction to him." She sent a page scuttling away for paper and ink.

"If I may make a suggestion," Hiram said, raising one furry finger. He had a streak of purple icing on his cheek. One taste of Hermalaya's layer cake had made him a firm ally of all things Reynardan. "Sebellum Oatis might be interested in such an experience."

"Who's he?" Massha asked.

"Well, he's not a monarch or world leader, though we've hosted him here a bunch of times," Bobbie Jo said. "He's stinking rich. He's in agriculture. He raises choconuts."

"That Oatis?" I asked. I had eaten choconuts. They were an absolutely addictive confection for sale in most civilized dimensions. "I didn't realize they were grown. I thought they were manufactured."

"No, sir, purely natural," Hiram said. "My cousin is his chief financial officer. Oatis has over four million acres on Pocalis. If you are looking for . . . monetary emoluments . . . he is someone you should approach."

"The Tanager family would love to meet you," a male chief boomed out.

"Lord Fetzaf—he's the chancellor of the exchequer of Simelian," an elderly chief suggested. "The Satnos of Simelian's gone completely senile. Fetzaf's been running the place for years. He *loves* cake."

Everybody else chimed in with suggestions. Hermalaya, Massha, Nunzio and I left with a pile of introductions.

"That was great!" I said. "How do you feel?"

"Tired but happy," Hermalaya said. "I feel as if I created some harmony in that place."

"Well, you scored something for the balance sheet," I said happily. I offered her the little box, which jingled appealingly. "Do you want to open it?"

The little box contained more than a hundred gold coins.

"Oh!" Hermalaya said, her large brown eyes welling with tears. "She's so generous! I could just cry?"

"Don't do that, honey," Massha said, offering a bright orange handkerchief to the girl. "This is just the beginning."

We arrived back in my office in high spirits. I bowed the ladies out into the anteroom, where Bunny was seated at the desk, filing her nails. Nunzio, who was trying to get Gleep to sit up for a fried lizard leg, with Guido stood up as we entered.

"Guess how we did?" I asked.

"Shhh!" Bunny hissed. She tilted her head toward the other room. I heard voices inside. I raised an eyebrow. Bunny shook her head.

I shrugged and passed over the box of money, along with other gifts the Octarooble chiefs had heaped on us when we left. Bunny looked them over carefully. She opened our ledger to a new page with my name on it and dipped a pen in indelible ink, one that neither Aahz nor I could alter with any spell available anywhere in the Bazaar. She wrote the number '117.' I felt a swell of pride. Guido took charge of the money, tucking the small box into the breast of his well-cut pinstriped coat.

"Nice job, boss," he said. He looked guilty for a moment. "I mean, Skeeve."

"And there'll be more where that came from, too. . . . Uh, has Aahz chalked up anything yet?" I asked in a quiet voice, trying not to sound eager.

Bunny frowned at me. "I don't think you need to know that. I'll tell you when it's all over."

"You are coming home tonight to stay with me in Possiltum," Massha told Hermalaya. "Skeeve and I both think it's better if you go somewhere with hot and cold running guards. Queen Hemlock won't mind putting up one noblewoman, particularly one without an entourage who makes pastry."

"Why, thank you kindly, but I'd rather be handy to Mister Skeeve?" Hermalaya said with an appealing look at me that made my chest swell. "I am relying on him as my protector?"

"We really don't have any lodgings good enough for a princess, even one in exile," I said.

"That doesn't really matter," Hermalaya said, raising hopeful eyes to me. "I'd just feel better if I . . . "

"Let's go see a couple of people here in the Bazaar to start," Aahz was saying as he pushed the door aside to let Tananda and his client step through. I was surprised to see that Aahz's subject was another Swamp Fox, this time a male with curly black fur and glasses perched on his long nose.

My surprise was nothing compared with his. He halted in the doorway and gawked openly, then dipped into a deep and courtly bow.

"Why, princess," the Fox said. "I must say I never expected to see you here."

Hermalaya sprang to her feet. She balled up her fists.

"Well, I didn't think it mattered to you any more where I was after you showed me my own border, you terrible man!"

"Border?" I asked. "Is this . . . your prime minster? The usurper?"

The black-haired Swamp Fox was aghast. "Terrible? I don't mean to be terrible!"

"Well, that's just what you *are*," Hermalaya declared, putting her long nose in the air. "How else do you want me to think of you?"

"Well, never as anything but respectful, ma'am. You've got to understand where I've been coming from . . . "

"Princess?" Aahz asked, his eyes narrowing. "No kidding! That's the little spendthrift herself?"

Hermalaya's eyes went wide with shock. "Spendthrift! Is that what you think of me! How dare you!" She recoiled with dignity. "How can you expect me to remain here for one more moment with that man! You're right, Miss Massha, I don't feel safe here any longer. Take me away! This minute, if you don't mind!"

"But, I . . . " Matfany began.

Massha gave us all a reproachful look and blinked out with Hermalaya in tow. Aahz pushed the black-haired Swamp Fox toward the door.

"Wait for me outside," he said.

Tananda grabbed Matfany's arm and towed him away. Aahz turned around, the orange veins throbbing in his eyes. Both of us rounded on Bunny.

"You knew," I accused her. "You knew they knew each other. You knew you were setting us against each other head to head!"

Bunny tossed her hair. "Of course I knew. I thought it was kind of poetic, having the two of you handle opposing sides of a sticky issue. *She* came in ahead of *him* by not more than a couple of minutes. She told me her problem, and I sent her in to see you, Skeeve. I had no idea the Swamp Fox behind her was her former prime minister, but once he told me what he was there for, I couldn't resist handing him over to you, Aahz. What are the odds that the two of them would arrive here on the same day at the same time, looking for help with the same problem? It's fate!" She blinked her long lashes at us.

"I don't believe in fate," Aahz snarled.

"Neither do I," I growled.

"Tough," Bunny said, folding her arms over her ample chest. "You both want to be president of M.Y.T.H., Inc. The agreement was that you have to take the assignment and do your best with it. You don't have forever."

"But his client's a black-hearted throne-stealer!" I exclaimed, pointing at Aahz.

His scaly hand pointed directly at me. "His is a brainless party girl who fiddled while Foxe-Swampburg fell apart!"

Bunny shook her head. "You know nothing's ever just black and white. Now, get going!"

With a glare at me, Aahz stomped out. Guido gave us an apologetic shrug and followed him. Bunny looked up at me.

"You, too."

"But this is my office!" I protested.

She shook her head. "This is neutral territory, and it's going to stay that way until all this is over. Nunzio, go with him." She pointed toward the door.

"Yes, boss," he said. "I mean, Miss Bunny." The Mob

enforcer took my arm. "C'mon. You know there's no arguing with her when she's being organized. We'll go see what Chumley's scared up."

With a groan, I went.

Chapter 18

___

"Hey, Aahz, good to see you." The Geek, a snappily dressed Deveel, started to stick out a hand, then thought better of it when he glanced at Tananda and Guido, unobtrusively holding up the wall. He sat down in his upholstered office chair and waved us to a couple of seats. "I don't owe you any money that I know of."

"Not to me," I agreed, after a quick shuffle through my memory. No sense in letting a debt slide if there was one, but there wasn't. The walk through the Bazaar had cleared my head. I'd deal with the concept of Skeeve working directly against me later. "I'm here with a business proposition for you. You'll thank me for thinking of you first."

The Deveel shook his head.

"It means you think I'm the biggest sucker you could think of, you mean," the Geek said.

"Now, how can you say that?" I asked, mellowing my voice out to the smoothest consistency I could.

"I know how Perverts think."

"That's Per-vect!" I corrected him with a snarl, then moderated my tone. You could catch more dragons with meat than a punch in the snout.

"Who's your friend?" the Geek asked.

"I'd like you to meet Matfany." I ushered the Swamp Fox forward to shake hands. "Prime minister of Foxe-

Swampburg. Nice guy. Runs everything. This is the Geek."

"You run everything, huh?" The Geek asked, with a grin.

Matfany gave him an uneasy look up and down. "I guess so," he said. "Right glad to meet you, sir. It's an honor." He gave a courtly bow. The guy seemed to have an inexhaustible supply.

The Geek eyed him suspiciously. "Is this a put-on?"

"They have manners in Foxe-Swampburg," I said. "Not like here. Listen, I didn't bring this guy here so you can insult him. He's got something for you you've never had before—brand recognition."

"You want to apply hot iron to my posterior, or someone else's? Not interested, Aahz."

"Not that kind of brand," I said. "The Geek brand. I want to set it up so that when people see your name, they automatically think of your style, your business savvy."

The Geek looked even more suspicious.

"And what is going to make people think I'm savvy and stylish?"

"When they see your name associated with a great place like Foxe-Swampburg."

"Foxe-Swampburg? Wasn't that the dimension that got hit with that insect plague about two years ago? I heard the place is a desert—culturally speaking."

I should have known he would have heard all about it. Well, when you can't hide something, minimize it. I shrugged.

"Just a hiatus. They like to think of it as a chance to clear out the old public relations material and come up with something new. That's why they want to align themselves with notable businesspeople such as you."

The Geek sighed and rested his chin against his fist. "I presume this is gonna cost me money. So, what do I get for it?"

"Naming rights," I said, proudly. "Landmarks with your name on them. Anyone who sees them will think of you as a Deveel of importance. You get your choice of any prominent location in Foxe-Swampburg: mountains, rivers, beaches, buildings. Anything you want—first come, first served, of course. That's why I brought Matfany here before anywhere else. We are offering you, and nobody but you, first crack."

"Naming rights?" The Geek looked thoughtful. "I dunno, Aahz."

"What's the problem? You get to be famous."

"I've already got all the recognition I can handle. But in a tourist spot, which as you admit hasn't been much of a tourist spot lately? I don't want to be associated with insects and bad food."

Matfany glowered at him. "Sir, our food is the top-rated by Dragon Rotay and the Witchelin Guide. We've got five four-star restaurants and four five-star restaurants."

"Yeah yeah," the Geek said, waving a hand. "Until some rival restauranteur sticks a cockroach in the canapés. And what about those bugs?"

I snorted. "The bug problem's under control. It's still a

beauty spot. Everyone knows it's spawned a million cheap oil paintings. And you could have your name all over it. Think of it. Geek's Peak. Geek Lake! Geekville! It's only limited by the level of your imagination—and your investment." I whipped out the portfolio from my inside pocket and unrolled the map, full color with magikal three-dimensional images, that we had bought from one of the waterfront shops. In spite of himself, the Geek looked intrigued. "The longest white sand beach in any civilized dimension. Crystal blue waters. Even the fish are friendly. Picturesque cliffs. Rivers. Canyons. And all a wagon's ride from the center of town which, as my pal just reminded you, has a bunch of five-star restaurants. What do you think? Sounds like the perfect investment for a guy on his way to the top."

I could tell the Geek was tempted, but no Deveel ever parted with a coin without examining every side of a negotiation.

"I dunno. It's not just me, Aahz. My capital's tied up at the moment. I've got partners. What about them?"

"Well, what about them?" I asked. "How much do you want to cut them in for? There's a mountain range just south of town. It's visible over the whole resort area. You could name the biggest peak after yourself and let them have the lower hills. And if you want to handle the transaction," I added, lowering my voice confidentially, "you could take a piece of the action as a carrying fee. I don't have to know anything about that. We don't have to be worried about anything except the bottom line."

The Geek's eyes brightened. I never knew a Deveel who

didn't like the idea of a piece of the action or adding himself as a middle man where there was a fee involved.

"Er, how many people can I bring in as partners on that?" he asked.

I didn't ask him how many partners he had. I knew that was an elastic number. Instead, I turned to Matfany. "How many peaks in that range?"

"Visible from town? Well, sixteen you can really see, only some of 'em's not real impressive . . . "

"There you go, Geek," I said, slapping Matfany on the back to make him stop talking. "Fifteen, not counting yours. Naming rights for the whole massif will run six hundred and forty gold coins. Renewable every year."

The Geek nearly coughed out his own teeth. "How much? You want me to starve? You have to be crazy! Six hundred and forty gold coins for a nontangible asset?"

"It's for immortality, Geek," I said.

"You're out of your mind, Aahz! A hundred is too much."

"We're talking about a whole mountain range!"

"For that much money I ought to get mineral rights, too!"

"Well, you don't," I snarled. "You get to name it. That's it."

"How much are you putting into this project?"

"My precious time," I snarled, "which you're beginning to waste." I grabbed Matfany and hauled him to his feet. "I can see you're not ready for the big time. Look, I'll just go over and talk to Gribaldi Enterprises. Grib knows a good thing, and he deals in souvenirs. It'll mean more to him than it does to you."

"Wait a minute, Aahz!" the Geek shouted. I could see that the image of a mountain with his name on it was still dancing before his eyes, not to mention lining up fifteen investors to buy the rights to the other peaks whose fees would no doubt cover the Geek's mountain and then some. "How long's this offer good for?"

"Until I get out the door," I said, towing the protesting Swamp Fox with me.

"Now, Mr. Aahz, just what's all the hurry?" Matfany asked.

"What's the hurry is that we've got a lot of stops to make. I thought the Geek would be happy to get first chance at naming rights. I'm not wrong that often, but, boy, did I blow it this time."

"No, you didn't, Aahz," the Geek said, lurching forward and grabbing my arm. "C'mon. Don't go away mad. We're old friends. Come and sit down." He gave me an ingratiating smile. "I mean, it sounds like a great idea, but where's the return on my investment?"

My mood changed in one second from fury to graciousness. I dragged the Swamp Fox back to his chair and dropped him in it.

"I'm glad you asked me that," I said. "Foxe-Swampburg's gonna come roaring back to life. You can get in on the ground floor. You've got business interests in the Bazaar. Maybe you've got some merchandise that the tourists can't resist. I'm sure Matfany here can fix you up with office space, vendors, whatever you need to make capital out of your investment. I don't have to tell you how. Telling you how to make money out of something like this is like teaching my grandmother to suck eggs."

The compliment wasn't lost on the Geek, but he was still hesitating. I leaned up and stretched out a hand for the doorknob.

"All right!" he blurted. "You have a deal."

I turned and extended the hand to him before he could change his mind.

"Pleasure doing business with you," I said. "Let's sign some papers. Half payable in advance."

Matfany loped alongside, looking worried, as I strode toward my next best prospect. Having the map marked up with the Geek's signature was the best spur I could put in front of another buyer. If they saw the good stuff disappearing, they would want in. I jingled the bag of coins in my pocket. The sound added to my good mood.

"Three hundred and twenty gold coins," Guido said. "That is a very nice hunk of change for the kitty."

"Pretty good," I smirked. The Geek had negotiated me down to half, but that was to be expected. "I bet I'm winning. Skeeve couldn't possibly earn that much that fast. He just isn't the operator I am."

"Don't count him out too fast, tiger," Tananda said, catching up with me and winding her arm into mine. "He's pretty creative."

"Yeah, but would he come up with a way to make

something out of nothing like we just did?" I asked. "And we're about to milk that nothing for a lot more money. All for the sake of Foxe-Swampburg, of course," I added, for the sake of the client.

Matfany's troubled expression finally broke out in words.

"Mister Aahz, I'm not sure I like this too much. The people in Foxe-Swampburg—they've always gotten by just calling things by their names."

"You don't have to use 'em," I pointed out. "No matter what you heard me say back there, naming rights doesn't convey any other rights to the sponsors. They get to put their names on a map. Whoop-de-doo. You don't hear about people trying to get ownership of the points they name in the Interdimensional Star Registry, do you?

"Never heard of that," Matfany said. "Kinda the same thing, is it?"

"You bet. Some bright thinker—I bet he was a Pervect—promised some sucker that if he gave him a couple of gold pieces, that he could pick out any star on the map except the fancy ones and name it whatever he wanted. By the last count there were about a million named for girlfriends, a hundred thousand named after pets and ten million named for NASCAR."

"What's NASCAR?" Matfany asked.

"Never mind," I said. "Look, the point is that we've earned three hundred and twenty gold coins, half of it in hand. How much does the kingdom need to get out of debt?"

"About twenty times that much to start with," Matfany

said, gloomily. "Mr. Aahz, there just isn't enough to sell to get that kind of capital."

"Leave that to me," I said. "I've got some more ideas."

"That, sir, is what I fear," Matfany said.

Chapter 19

_____

"There's no problem with deficit spending."

—Weimar

Hermalaya held out one slender hand to the choconut tycoon. He took it in his big paw, looking dazed and pleased.

"Mister Oatis, it has just been a pleasure?" she said.

"Oh, no, pretty lady, the pleasure was all ours!" he exclaimed. "What a day!"

Nunzio, Chumley, and I had all of Hermalaya's ceremonial gear packed up in cases. Massha stood beside the princess, an honorary lady-in-waiting. We had the system down to the point where we could get the Cake room cleaned up in under half an hour, including magikal deep cleaning, thanks to a trumpet-shaped gadget Massha had unearthed in a wizard's estate sale in Plupert. Sebellum Oatis's nine children were lined up wide-eyed and quiet, waiting for their chance to say goodbye to the princess.

"I don't know how you did it," Oatis's wife whispered to her, "but they've been good all afternoon! And all with a few little pieces of cake!"

"It's not what Cake is," Hermalaya said, smiling, "it's what Cake _means_."

"I know. You have triumphed over such adversity thanks

to Cake. I read it in your diary. I bought a dozen copies for all my friends!"

"Well, that's just so kind," the princess gushed. "I mean, I didn't want to share my private thoughts all over the dimensions? But Skeeve here told me that a lot of people would find the story moving? I kind of guess they have."

I grinned a little sheepishly. The publication of *The Princess's Diary* had been a hard sell with Hermalaya, but I had pointed out she had already given copies not only to Massha's friend Bobbie Jo, but also to several of the clients who had requested them as mementos after their Cake ceremonies. I suggested that she find a good publisher who would present the princess's own words in her own voice, all the better to drum up support for Foxe-Swampburg. She agreed, but only for the sake of her kingdom. It had sold thousands of copies already. Bunny was keeping track of the royalties.

" . . . I wish I could take Cake ceremony lessons from you. And I think my two older daughters are interested, too."

"Maybe later on, when things get settled out?" Hermalaya said, grasping her hand courteously. "I just love children, you know. I'd be happy to help you all on the path."

"I admire you so much, princess."

"Thank you. You're just too complimentary?"

"Uh, here," Oatis said, offering me a box. "Thanks."

The goodbye looked like it was getting protracted, so I grabbed Hermalaya's arm.

"Sorry, but her highness is getting tired."

"I'm sorry, but we have to go?" Hermalaya said, taking my cue. "You are just all so kind."

We hadn't even BAMFed out of there before the herd of children started clamoring and running around. I felt sorry for Oatis's wife. But it was another two hundred and fifty gold coins for me—I mean, the treasury. Oatis found Hemalaya charming, but he didn't have any economic hold on Reynardo or Foxe-Swampburg that was of any help. He did, however, have friends who did.

I had met a lot of royalty during my stint as a Court Magician. One thing that I realized about them was that most of them didn't have access to their countries' wealth. That power lay in the hands of merchants, landowners, and ministers. I'd known a number of tightwads among them—understandable, since the way to stay wealthy was not to spend the fortune they or their ancestors had spent lifetimes amassing—but I had underestimated the curiosity value of royalty to those very people. Among those willing to listen to the Princess's diary, more than a few were eager to experience the famous Cake ceremony, as conducted by the exiled Hermalaya herself. Those who enjoyed it passed the word on to others.

"Who've we got next?" I asked Massha, who was keeping track of the letters of introduction and callbacks once I'd let them see the diary spell. We had set up a command center in one of my old chambers in Hemlock's castle. As long as only Hermalaya was imposing on Hemlock's hospitality, the queen let us come and go as we pleased. I transported Nunzio and Chumley in daily from the Bazaar. I was staying in the lonely old inn in the woods there in Klah.

"Ooh, this is a hot one," Massha said, holding up a gilt-edged piece of parchment. "Oatis tipped us off to him. Bobono Macullis Lupercalia. Hey, he's right in Reynardo. He's a Swamp Fox. You would think he has seen the Cake ceremony before."

"He might have," Hermalaya said. "I think I've heard the Lupercalia name before?"

Nunzio and Guido had been doing some research for me into kingdom finances. I plunged into the piles of papers.

"Oh, yes," I said, my eyes narrowing on a document. It was a copy of a loan agreement negotiated on behalf of the royal house of Foxe-Swampburg and signed by Matfany and Lupercalia. "This is great. Matfany's been buying building supplies on credit from this guy. He's months behind on payments. Thousands of gold coins! If we can persuade him, he might be just the straw that breaks the camelpaca's back. Let's see when I can get an appointment to visit him."

"Well, you can't go tomorrow. Both of you have got an interview with Boccarella for the Crystal Ether Network in the morning. The Overseer of Mirth in Killinem is expecting Skeeve in the afternoon."

I made a note on a scrap of paper. "No problem. Day after tomorrow or later. If that's all right with you, princess? I don't want you to feel burned out. I know we're having you meet a lot of people, but I think we're gaining some terrific allies."

I turned to Hermalaya, who sat on the window seat, turning her Cake server over and over in her fingers.

"Are you okay, honey?" Massha asked, floating over to sit

in the air by her. Massha preferred to be weightless whenever possible, and her gaudy flying ring provided all the buoyancy she needed. The Swamp Vixen turned a wistful face toward us.

"I just miss my friends, and all my ladies, and the Old Folks," she said with a heartbreaking little sigh.

I knew just how she felt. I had been exiled, too. Bunny wouldn't allow me to stay in my new office more than a few minutes at a time. On my rare visits back to drop off money and gifts meant to replenish the Foxe-Swampburg treasury when Hermalaya was restored to the throne, Gleep greeted me with a tongue-sliming as if I had been gone for years. He and Buttercup were lonely hanging around a half-empty office. Nunzio volunteered to stay behind sometimes and play with them.

"Beneficial and educational exercises," he told me. "It helps increase their intelligence."

I knew he'd be surprised if he knew just how intelligent both Gleep and Buttercup really were. Buttercup was still keeping an eye out the back door for assassins. Each time I checked in with him he dropped a wink of his heavy white lashes to tell me that no strangers had yet tried to invade from the extra-dimensional side of the tent. That information was all the more important now that I knew Aahz was working against my client's best interests. If he managed to stabilize Matfany's position, poor Hermalaya would never get to go home.

The best weapons we had were outrage and financial securities. I'd asked the creditors we had met and impressed so far to hold back until we were ready. I figured that public outcry, mixed with a massed call for repayment of capital I knew Matfany didn't have, would force him to resign and allow the princess to come home. I just hoped we could outdraw whatever Aahz was bringing in for the prime minister. No one would tell me how well he was doing, or even what he was doing.

Chapter 20

"You don't need to know anything, Aahz," Pookie said without even looking fully at me as I slid onto the bar stool beside her.

It had taken me a long time to hunt down my younger cousin and Spider, the Klah woman she had taken on as a business partner. The two of them had the far end of the room to themselves. No points for guessing why: Pookie was dressed in a skintight silver jumpsuit crossed with bandoliers studded with pouches and holsters, and shiny black boots that had sharpened points for heels. Spider wasn't as flashy. Her faded fatigues had the air that she had been the one who wore them out, instead of buying them from an army surplus store. Either way, no one in the room was going to mess with them without permission. I suppose that also meant me, but I had no intention of taking the hint.

"C'mon," I wheedled. "You can at least tell me if he's in trouble. You know what the kid's like."

"He's not in trouble," Pookie said, her yellow eyes favoring me with a full glare. "Satisfied?"

"No. What's the big problem with helping me find out what direction he's taking?"

"You don't need my help for that, cousin."

I narrowed my eyes at her. "Are you working with him?

Any chance I can get you to come over to my side? Spill what you know for the sake of blood ties?"

Pookie emptied her glass and signaled for a refill. "I'm not on his side or anyone else's side. If you want us to do research, you know our rates. Personally or professionally, we're not interested in this one. Final answer."

"Did the others tell you to stand down, or was this your idea?"

"Whether or not I subscribe to it, your friends there hold to a code. No double-crossing. No dirty tricks."

I shrugged. "I've always thought of it as more of a suggestion, myself."

"Whatever. Now, get lost, cousin. We're waiting for a client."

Perturbed, I drummed my fingers on the bar top. The innkeeper gave me one look and stayed back out of reach. I could start tearing the place up, but what good would it do?

"You ought to be more careful about the people you let in here," I informed him. I slid off the bar stool and headed out into the town.

Pookie had been my last chance to pry information out of any of my partners or temporary associates. I decided to stretch my legs and see if I could come up with some ideas.

I stalked through the busy streets, dodging other pedestrians and magik-driven traffic. The locals were at least a foot taller than I was, but thin as fence rails. Skamital wasn't the end of the universe, but nothing was, these days. With the growing availability of travel gadgets and spells, it seemed like there was no place I could go where I didn't encounter a familiar face.

As I passed by a shop window, I thought I recognized someone.

I backed up a couple of paces and peered through the glass. Yeah, there she was! Matfany's pretty little nemesis, Hermalaya. Not the girl in person, but a portrait of her, on a card standing on top of a pile of thin books on a display table. "*The Princess's Diary*," the poster said. This was definitely Skeeve's doing.

I went inside. The table was surrounded by shoppers, both male and female, in animated discussion. More to the point, they were *buying* the book. I sidled over to take a look for myself.

Somewhere in size between *War and Peace* and the latest graphic novel, *The Princess's Diary* had been bound in shell-pink leather tooled with leaves and thorns intertwined around a tilted crown. I nudged open a copy and started reading.

In spite of my requisite partiality toward my client, I fell into the story. The first few entries were the usual girly stuff: comments about official functions and what dresses she wore. When the first pinchbug problems surfaced, far from being unaware, she had her finger on all the facts. The Swamp Fox who had imported them was in deep trouble, but the problem had to be taken care of. Trouble was, the bugs were breeding like crazy. Since they weren't native, they had no natural predators in Reynardo. The cabinet, acting on advice, made the decision to try and keep the problem confined to Foxe-Swampburg. Heroic, I thought. Hermalaya didn't say so directly, but I got the impression she might have been behind the suggestion. She came across in print a lot smarter than she did in person, though I still didn't see that she had what it took to rule.

I could see that the girl could get a lot of popular sympathy. She had a future as a storyteller, but as a monarch? Matfany had done the right thing in putting her out the door. You can go only so far on charisma. At some point, you have to have real savvy and business sense to prosper.

I wasn't too obtuse to see a parallel between my client and my own situation. I could tell by the looks on the faces of the others in the office the other day that some of them thought I was overstepping the bounds in stating that I wanted to be the president of the company. If they had wanted to work for me, they would have said so after Skeeve left. Well, I never asked them to. At that time, the last thing I wanted to do was lead. I missed the opportunity then, but not a second time. Pervects aren't used to coming in second place. If the company was going to rebuild with all of us as partners, this time I wanted to be first among equals. Enough was enough.

I had always kept my association with the others loose because it wasn't my intention to start an organization in the first place. Like them, I only came in because of Skeeve.

Maybe that was the problem. They knew I wasn't committed to a group. They were more inclined to be cohesive. Maybe it was a herd thing. Pervects don't have a lot of herd instinct, or trust, for that matter. When we see a crowd of people running away screaming, "fire," we always go back to see if there really is one. And if maybe anything interesting got left behind when everybody else fled. I never intended to be an employee of anyone, not then and not ever again. Standing aloof kept me from being vulnerable. Now that the status quo had been shaken up, I was ready to take the lead. I had the most business experience of the group and the most leadership potential, so why not? This was my shot to prove it.

"And did you hear?" one woman beside me told another, as they giggled over a shared page. "Princess Hermalaya is personally going around the dimensions and inducting people into a secret society!"

"No!" her friend exclaimed. I aimed an ear in their direction. "What do they do?"

"I don't know! I heard about it from my sister-in-law. Her aunt's father travels on business. He said he was in a dimension where the entire royal family was inducted. It was a big secret, held in a dark room with candles and chanting and glitter!"

"How did he hear about it?" the friend asked.

"Oh, well, all the servants knew. *They* told him when he made his delivery. It just sounds so romantic!"

"Oh, it does," the friend said. "Ooh, I wish I could join!"

So that was what Skeeve was up to.

"Excuse me," I said, favoring them with my most ingratiating smile. They backed away a couple of paces, so I held up my copy of the book to show I was in the princess-admiring club along with them. "What dimension was that your uncle went to? I was just visiting a place, and I heard rumors about this society. Was it Imper?"

"Oh, no!" the first female said. "It was Octaroo. Did she go to Imper, too? Oh, I wish I could travel all around like she does. I bet she has a fancy car and servants and a tiara!"

Glamour and mystery, I mused, moving away from them. You can't fight against a couple of concepts like that. If I knew Skeeve, he had figured out a way to make money, substantial money, from it.

Thinking of herd instinct gave me an idea. I edged toward the clerk and bought the little pink book.

I had to counteract Hermalaya's appeal somehow. I ought to set a back fire, or at least start some rumors, get a little negative chat going. Secret societies are great for making feeble-minded people do things they'd be too embarrassed to unless they had drunk at least six beers. I grinned. Exclusivity was only desirable unless it wasn't any longer. Maybe I could make her more popular still. Too popular, in fact.

In the meantime, I had some unreal real estate to move.

Chapter 21

―――

"Nothing else is like dining with the original."

—Count Dracula

Hermalaya was as gracious as ever as we showed the final set of guests out of the reception room.

"Thank you for working us in at the last minute," said the chief operating officer for Pangallobank, Interdimensional. He shook my hand energetically with five or six of his own spindly little limbs. "I heard about you all from my financial wizard. She watches the Crystal Ether Network on her scrying ball. The writeup was so enthusiastic, I had a hard time believing it, but I checked in with a few of my friends. Word on the street, you know, isn't always trustworthy. Know your sources, that's what I say. Ruty!"

"Yessir!" A yes-centipede with a go-getting attitude appeared at his boss's side. He handed me a silk envelope that jingled satisfyingly. "Wove it myself, sir! Enjoy it, sir!"

"Thanks a bunch," I said, tucking it into my belt pouch. "And if you give any other thought to what I mentioned earlier . . . ?"

"I will," said the COO. "We hold paper on a number of small banks across the dimensions—nothing as big as the Gnomes of Zoorik—yet. I'll let you know. Meantime, you tell me if I can help out this lovely lady in any way."

One of Massha's gadgets moped around the floor, picking up glitter and stray crumbs. I drew out the small package and counted up the coins.

"How are we doing, boss?" Nunzio asked.

"Pretty well," I said. "Another two hundred coins."

"Jolly good, what?" Chumley asked. "Where to next, Massha?"

"Well . . . " My former apprentice looked embarrassed. "I didn't want to mention this while everyone was getting ready for these visitors, but there aren't any more."

"Why?" I asked. "But we were booming just a couple of days ago! We got all sorts of good interviews in half a dozen dimensions. Hermalaya's diary is about to go into reprint."

"I know," Massha said unhappily. She thumbed the jewel on her bracelet. A list sprang into view against the wall. I peered at it. All the names on it were crossed off. "I got a bunch of cancellations just this morning. I'm sorry, Skeeve. I have no idea what has gone wrong. Everyone loves her, but it looks like no one wants to do the Cake ceremony any more."

"Why? I thought that the 'princess in exile' angle was the best draw around."

"It is! The flow's been everything we could have hoped for, up until right about now."

I drummed my fingertips on the chair arm. Good publicity plus good word of mouth couldn't equal no interest. "That means something's actively interfering," I said.

"That would be my assessment as well," Chumley said. He

had suspended his persona of Big Crunch around Hermalaya. It was too difficult to discuss strategy in monosyllables.

"Me, too," said Massha.

"Why, who would want to stop people having Cake?" Hermalaya asked, distressed. "It's so beneficial! Unless it was that rapscallion Matfany!"

"That's it! You think Aahz has anything to do with this?" I asked. "I know he wants to win."

Chumley fixed his odd-sized eyes on me. "I say, Skeeve, how could you even think such a thing of him?"

I felt ashamed of myself. "I guess I'm just so fixed on this contest that I'm convincing myself of anything. Sorry."

Chumley guffawed, an unusually crude noise for a refined person like him. "I say, no, that's not it at all. He's convinced he can win this without scuttling you, old chap. Doesn't need to. Good heavens, what? You know Aahz perfectly well. If he thought he had to spike your guns, he wouldn't hesitate for a moment, would he? Has he ever had mercy on a rival?"

I glared. "So he doesn't think I'm much of a rival, huh?"

"Well, pride and all, what? Come, come, Skeeve. When has he ever overestimated you, eh?"

I forced myself to calm down. That was true. He always thought I would goof up, no matter how many times I managed to succeed. Why would this time be any different?

"So, if the problem's not Aahz, then there's someone else. Who?"

Massha handed the stack of cancellations to me. "Ask the people who turned us down."

———

Killinem stood only second to Vaygus as the dimension to visit when you wanted a good time. I passed by the comedy clubs, the circus tents, and hundreds of street buskers. A stilt walker blew a long stream of fire just where I was going to walk. I diverted it with a flick of magik and sent it back to him, to the roar of the crowd gathered to watch. I wasn't in much of a mood for pranks.

"The Overseer of Mirth does not have you on his agenda," a red-nosed clown informed me when I identified myself and my party at the desk.

"He did," I said. Reading upside down was something I had gotten good at during the time I had worked with M.Y.T.H., Inc. "Right there. Princess Hermalaya and coterie."

The clown looked down his round, rubicund nose at me. Unlike in Klah, his wasn't stuck on; it was real. "You've been cancelled, friend. Forget it."

I leaned confidentially over the desk. "Look, our appointment was for this afternoon. I see that he hasn't got anything else at the moment. This is Princess Hermalaya herself." I nodded over my shoulder. Hermalaya wiggled two fingers at him. The clown grinned uneasily at her. "Let me just ask him a couple of questions? For the fun of it."

No humorist in Killinem was going to let a challenge like that go by.

"All right, friend. I'll see what I can do." He mounted a foot-high bicycle and rode toward the brightly colored doors at the rear of the room. A trunklike nozzle reached out of the ceiling and *whoosh!* He was sucked up off the floor like a house in a windstorm. I stared at it in delight.

Just as I was wondering how I could incorporate that trick into my own office, the nozzle reappeared and spat the clown and his bicycle back into the room.

"The Overseer will give you a minute of his most valuable time," the clown informed us.

"I don't know why you bothered to come," the Overseer said. His red nose was more patrician in shape than his secretary's, and his floppy suit and shoes were all made of white silk. "We have our own cheap acts here in Killinem. I don't need to import any."

"Cheap!" I sputtered. "You cried when I let you hear the Princess's own words."

"The tears of a clown are sacred to us," the Overseer said. "Yes, I was moved by her plight. I was even willing to give you an audition to see if your act was something I wanted to give wider attention across this dimension. But then I see it's just a derivative. Commonplace. You trifled with my emotions. That's a crime here in Killinem. You will be fortunate if we don't have you publicly beaten with a slapstick!"

"Cheap?" Hermalaya demanded, her eyes round.

"Derivative?" I echoed.

"No one is delivering any beatings to Mister Skeeve or anyone else," Nunzio said, putting his hand into his breast pocket.

"Hold on," Massha said, intruding her large presence into the midst of all of us like an orange thundercloud blocking out the sun. "Don't all of you get your panties in a braid. Just what changed your mind?" she asked, fluttering her wealth of false eyelashes at the Overseer.

"Not long after you visited me, I heard thousands of citizens here were offered invitations to a Cake ceremony. I received one myself. I thought it was rather . . . tacky."

I raised my eyebrows. "Who else could be offering the same experience so soon?"

The Overseer matched me lift for lift. "I see you don't believe me." He turned to a page in harlequin tunic and belled cap.

"Pidrol, go get those flyers."

A page in a harlequin tunic and belled cap went running out of the room. He returned in a moment with a couple of scrolls in his hand. One I recognized as ours, on cream-laid parchment with embossed calligraphy, a copy of the cover of *The Princess's Diary* with a really good image of Hermalaya in the corner holding her Cake server. The other had been run off by some handbill press or a shutterbug printer. Superficially, they resembled the letters we sent out requesting interviews, but they were more on the order of handbills.

"Cheap," Massha said. "Looks like an ad for a bordello."

The Overseer nodded. "I agree. That is why I rejected both."

I pressed him. "But you can see that Princess Hermalaya offers the real thing. So, why not come and enjoy her ceremony?"

"Well," he said, as if reluctant to embarrass me. "It didn't seem so . . . exclusive any longer. Not when it was being held in *the Bazaar*. And *these*," he added, looking less like anyone associated with mirth I have ever met. He produced a small carton from the box of documents presented to him by his page. "These dolls. Vulgar. I can't believe that anyone of quality could possibly grant their countenance to such things."

"Cake Queen Action Figure," I read off the side of the carton. The cardboard was cut away to show the foot-high doll inside. It resembled a miniature Swamp Vixen with white fur and black markings. She had a miniature Cake server in her hand. When you pushed a button on the back, it slashed its tiny arm back and forth in a pretty good imitation of Hermalaya's impressive Cake-cutting action.

"You have to admit it looks like her," Nunzio said.

"They're selling images of me?" Hermalaya asked. She snatched the box out of my hands and gazed at it with growing horror. "Mister Skeeve, this is outrageous of you! Is absolutely nothing sacred where you are concerned?"

"I didn't authorize this," I said. I flipped it over, looking for a company name or an address. "Asfodeel's Novelties, Paperhanger's Lane. This also came from the Bazaar!"

Massha shrugged. "No surprise. Anything that rips off a good idea is almost guaranteed to be run by Deveels."

I had a sudden inspiration, and I didn't like it. "Or someone tipped off by Deveels," I said. "We'd better go see what's going on. Thanks for your time, Overseer."

"My pleasure," the white-clad clown said, waving us toward the vacuum ejector. "Come see me when you have something really original to show me."

Chapter 22

————

"It doesn't really look like me."
—Barbara Millicent Roberts

I was so mad I could hardly think. I BAMFed us into the Bazaar so fast that I didn't even bother to figure out where we would land. Fortunately, my instincts were smarter at that moment than my conscious mind. We appeared in front of M.Y.T.H., Inc.'s own tent. I had automatically gone toward my old stomping grounds.

"Uh," I said awkwardly, unable to offer a legitimate excuse to my companions for my choice. "This could get kind of ugly. I don't think that the princess ought to get involved in it. I'd like to put her in a safe place."

"She could hide out in our tent, boss," Nunzio said. "No one would dare interfere with her in our own territory."

"I say, would you like a spot of tea, your highness?" Chumley asked her with a bow that was a triumph of grace for someone his size. "I am afraid I won't be as elegant in my service as you are, but I am sure refreshment would not go amiss. Perhaps you would like a moment to rest. You have had a most strenuous day."

Hermalaya was torn. "Well, I am sure you are the most courteous thing, but I should go along with Mister Skeeve?"

"Better not, honey," Massha said. "Even if this was legitimate, you don't want to be around for the nitty-gritty. Let Chumley take care of you. We'll be back."

"But, I ought to come with you," the Swamp Vixen protested. "Isn't it my countenance that they are messing with?"

"Better not to involve you, doll—I mean, princess," Nunzio said, giving her a pat on the arm. "Don't worry."

Chumley led her firmly into the tent. "This way, your highness. Perhaps you and I can discuss other customs of your most fascinating dimension. . . . " The flap swished shut behind them.

The three of us stalked toward Paperhanger's Lane. I assumed my disguise as the ancient and powerful wizard. Massha put on all the magikal jewelry in her shoulder bag. Nunzio put a hand in his pocket. I knew he was counting bolts for his miniature crossbow. We were taking no chances.

All along the way I kept noticing copies of the handbill that the Overseer of Mirth had shown us offering "The Famous Reynard Cake Ceremony! Fun for the Whole Family. At Reasonable Prices!" Somebody had plastered the Bazaar with them. I saw all our advantage leaching away. Was this an onslaught by Aahz to cut off our source of capital?

When we reached the flap of Asfodeel's tent, there was no doubt at all that we had found the source of the action figures. Dolls of every species and shape were pinned to the leather curtain. Right in the middle of the display was the Hermalaya doll, complete with its silver accessory. Small Deveel children, mostly girls, fingered the toys and clamored for their long-suffering parents to buy them. The red-skinned Deveel behind the heaped table, a narrow-faced, narrow-eyed individual with a forked beard, turned to grin at me.

"And how can I help you, honored sir?" he asked, in a silky voice.

I ripped the Cake Queen action figure from the display and brandished it at him.

"For a start, you can stop selling these."

"Are you out of your mind?" the Deveel screamed, going from a baritone to a soprano in one sentence. "Why should I?"

"Because you don't have permission to use this lady's image," I said. "This is Princess Hermalaya of Reynardo. I am her representative. Maybe you've heard of me? I am Skeeve the Magnificent."

"And I am Asfodeel the Totally Unimpressed! Do you see?" he demanded of his potential buyers. "I sell you dolls of a real live princess, and this fool wants me to take them away from you!"

"Princess?" the little girls asked, their pointy ears perking up. "A real one?" They went for the display on the table, grabbing up the cardboard boxes.

"No!" I said, taking the dolls out of their hands. The girls burst into tears. Their parents rounded on me in fury.

"What are you doing to our children?"

"Thief! Thief! We'll call the authorities!"

"Just a minute, Skeeve," Massha said, gently, taking the boxes away from me. She dealt them out to the girls as smoothly as a card shark. "You're solving the wrong problem."

I turned my scowl on Asfodeel. "Where did you hear about Hermalaya?"

The Deveel looked at me as if I was feeble-minded "She's all over the place! I saw her in the crystal ball at breakfast yesterday, and got a shipment from my factory on a crash basis. I mean, there's instant publicity. Why shouldn't I cash in—I mean, provide a figure from current events for these lovely children?" He beamed at the eager little girls.

"Because," I said, pushing in on him from one side as Nunzio did from the other, "there might be some severe repercussions for doing it."

He felt Nunzio's crossbow bolt poking him in the ribcage. Deveels might have been loud and dishonest, but most of them were also cowards.

"Well, if you put it that way . . . how about I cut you in on the action? Say . . . two percent of net?"

I had a different offer. "Say . . . you stop making these, and you get to keep your factory and your shop?"

"And who are you to threaten me?"

"He's Skeeve the Magnificent," Nunzio said. "Like he told you. I thought you were listening."

"Your name has no meaning any more, old man. Nothing you can do will stop me. Your Hermalaya is a public figure. She's got no special rights to her own image. I got advice."

"What kind of advice?"

Asfodeel smirked. "A guy told me you was a has-been. He says there's no fight left in you. You've lost all your influence. All you're breathing is hot air."

"Who told you that?"

The Deveel shook loose from our grasp. "Forget about it. I don't blab my sources."

I fumed. "Aahz."

"You don't know that, Hot Stuff," Massha said, but the look on Asfodeel's face told me I had hit gold. Aahz had told this guy I was a has-been. He was actually talking me down in the Bazaar! The . . . the Pervert!

"I'll show you how powerless I am," I said, throwing back my sleeves. Asfodeel stuck up his chin.

"Come and take me on, big Klahd. I'll tell everyone the Great Skeeve is afraid of competition. You haven't been around much lately. Word on the street was that you lost your nerve. How about that? Are you willing to attack one of the little guys? In front of witnesses?"

I stopped short. The fact he was taunting me meant he wanted to cash in on the controversy. I knew all the earmarks. I'd been in this position once or twice before. I didn't like it, but I held on to my temper.

"You're not even worth my discussing it with you," I said haughtily. "Come, my friends. Let's go."

I withdrew, hating him with all my being, but absolutely unwilling to give him an inch. Within three steps, Asfodeel was at my side.

"But what about a percentage? You're just going to walk away? When I'm *unauthorized*?"

I allowed myself a tiny grin. He *was* hoping I'd fight him or partner up. What he never counted on was neither. Maybe I had learned something.

"Unauthorized, unappetizing, and unimportant," I said. I

left him in the midst of a crowd of clamoring little girls and their parents. When I walked away, they sensed a bargain. I covered half a block before I let the grin take over my whole face.

"I figure Asfodeel's going to lose some money on the crash basis."

"But what about the dolls?" Nunzio asked. "He's gonna get more."

"As much as I hate to say it, we should just ignore them," I said. "We . . . I made her a public figure. It's my fault. But if we make a big deal about these dolls, it will draw more attention to us."

"Let me go back there and negotiate with him, boss," Nunzio pleaded. "Something ought to befall him for violating our copyright."

"Something's going to befall him, but not directly," I said. "I think I'll take Gleep for a walk here later on."

Nunzio grinned. "Perhaps this is the day that his obedience training just happens to fail."

"I'm counting on it. The Cake ceremony imposters, though, have got to be shut down. That affects our very bread and butter, so to speak."

Chapter 23

———

"Imitation is the sincerest form of flattery."

—Chinese copyright enforcement agency

"This is the address," Massha said, after we had turned about eight corners.

It looked like an ordinary bakery. I ducked my head to pass underneath the flour sack towel that had been nailed over the doorway. Inside, a bunch of blindfolded Deveel children were playing Pin-the-suit-on-the-Imp. Each tot had a cutout of an incredibly ugly suit and were trying to tack it onto the image of an Imp wearing a red flannel union suit. He didn't look any more embarrassed than I was.

"Hi, there!" called a nice, middle-aged Deveel woman. "Are you one of the parents? Oh, wait, you're a Klahd. No offense. Can I help you?"

I looked around. This was definitely the place. Imitations, and cheap ones at that, of all of Hermalaya's beautiful ritual objects were arranged throughout the big room, but it was a far cry from her oasis of peace.

"Are you the one running Reynardan Cake ceremonies?"

"Sure am! You just missed one! We're all done now." She caught one of the children as it raced by and wiped frosting off its smeared face.

"But . . . all these are children," I said, looking around.

She planted her big hands on her hips. "But of course it's for kids!" she said, looking at me as if I was out of my mind.

I fumbled for an explanation. "Yes, but, Dragon-pinning is part of the sacred rites of Foxe-Swampburg. You're cheapening it by using a different image. You're devaluing a historical rite!"

"Pal, I'll rip off your arm if you don't keep your voice down. These kids are having fun!"

"I am Skeeve the Magnificent. I am here as a representative of Princess Hermalaya of Foxe-Swampburg. You shouldn't be doing all of this."

The woman glared at me. "Buddy, I don't care who you are, but if you frighten these kids off, I will give you a black eye so large it will cover your whole body."

"Now, see here," I started.

The woman lowered her horned head until we were eye to eye and nose to nose. "*You* see here, you skinny Klahd. The kids love it! I'm not stopping just on your say-so."

"Take it easy, take it easy," Massha said.

"I'm not giving up on this one, Massha," I declared. "Not twice in one day!"

"You don't have to, Skeeve. Excuse me a minute."

She put a huge, meaty arm over the shoulders of the Deveel and led her away quietly. I tried to listen over the din the children were raising.

I heard the words " . . . genuine . . . adult . . . contractor . . . Bazaar exclusive . . . children." When she returned to me, the Deveel was grinning broadly.

"Mr. Skeeve, your associate told me all about what you're doing. I am so sorry to interfere with such a worthy enterprise. My name's Hepzibiltah, by the way." She seized my hand in both of hers and pumped it up and down. "Forgive me for not introducing myself, but these kids make me crazy. It's a wonder I can remember to go home at the end of the day."

I tried not to look suspicious. Deveels didn't act solicitious and placatory unless you had them over a barrel, one in which they could see an advantage for themselves.

"So, my associate, did she agree with the terms we proposed?" I asked Massha, trying not to sound as though I was totally in the dark.

"Well, master, she walked right into it . . . I mean, she likes the idea a bunch. Who wouldn't?"

"Indeed?" I inquired imperiously.

"Yeah, well," Hepzibiltah said, a little awkwardly. "I mean, I heard about it on the Crystal Ether Net, and it sounded like something the kiddies would like. I mean, I am already running a bakery. Having the kiddies come here to have a party just seemed like a natural extension of my business. I didn't mean to move in on your territory. I mean, you're Skeeve the Magnificent! I forgot all about y—I mean, it's been a long time since you've been around. I guess I thought you moved on."

That stung, but it wasn't her fault. I regarded her with a benevolent face.

"I am sure you did not mean to offend. Then it is agreed?"

"You bet," the matron said heartily. "I get two-year exclusive Bazaar rights to run this operation for kiddies, option to be renegotiated at the end of that time. And I will study to become a real Cake Master. I'm looking forward to it. It's been a hoot so far. Er . . . you won't mind if the definition of kiddies gets expanded a little? Sometimes I get teenagers in here, the occasional frat party . . . ?"

"As long as they don't have kiddies of their own, they can count," Massha said. "You know, twenty-nine is the new nine."

"Uh, okay," she said, doubtfully. "Sounds fair. But your fee? Twenty percent of the gross sounds a little, er, hefty."

"In exchange for calling yourself an official representative of the Foxe-Swampburg Cake Ceremony, it is minor. But . . . since you seem to be operating in a friendly and hygienic setting . . . " I glanced at Massha for her approval and got it. "Fifteen percent will do."

"Still a little top-heavy. Ten?"

I spread out my hands. "Twelve and a half. Skeeve the Magnificent does not haggle."

"That is what they all say, buddy. But all right. Weekly collection is okay. That's when I pay all my suppliers."

"Enforcement of exclusivity will be handled by you, I assume?" I eyed her under my lowered brows.

"Honey, you can count on it. My husband's Mettro. You probably have heard of him?

Mettro ran a large underground network of enforcers that worked in the Bazaar but had hired out to other dimensions for a fee. I had never needed his services, but I heard he was reasonably priced and would go anywhere. I raised one eyebrow. "Yes, I have."

"So, no problem. The kiddies get their Cake and eat it, too." Hepzibiltah burst into hearty laughter which shook her ample flesh all around. "Get it?"

"I . . . got it."

Massha beamed as I shook hands with my new partner. We swept out of the shop and turned into a side street, where I dropped my disguise.

"Whew," I said.

"Not too bad," Massha agreed. "A little extra in the kitty. I looked at her books. She's pulling in almost ten gold coins a week profit already."

"Sounds kind of marginal to me," I said. "Around here, ten gold coins is nothing." I started to turn back. "Maybe we could just make do with ten percent. Or five."

"Hold it right there, Hot Pants," Massha said, dragging me back by my arm. "Don't let your heart get in the way of the real reason we did that. Hermalaya needs the bucks, and you don't want anyone to get the idea that you're a pushover. You handled one difficult situation pretty well. Let's go back to Bunny and turn in this money. We're doing pretty darned well right now. Don't forget that."

We went back, handed over the funds. Bunny tilted her head as we explained the day's work.

"I wonder if you should get credit for the subsidiary rights, Skeeve," she said. "No offense, but you didn't strike the bargain."

I felt my face go scarlet, but she was right. I couldn't take Massha's glory away from her.

"Okay," I said. "Chalk that contract up to experience. Hermalaya gets the money no matter who gets credit for it."

"No," Massha said. "It's his. We work as a team in the field, Bunny. We always have. We play off each other's strengths and weaknesses. I was there. I just jumped in. He would have gotten around Hepzibiltah in the end, but he was starting off from the wrong place, and it would have taken much longer. I just cut through some of the thicket. He did finish off the negotiation in the end."

Bunny smiled at her. The two of them had become very good friends over the years.

"Okey-dokey," she said. "I get it."

I breathed a sigh of relief as she inked in the profit under my name. In spite of setbacks and disappointments, I was collecting a pretty impressive sum. I just wondered what other booby traps Aahz was setting for me. I might have to lay a surprise or two of my own.

Chapter 24

"Come on," I said, pulling Dervina along through the dank, chilly corridor of the Foxe-Swampburg castle. Centuries of Hermalaya's ancestors glared down from fancy gold frames in between sconces giving off a faint, blue light. "He'll be glad to see you."

"But aren't we expected?" the Gnome asked. The fussy little creature kept tapping her fingertips together over her little round midsection.

"Constantly," I assured her.

Most of the hallway was deserted, now that about half the servants and almost all the courtiers had been dismissed. I knew where we were going because I could see the two guards flanking the door two-thirds of the way up the hall. Dervina looked nervous as we passed them, which I put down to the local livery. Over their already feral faces, the guards wore helmets of bronze cast into the likeness of insane wolves with slavering jaws and anatomically correct dentition, giving them almost as fearsome a snarl as a Pervect. The fur cloaks over their shoulders looked like they might have been skinned off the backs of defeated enemies. Dervina gulped.

"Hi, boys," I said, slapping the one on the right as we went by him. "The big guy's expecting me."

Theirs was not to reason why, I figured, since they didn't

stop us. On the other side of the door, we were halted by an ice-cold look from Matfany himself.

"What are you doing here, Mister Aahz?"

"Business," I said amiably, hoping to engender the same mood from him. It didn't work. The gaze grew even more chilly.

"Mister Aahz, I informed you that it would be best if you made an appointment before bursting in. I am very busy most days and don't have time to drop everything on a whim. Perhaps I didn't impress you enough with the importance of my position here and the respect that derives from it?"

"Sure you did, sure you did," I assured him. "And that is why Dervina here wanted so much to meet you in person."

I stepped aside. The Gnome bowed over her folded hands. Matfany peered at her over his glasses and rose to his feet.

"Ma'am, I apologize. I am afraid I didn't see you there."

"Perhaps we should leave, Mister Aahz," Dervina said nervously. "If Prime Minister Matfany is too busy . . . ?"

"Not at all, ma'am," Matfany said, automatically turning on the courtesy. He came around the document-strewn desk with his hand extended. "Please, be welcome in Foxe-Swampburg. How may we serve you?"

"She's looking for a little something in a library or a symphony hall," I said. "What have you got?"

Matfany put on a pained smile. "We have a couple of fine libraries, ma'am," he said. "The Orchestra Hall is where the orchestra plays, but we've also got an opera house. Both of those are pretty popular."

"I can show them to you on the map," I said, brandishing

my chart. I glanced at his desk and at my prospect. It had taken me weeks and half a dozen favors to get an appointment with anyone in the Zoorik banking industry. Dervina was the only banker willing to talk to me about Foxe-Swampburg. Evidently their bond issues were down below an F- rating, and no one in Zoorik wanted to even talk about Foxe-Swampburg and money in the same sentence. She liked the idea of a cultural center with her name on it, but being more cautious than the Geek or Gribaldi, she wanted to see the place first. We needed to wow her. "You haven't got a lot of room here. Let's move into the throne room and take a look at the map in there."

"Let's not, sir," Matfany said, just as firmly. "This is my office. It is where I do business. Pray allow me, ma'am?"

He escorted Dervina to his chair and helped her to sit down. He rang a hand bell on his desk. When one of the masked guards looked in to the room, Matfany beckoned to him.

"Will you go ask the kitchen to bring this lady some refreshments? Would you like coffee, tea, or a little something stronger?"

"Oh, tea, thank you!"

I would have liked something a lot stronger and in decent quantity, but Matfany ignored me and my wishes. Efficiently, he tidied everything off his desk and spread out the map facing our guest. When the tea arrived on a cart pushed by a surly maidservant in a frilly pink apron, Matfany took it from her. He fussed over Dervina, fixing a cup for her just the way she liked it. I finally caught him alone by the door when he went out to ask for a few more lamps over his desk.

"Look, pal," I hissed at him, "this gal could mean a bucket of money. I don't want her to think the two of us don't get along. You have been torqued off at me for days. You have a problem with me? Let's hear it. You want my help, or not?"

Matfany pulled himself up to his full height and looked down his nose at me.

"That encounter in your offices continues to trouble me, sir. I need your help for the kingdom's sake, sir, but I will not have you blackening the name of our princess."

I blew a raspberry. "Former princess, pal, let me remind you, since it was you who booted her out. Remember?"

Matfany looked pained. "Also for the sake of our nation, as I told you, but you must understand, I still have the greatest respect for her."

"Fine!" I snarled. "I won't insult her any more. But this Gnome is a serious prospect who wants her name on a feature in Foxe-Swampburg. Keep the charm going, and it'll pay off in gold, remember? Prosperity equals respect?"

"I have to talk to you about that, Mister Aahz," Matfany began.

"Later," I said. "That tea okay, Miz Dervina?"

"Yes, yes," the Gnome banker said, blinking up at us. "This is a most curious opportunity, Prime Minister. I have to admit that it intrigued me. There are few intangible assets that carry value. I intend to retire next year, and having my name on a building would be a legacy I should enjoy in my retirement. Can you show the options to me?"

"Why, they are right there," Matfany said. "That is the old library, right here facing the castle. The new library is the building here next to the university on the edge of town. The other new library's over here. Which one do you like?"

"Oh, I'd have to see them to decide," Dervina said. "I never buy a property without a thorough inspection. We Gnomes are cautious by nature, you know."

"Ma'am, you do understand that you aren't really buying the item in question?" Matfany asked, with more emphasis than usual. "You're providing a name, in exchange for a consideration?"

"I do understand, sir," Dervina said. "But, perhaps also, with an additional honorarium, I might be allowed a tasteful plaque with my name on it affixed to the edifice in question, the fee to allow that designation in perpetuity? I would be prepared to go as high as a thousand . . . ?"

A thousand! I tried to keep from whooping out loud.

The prime minister's face cleared. "That would be quite all right, ma'am. I'd be happy to escort you around to the various sites you want to see. May I warn you in advance that there's been some little trouble as of late? You might see things that I hope won't upset you."

"I know all about the pinchbug infestation, Prime Minister," she said.

"Well, it's not exactly *that*," Matfany said, with a significant look at me. I could see more discussion coming my way, but I had no idea why. "Ah, but if you please, your time is valuable." He pulled back her chair and stuck out his elbow. "This way, ma'am."

I trailed along behind him. The heralds in the hall raised

long trumpets and blew a fanfare, and the guards threw open the big main doors as we approached them. Matfany marched proudly out with Dervina on his arm. I followed, and stopped short.

When I saw what he called 'some little trouble,' I had to hand it to him for understatement.

"What the hell is this?" I asked.

"Clearly, you did not come in this way," Matfany said.

I whistled. "No kidding."

The courtyard wasn't distinct in any way from thousands of enclosed spaces of fortified houses and citadels across the dimensions, except in its present population density, which had to comprise a good quarter of the Swamp Foxes in Foxe-Swampburg. As soon as they saw Matfany, they raised protest signs over their heads and shook their fists at him. The signs were badly lettered, but I could read most of them.

"Bring Back Hermalaya!" and "We Want Our Princess!" was the gist of the majority, but "Keep Foxe-Swampburg Beautiful!" was on a good third of the placards out there. Other gripes filled the rest, but I got the point. They surged up the stairs and surrounded us. Dervina cringed.

"Get back!" I roared. The Foxes crowding me recoiled slightly, but kept pressing in. The next one that touched me, I heaved into the air. He landed on six or eight of his fellows. I lunged for the next one, but he dodged out of reach. I grabbed two more and banged them together. They fell down. The Foxes behind them tripped over the bodies and whacked each other with their signs.

The prime minister maintained a dignified mien down

the long staircase, Dervina on his arm. A group of Vixens came running toward him with their signs up.

"Bring back the princess!" they cried.

Matfany flung up a hand. They barreled to a stop. He lowered his head so he was looking over his glasses at them. He dropped his fingers and flicked them twice. The females scrambled backwards, retreating into the crowd. He started walking forward. A path cleared before him. The protesters started shouting again, but they never got closer than arm's length. It only took a glare to make them back off. If I could have bottled that look, I would have been the wealthiest merchant in the Bazaar.

"When did this start?" I shouted at Matfany.

"Not long after I saw her highness in your office, sir," he said. "But it has gotten considerably worse after *those* started appearing." He pointed toward a distraught vixen who waved a copy of *The Princess's Diary* at him. "Is this the work of your rival? Is he trying to destroy what is left of our fair country?"

"I'm taking care of it," I promised him. "What's the deal with the others?" I aimed a thumb toward the "Keep Foxe-Swampburg Beautiful" contingent.

"You will see, sir," Matfany assured me.

I did.

From the castle gates, which overlooked the resort and the seaside, I could see the range of mountains that the Geek had put his name on.

"It wasn't supposed to be literal," I said.

"It seems your friend misinterpreted that concept," Matfany said.

The whole range looked as though it had been hit by a squad of giant, hyperactive subway taggers. From one end to the other, the sixteen peaks were covered with brilliant designs in colors that gave me a headache, even at that distance. In the middle of the largest and most prominent peak, the words "The Geek" flashed on and off in a blaze of orange light. I gawked.

"Oh," Dervina said. "I thought this was a quiet beauty spot."

"It was, ma'am," Matfany said. He glared at me. "And it will be again. Mister Aahz, I believe that's your problem."

"Down with the outsiders!" someone bellowed.

That's when the tomatoes started flying. The last I saw of Dervina, she vanished before the first one splatted just where she had been standing. I groaned.

There went my thousand gold coins.

Chapter 25

———

"What is the matter with you?" I bellowed at the Geek. He retreated to the back room of the tiny office he had rented on the resort's main street and tried to slam the door on me. I threw my whole weight against it and it banged open. The Geek cowered against the rear wall.

"You . . . you don't like it?" he said, attempting a shaky smile.

"Like it?" I slammed my hand against my forehead. "What part of 'you only own naming rights' was so hard to understand? What is all that out there?"

"Well, Aahz, you can't blame me for that! I didn't start it. It was my partners."

"What difference does that make?" Matfany asked, looking down at him like a stern professor. His sleek, black fur was amazingly untouched by the rotten vegetable cascade thrown by the crowd. On the other hand, I was dripping with liquescent salad. "A contract is a contract."

The Geek scowled at us. "Look at it from my point of view. I got a lot of other people . . . I mean, my business partners, to put down money. I had to cover my own . . . I mean, a lot of expenses, so I made them some unimportant little promises."

"Like what?"

"Well, I said they ought to be able to designate their

206

purchases in some way. I mean, it's a lot of money. No Deveel with any pride is going to pay something for nothing. So, I thought maybe a nice small sign with each person's name on it on top of their own peak. Not as big as my sign was going to be, since I'm the senior partner. It kind of . . . escalated a little."

"A *little*?" I bellowed. The Geek recoiled from the gust of wind. "You want to tell me why your name is written in Salamanders covering five or six square miles of terrain?"

"The first guy who arrived to see his mountain, he wasn't happy, but he was okay with the sign. The next few guys didn't like it. They said they wanted something different than the first guy. So I let them design their own signs. Bo-Fort, you know him?"

"Yeah."

"He came to me and said he was going to write his name in Fireflies on the mountain."

"That's not in the contract!"

"I know! He said to me, 'Well, how is anyone going to know that I own it?' I said, 'That's a good point.' "

"You don't own it," I said. "It's named after you. Owning it would cost about ten thousand times more."

"So, what did I buy?" the Geek asked, abandoning his imaginary partner's arguments. "I want my name on it. If I endowed an arena, my name would be right over the door."

I threw up my hands. "All right, we'll discuss it, but you are going to have to turn off the Salamanders!"

"I can't do it right away, Aahz," the Geek whined. "I paid for the first month in advance."

"Too bad. You can go as far as having a tasteful label with your name on it. So can your other suckers."

The Deveel frowned. "I don't want tasteful, I want readable. The range is more than ten miles from town. A tasteful sign isn't even a dot in one of those coin-operated telescopes! Not that there's anyone here to look at it. This place is as deserted as a shop offering free tax audits! We want some satisfaction for helping bail it out."

"Satisfaction! Did you see the protesters out there?" I pointed through the window. The picketers had followed me. They were shaking their fists and pointing. Any minute, they were going to start throwing things again. I was pretty sure they were out of vegetables, so they'd have to resort to dead animals and dung.

"I figure that's just their little way of welcoming us to town," the Geek said. "I could tone it down a little. Have the Salamanders only operate at night?"

"What about the size of the displays? You could feed a starving country on what you're spending to cover that kind of real estate!"

"I must tell you, Mister Geek, that I am disappointed in your lack of restraint," Matfany said in a quiet voice that impressed the heck out of the Deveel. "Some of your partners have actually put up signs that are larger than the feature itself that they have named. Is that sponsorship as you know it?"

The Geek rose to the occasion. "Uh, well, I could go down a half."

"You can go down to nothing," I countered.

"Forget it, Aahz! This isn't the deal we agreed to."

"If you read the contract, that is exactly the deal you agreed to."

"Then I want out! I want a refund!"

I felt as if my heart was being torn right out of my body. "You want . . . a what? No way!"

"That sounds like a reasonable response," Matfany said. "You can take all that nonsense off our mountain. I will find a means of returning your funds to you at once."

"What?" the Geek asked, off guard. "What about my investment? What about the money I put into that display? What about all the subsidiary rights I sold on the logo? What about the advertising I paid for to get people to come and visit Geek's Peak?"

The prime minister shrugged. "I suppose that we are both going to suffer a loss. That's business. We've been broke before. As you so tactfully point out. We will give him back his money, Mister Aahz."

I was still hyperventilating. "Give . . . it . . . back?" I saw the president's desk gallop away from me on little wooden legs. "I can't do that!"

"Then what's your offer?" the Geek asked.

Matfany peered over his glasses at him. "I want you to lessen your . . . logos to something not so intrusive, is what I want."

"Intrusive's the name of the game, pal. Where did subtlety get you? In the hole, that's where. This is the way out."

"I'd rather be in the hole than desecrate our landscape, sir," Matfany said. "I thought you understood the nature of our agreement."

"You wetlanders are all alike," the Geek yelled. "You don't know what civilization's really like."

"Wait a minute, wait a minute," I bellowed. I pulled Matfany aside. "What's the harm in letting him have a few little fireworks? When the crisis is over, you can nationalize all the geographical features again. In the meanwhile, it's a way of drawing people back here and getting some serious cash flow going. After all, you are going to have to figure out a way to pay M.Y.T.H., Inc.'s fee, aren't you?"

Matfany's proud shoulders slumped a little.

"Necessity makes traders of us all, Mister Aahz. Very well, then."

After two hours of solid and loud negotiation, Matfany agreed that the Geek and his partners could have a display on each of the items they sponsored, but such displays were to be limited to a standard billboard in size. The Geek's Salamander crew could operate for three hours after sunset every night, no more. Neither side was happy, but at least no refunds had to be issued.

Matfany shook his head when the Geek disappeared to inform his partners of the changes.

"I don't like it, Mister Aahz," he said.

"Don't like what?" I asked peevishly. This investment was saved, but I was still feeling the sting of losing Dervina. That thousand coins was going to be hard to replace, and I would never get another appointment with the Gnomes over Foxe-Swampburg.

"I must say I doubt that those Deveels are going to stick

to the agreement we just made. Just a feeling I have."

"A newborn baby would get that idea from talking to a Deveel," I said. "Look, the Geek agreed to tone down his fancy sign. You'll hardly know it's there."

"I would have preferred to have no lights at all. *I* understand why we have got to put up with it for the term of the contracts, but it is gonna upset the Old Folks. They like the way things were."

"So what?" I asked. "I can talk to a bunch of senior citizens. Where are they?"

"Well, that's kind of hard to explain. They're just around. They sort of enforce the old ways."

"Are they Swamp Foxes?" I asked.

Matfany nodded. "Yes, sir. Well, they were Swamp Foxes. When they were alive."

I felt the scales at the back of my neck prickle. "They're dead? Are they undead now?"

"No, sir, they're just dead. But they don't go away. Why would they? Foxe-Swampburg is their home. They like it here. And I don't think they're gonna like your changes too much, even if you do think the Deevils will tone it all down."

"What can a bunch of ghosts do?" I asked with a laugh. I opened the door.

SPLAT!

A long-dead fish hit me in the face.

"Who threw that?" I demanded.

"I beg your pardon, sir," a courteous voice shouted from the middle of the crowd. "I meant to hit that rapscallion next to you. This one's for you!" A hunk of decayed seaweed smacked into me.

I BAMFed out. I had had enough of Foxe-Swampburg for one day. I had to locate some more prospects to replace Devina. At least the investment here was safe.

Chapter 26

"With friends like these, who needs enemies?"

—Romeo Montague

I frowned at Gimblesby Ockwade. "So that's your final word on it? You won't even listen to the transcript of the Princess's diary? Your letter to us was downright enthusiastic."

"That was before I heard more about it." The Imp tycoon crossed his arms over the breast of his blue houndstooth suit. "I don't really go in for *prurient* literature."

"Prurient?" I repeated, not sure I had heard him right. "But it's just the observations of a young woman . . . "

"Enough!" he said, raising a hand. "I don't want to hear any more. I have a weak heart, and I can't take too many shocks. Just go away, please."

"May I just ask who told you what was in her diary?"

The Imp turned pink. "I have my sources. I consider them reliable."

"You know my reputation, don't you?" I asked, though I knew it was a lost cause to make any further appeal to him. "I'm considered very reliable, and I think you should reconsider using that source. He's lying for his own purposes."

Ockwade turned pinker. "I don't remember giving you a name."

I allowed myself an imperious smile. "I am a magician. I have ways of knowing."

"Reading minds without permission is rude! Goodbye, Mister Skeeve. Good to meet you, Mistress Massha."

"Just Massha," the court magician of Possiltum said with a wicked wink. "Gave up being a mistress a long time ago, when I got married."

The Imp's bright pink cheeks turned even pinker. He glanced at Nunzio, but thought better of addressing him.

"Thank you for dropping by," he said, all but pushing us through the ornate doors of his office. "Miss Selquiff, send in my three o'clock appointment."

"What a disaster," I said, as we got outside the gaudily-painted office building. I ducked around the corner and leaned against the wall.

"You said it, Big Shot," Massha said, fanning herself with a length of the filmy violet cloth she wore around her ample form. "That's four in a row."

The Imp tycoon had been nice enough to listen to my explanation of the difference between the princess's Cake ceremony and the knockoffs that Aahz had spawned across the dimensions, but he had flat-out refused to reschedule Hermalaya's appearance. Most of those who had cancelled wouldn't even take my calls. The people I did speak with were apologetic. Some of them renewed their invitations, but most didn't want anything to do with me. The controversy and the sudden onslaught of imitators had poisoned our appeal.

"This is all Aahz's fault," I said, shaking my head. "How could he do this to me?"

"Now, boss," Nunzio said, with a bitter kind of satisfaction. "He sees you as a threat."

I slammed my fist into my palm.

"We've just got to keep going," I said. "Hermalaya said she trusts us. She'll keep doing the ceremony as long as we can get anyone to host us. I'm just afraid of falling behind in income. I'll have to think of something else. I don't want Aahz to get ahead."

"No problem there," Massha said. "Why, the royalties on *The Princess's Diary* alone should cover . . . "

Massha's words were cut off at the same time as my eyesight. I never saw it coming. Hoods fell over our heads and light bonds dropped around our arms made it impossible for me to do anything but try and kick loose, which I did. To no avail. Whoever had grabbed us outnumbered us about ten to one at least.

I heard the explosion of air that informed me we were being moved to another location, if not another dimension.

The arms holding me shoved me forward, then pushed on my shoulders to force me to sit down. My bottom hit a flat surface that creaked under my weight. The hood was swept off my head. My eyes narrowed in the light of a fiercely burning candle that made me wince and draw back.

Shadows stood behind the candle. One of them leaned in toward me, but not enough so I could really see its face.

"So, you're Skeeve the Magnificent," it said. I thought it sounded female, but I couldn't be certain.

"Who wants to know?" I asked.

"Just answer me." Out of the darkness, an object flashed and came down on my head. *Honk!*

"Ow!" I yelled. The object fell at my feet. It was a bright blue and yellow rubber hammer, the kind used to play Whack-a-Gnome. Suddenly, I saw something silver leveled at my nose. It was a cake server, a very fancy, heavily ornamented solid silver handle with a well-sharpened blade, even more venerable-looking than Hermalaya's. I looked up into a pair of glittering black eyes. A black cloth concealed the rest of the face.

"Are you Skeeve the Magnificent? Answer! I don't have time to play games with you!"

"I'm Skeeve. Where are my friends?"

"In the corner with a couple of *my* friends. They're fine for now, as long as you answer my questions."

Another candle flared into light. I saw Massha near the wall. Her filmy veil had been tied over her mouth, and colored streamers bound her wrists. Two black-clad figures stood by her with servers at her throat. One of them held up a filmy bag that contained all of Massha's magikal jewelry. I winced. Without her toys, as she called them, Massha was almost as helpless as an ordinary person. Nunzio was dwarfed by an enormous figure who held his miniature crossbow by two fingers. The Mob enforcer was tied up with green cloth streamers that I recognized as Dragon-pinning tails.

We could escape from this situation, no matter how badly outnumbered we were, I thought. I reached out for a force line to gather some power to untie them. I ran into a magikal wall. I tried again. Nothing.

Although I could picture at least two nearby lines in my mind, I couldn't touch either one. There was a dampening spell on the room. Both of us were powerless, at least for the moment. I tried to keep calm.

"I don't want any trouble," I said amiably. "May I ask who I'm speaking with?"

The mysterious female loomed over me.

"My name is Ninja. I am a sixteenth-generation, nineteenth layer Cake Master."

"Nineteenth *layer*?" I asked. "I've never heard of that."

Ninja recoiled as if insulted. "You doubt me? Bety! Kroka! Prepare . . . the layer!"

Two black-aproned and masked females came forward, bearing between them a solid silver platter with a single, unfrosted chocolate cake on it.

"Hiayah!" Ninja swung the server at the cake.

Whisk, whisk! Whisk, whisk! Crumbs flew in all directions. I pulled back out of the way. A claw caught me by the nape of the neck and pushed me forward.

Ninja halted with an impressive economy of movement and drew the server back. She wiped it very carefully upon her apron tie and slid it into a sheath at her belt. She gestured to the others, who brought the cake close enough for me to examine.

"Count them," she said proudly. "Nineteen."

Gingerly, I ran a thumb up the edge of the cake, and the edges flipped back like very soft playing cards. I could see that it had been sliced thinly but so evenly that it looked like the side of a children's board book. There were exactly nineteen.

"Gosh," I said. "That's amazing."

"Gosh? The Great Skeeve says gosh?" Ninja sounded scornful.

"Sure," I said. "When I'm impressed. But why kidnap us? We're trying to help one of your, uh, society. Princess Hermalaya of Foxe-Swampburg."

"We have heard of your so-called *help*," Ninja spat. "We Cake Masters are disgusted by it."

"But why?" I asked. "Hermalaya has been doing everything according to the rules, isn't she? You couldn't ask for a more dignified representative of your . . . association. We've done what we can to make sure the fakes get closed down. And the rest have agreed to start taking the training courses."

I was hauled off the stool and smashed face first into the wall. Nunzio stood up, but the huge Cake Master shoved him down again.

Ninja hissed in my ear. "We hate fakes, but we also do not care for the sacred practice of hospitality and enjoyment being prostituted for money!"

"How do you support yourselves, then?" I asked in what I thought was a reasonable tone, as much as I could with a cake server pressed against the back of my neck while my face was buried in a silken Pin-the-tail-on-the-Dragon chart. "If you don't receive any, uh, gifts, you're not earning anything on your historic culture and experience."

There was a long pause.

"Well, I don't suppose we do," Ninja admitted. She backed off and took off her veil. I saw that she was another Reynardan, like Hermalaya. "We have patrons."

I spat out silk. "So, how's that different? You only support yourselves, if you can. Can you?"

Ninja sounded embarrassed when she finally answered. "Well, we all have other jobs. I decorate cakes in a hotel on Lux."

"I deliver pizzas," said one of the other black-clad figures. Behind her veil she was a Kobold.

"I'm a nanny," grated a Gargoyle.

"I'm a stockbroker," added a Gnome.

"Really?" I asked. It looked as if Cake Masters came from nearly every race in the dimensions, and almost every profession. "You do all that to support your hobby?"

Ninja whipped out her server again and brandished it at me. "It is not a hobby. It is a sacred calling! Cake has shown us peace and beauty in the world. If the Princess has prostituted that calling, then she must be punished. She is a Cake Master. She ought to know better!"

"Look, the Princess believes in all that!" I said. "I'm the one responsible for making it commercial. If you have to punish someone, punish me, not her. The only reason I got her to offer Cake ceremonies in exchange for favors is to rescue her kingdom. Maybe none of you know what happened to her?"

"Oh, we do," the Kobold said. "I bought a copy of her diary. We all read it. We cried like babies!"

"The Princess has never had another job. In fact, she's trying to get her job back. Princessing is a tough gig, as hard as being a nanny." I glanced around the circle of black-clad figures. "Maybe worse."

"It couldn't be worse," the Gargoyle replied. "Not with *triplets.*"

"Hmmm," Ninja mused. "I never thought of it that way. You say that she is a sincere student of the art?"

"She throws me out of the kitchen every time she bakes a Cake," I said, making certain to pronounce the capital letter. "She spins every attendee around three times before they try to pin the tail on the Dragon. Nobody gets more than one scoop of ice cream on their piece of Cake."

Ninja drummed her fingers on her lip. "That is strictly traditional. Possibly even orthodox."

"See?" I said. "How do you get more sincere than that? I promise that as soon as she's back on the throne, she will never accept money for doing the Cake ceremony ever again. In the meantime, I've got to ask you to be patient. We still have an uphill battle to get her back safely to her homeland and restored to the throne."

Almost in unison, the society of Cake practitioners sighed.

"It's so romantic," the Gargoyle said. "I can't wait to see how it ends. Is she going to publish a sequel to her diary?"

"I have no idea," I said. "Will you let me and my friend go now? Can Hermalaya keep practicing the way she has? Maybe if you think of her guests as patrons it wouldn't sound so bad?"

Ninja gathered her companions around her, and they had a quiet but very animated conference. It broke up. Ninja turned back to me.

"You have a deal, Skeeve." She clapped her hands, and three

of the women ran to untie Massha and help her re-bling. The Gargoyle returned Nunzio's crossbow and helped him brush down his suit. "Let's see how Princess Hermalaya does, and maybe we'll even throw some business her way. Please tell her we are at our sister's service. If there's ever anything we can do to help her, all you have to do is call. Uh, after four o'clock, if you don't mind. That's when I get off work."

Chapter 27

———

"It seems my reputation has preceded me."

— Viktor Frankenstein

Massha, Nunzio, and I bounced into the office. Bunny smiled up at us from the book she was reading and reached for the ledger.

"Not that," I said, holding up a hand. "I don't have any income to report at the moment. In fact, I have a complaint."

"A complaint?" Bunny asked.

"Gleep!" My dragon had heard my voice and came running to express his joy that I was home again. He charged into the room, and before I could yell 'No!' he had launched himself in the air and knocked me flat on my back. He held me down with both forepaws as he slathered my face with his long, stinking tongue.

"I hope this contest is over soon," Bunny said, shaking her head disapprovingly. "He never behaved like that in the inn. Bad! Bad dragon!"

My dragon stopped sliming me and sat back on his haunches. He favored Bunny with a reproachful look.

I sat up. I wiped my face with one hand and scratched the dragon behind his eye ridges with my other. Gleep crooned.

"I almost wish I was back there now," I said. "Look, when everybody agreed that the contest was to amass the greatest wealth possible for our respective clients, right?"

"Right," Bunny said. "What's the problem?"

"Aahz is sabotaging us," I said. "He's interfering with practically everything we're doing to try to earn money for Hermalaya. Someone told a toymaker here in the Bazaar he could make dolls in her image. Somebody went around selling the idea of ripping off the Cake ceremony. All of that points to Aahz."

"That's a pretty hefty accusation," she said. "Do you have any tangible proof? Has anyone actually named Aahz?"

I grimaced. "Well, no, not used his *name* . . . but I know it's him! Who else would have all the details of Hermalaya's life at his fingertips so he could lie about them?"

"Well, anyone who has a copy of her diary, for one," Bunny said. She held up the book on her desk. It was *The Princess's Diary*. "This is a third printing. We're talking about thousands of copies across the dimensions. And Hermalaya doesn't spare the ink when it comes to setting down her thoughts. I know everything about her except her lingerie sizes. As for the rest of the copycats, you have been getting a lot of publicity. People talk. And people who want to make money use new ideas. Didn't you?"

"Yes, but . . . "

BAMF!

"There he is!" Aahz pointed a claw at my nose. "What do you think you're doing, making a mess of my assets like that?"

"What?" I goggled. "I never touched your assets. What assets?"

Tananda, Matfany and Guido all appeared behind Aahz, looking at me reproachfully.

Aahz turned to Bunny. "It's like I don't have enough problems trying to revive a has-been resort town in a hick kingdom in a backwater dimension. And it's not like I don't have enough problems dealing with people who can't take no for an answer, or poker-up-the-rear bureaucrats, or angry peasants throwing last year's produce at me, that I have to deal with *you* short-circuiting my efforts to make things work for my client." The finger came around and poked at my nose again.

"Me?" I knew my voice went up to a squeak.

"Yeah, you! Who else would want to ruin the displays when I finally got everything negotiated to run like a top? Who has a stake in seeing my enterprise fail? You."

I felt steam come out of my ears.

"I would never do anything like that," I protested. "I never saw your displays. In fact, I have spent the last week trying to deal with the damage you did to me and *my* client. Poor Hermalaya hasn't been so embarrassed in her life. People are calling her a phony. She's the most genuine person in the world! She used to be a respected head of state, and now she's an *action figure*. I feel responsible for setting her up—for putting her in a position where someone I used to trust more than anybody could make her feel like a fool."

"Used to trust?" The veins in Aahz's eyes burst into relief. "Listen, you Klahdish pipsqueak . . . !"

A piercing whistle knifed my eardrums. Both of us stopped talking. Bunny removed two fingers from her mouth.

"Gentlemen! If I may use that term without bursting into cynical laughter. You," she pointed at me. "I already heard from you. You!" she pointed at Aahz. "What is Skeeve supposed to have done to you?"

Aahz glanced sideways at Matfany, who was holding himself aloof from interacting with any of us. He looked pretty disgusted, not that I cared what he thought. I was glad that Hermalaya wasn't safely back in Possiltum.

"I . . . made deals with a number of prominent businessmen who would take an interest in Foxe-Swampburg in exchange for financial consideration. It involves a certain amount of visible advertising on local landmarks."

"Glaring, vulgar displays," Matfany added.

"Yeah, it all depends on how you look at it!" Aahz snapped. I could see the honeymoon was long over between the two of them. "I conceded to local interests to . . . "

" . . . Tone them down a little," Tananda put in, when Aahz had hesitated too long.

"Yeah! They were toned down!"

"To a dull roar," Matfany put in.

"Let me finish!" Aahz bellowed.

Bunny held up a thumb and forefinger and brought them together. Everybody else closed their mouths.

"Go on," she said to Aahz.

He frowned. "From that point, they should have been fine. Then, all of a sudden, the images started fading right off the rocks and buildings. Whole billboards disappeared overnight!

Salamanders started going out, or they lost their grip and fell. The Firedrakes' Union steward complained to the Geek, and he came to me. Matfany's guards questioned the protesters . . . "

"Protesters?" I asked.

"Shut up," Aahz said. "They didn't have anything to do with it. The whole mess smacked of magikal interference." He glared at me. "And who has the greatest interest in seeing me fail? Skeeve!"

"I didn't do anything!" I said. "Bunny, you have to believe me. I haven't been in Foxe-Swampburg. I never got near any of his arrangements. What about Matfany? From what I hear, he's underhanded enough to cause trouble! Look what he did to Hermalaya!"

The Swamp Fox was outraged. "Sir, you have no right to make such accusations."

"He's just trying to misdirect you," Aahz said. "Typical behavior of someone who is guilty."

"How could you, Skeeve?" Tananda asked, woe in her dark green eyes. "Attacking someone you don't even know. It's just so unlike you."

"It's unlike me because it wasn't me! I mean, I thought about it. Who wouldn't, after everything started to go wrong with our plans?"

"Your plans went wrong because you set them all up wrong," Aahz said with grim glee. "Everything I ever taught you about exploiting a situation to the fullest, you seem to have forgotten. Sitting in that inn seems to have rotted your brain. Such as it is. Klahds just don't have a lot of basic intelligence."

The whistle called time-out on our argument again.

"Enough with the personal remarks," Bunny said. "Some of the rest of us are Klahds, too, you know."

"No offense," Aahz said.

"I didn't sabotage anything," I said. "How can I prove that? I can't prove a negative. Look, I have been with Massha, Nunzio, Chumley, or Hermalaya almost every minute I haven't been in here."

Chumley raised a forefinger. "I say, he's right, but it doesn't take long to upset the apple cart, what? I have to be fair, Skeeve, old boy. You did dash in and out a few times. I'd be very disappointed if you were going off to interfere with the other side, what?"

I felt more alone than I had ever been before. "I don't know how I can convince you. I didn't do anything wrong. You have to believe me. I give you my word I wasn't involved in anything Aahz did failing."

Aahz was gloating. "If that's your story, then I didn't do anything wrong, either."

"All right, all right," Bunny said, holding up her hands. "Then, here are the new ground rules: both of you stay away from each other. Don't interfere in what the other one is doing. Don't go near each other anywhere except here. Any conversations you have from now until the end of this contest will be held in front of witnesses, preferably in this office. Any more bad behavior means you automatically concede the contest to your opponent. Do I make myself clear?"

Very grudgingly, I choked out a yes. So did Aahz.

"Good. Both of you go away. You've been in here too long.

Help your clients. Stay out of trouble. That's all. Beat it."
Bunny sat down at her secretary desk and opened her copy
of *The Princess's Diary*.

We all looked at each other. Aahz gave me a smirk.

BAMF! He, Matfany, Tananda and Guido disappeared.

I regretted the day I gave him that D-hopper.

Chapter 28

"Mister Aahz, I have to say I believed your colleague, Skeeve," Matfany said. We were following an indignant foreman— or really fore-Salamander—Pintubo, and his fireproofed Reynardan escort, back to the damaged displays in the hills to get a good look at them. "His countenance did not seem like one who dissembles, and as an administrator, I must say I see my share of dishonest faces."

I growled without looking at him. The uphill slog was complicated by thick, cementlike mud on the path that was building up under my feet like platform shoes.

"I believed him, too," Tananda said, tripping along lightly. "I might have jumped to the wrong conclusion back there. It's not the first time Skeeve has been innocent when we believed the worst about him, Aahz. Look what happened on Imper."

"I don't want to hear it," I said. "The kid knows I put a spoke in his wheels, and he got back at me. Big deal. It's over."

"Unless he didn't," Guido said. "You gotta look at the bigger picture. More people than Skeeve don't like what we're doin' here."

He aimed a meaty thumb backwards. We weren't the only people on the mountain path. Some of the more determined protesters were following us, at a distance enforced by a whole troop of the castle guards. By then, the townsfolk were using their signs as staffs to help them up the steep slope, but they were determined to let us know that they weren't happy with the status quo—as they knew it. I realized we had let an important facet of Matfany's reform slide.

"We have to give the people an update when we get to the top," I said. "We're doing all kinds of publicity, but no public relations."

"And what will that involve?" Matfany asked.

"A speech," I said. "By you. Start thinking about bullet points: how you are doing your best for the country, how what's happening up here is beneficial to them, and how tourism is going to start coming back. It's already happening."

I spoke with confidence because I had been keeping up with the hoteliers in the resort. All of them reported bookings from a dozen dimensions, including some large tour groups. I had made a mental note of which ones had the fewest rooms left to rent, with an idea toward sending auditors in to scan the books. I figured I could count the taxes the hotels and inns paid on profit to the kingdom as part of my total. I was sure I could talk Bunny into it. As mad as the Geek was about the vandalism, his new trade in knickknacks was also paying off, with a percentage on all sales to be paid to me—I mean, the treasury. That ought to boost my takings so far over Skeeve all he'd be able to see was the bottoms of my feet.

The prime minister considered the request gravely. "I believe I can do that."

I expanded on my topic. "Don't forget, you have to stress that things are only better *because* you took over. That Pixie-headed princess of yours threw the whole country into a financial crisis on top of your environmental disaster. But you're the one pulling it all out again. Get it?"

"Now, just a minute, sir!" Matfany said, coming to a halt. "I have asked you not to lay tongue to our monarchy!"

"Only if they really need a licking," I leered at him. He looked shocked. "Look. People might like the fact that money is coming in, but no one can get past the idea that you threw the royal house out and took over. If you don't get people on your side pronto, you're not going to be a popular ruler when the crisis is over. I don't want you to have to keep looking over your shoulder for the rest of your life. Hermalaya may have been featherbrained, but people liked her. It's gonna start affecting the bottom line if we don't do something."

Matfany looked glum. "I know it, sir. I am just about ready to go back on bended knee and ask her to return."

"No!" I roared. The force of my voice knocked him back about five paces.

"Mister Aahz, whyever not?"

"She's the reason you had a problem, isn't it?"

"Well, sir, of course she's not," Matfany said. His face softened from its usual stern expression. "It was the bugs that caused all the problems. She kinda made things light up, really. She cheered people up even when things got really bad. Even me."

"Aw," Tananda said, throwing her arms around him. "I

get what's going on here. You had to send her away because you're in love with her, aren't you?"

"Ma'am!" Matfany exclaimed, taken aback. "I do not appreciate having my feelings discussed in public."

"We're not in public," Tananda said, cuddling into his arm and looking up at him. I'd seen men made of stone melt at that look. "Is it true?"

"What has that got to do with public relations?" I growled.

"Nothing," Tananda said with a grin. "It has a lot more to do with private relations. Matfany, what would you do if you didn't have the kingdom to consider?"

The prime minister pulled away from her. "Ma'am, my whole life is service to the throne!"

By now, even I could see he was evading the question. If I hadn't been fixed on the job at hand, I might have had some sympathy for him.

"Forget it," I said. "We're there. Hi, guys! Great to see you."

We had been met by not only the Geek and some of his business partners, but the entire Salamander workforce, all of them bright orange-red hot and boiling mad.

Salamanders are small but dangerous beings from a dimension called Salamagundi. They like to visit other places because they're social by nature. Trouble is, they can set almost anything on fire just by touching it, which makes having one for a house guest a real pain in the posterior. Gus, our Gargoyle buddy who worked in the Golden Crescent Inn and did side jobs for us, had a Salamander pal named

Berfert, who had also worked for M.Y.T.H., Inc. once in a while. Being made of solid stone, Gargoyles don't have the problem with flammability the rest of us do. That was also why I hadn't panicked when the Geek told me he had hired a Salamander advertising firm to run his billboard on Geek's Peak. There should have been no problems with the little lizards on a bare rock face.

'Toned down' in Matfany's terms, or even my terms, came nowhere even in the same ballpark with the Geek's, but the whorls, flourishes, and fancy typography had been reduced by over three-quarters of the mountainside. Within the newly defined borders, I could see wild streaks and black burns, evidence of Salamanders being surprised by something.

"Look at that!" Pintubo shrieked in his shrill little voice, waving his tiny forefoot upward. "Hazardous conditions! My lizards don't have to work like this."

"Right!" the miniature crowd of Salamanders cried.

"What do we want?"

"Safety harnesses!"

"When do we want them?"

"*Now!*"

"But you guys can melt yourselves into solid stone," I said, interrupting the chanting. "There's no reason you should be falling off. That's not even a vertical slope."

"It's some kind of magic!" the forelizard said. "Either you fix it, or we're going on strike. We'll take down the other displays around town, too."

"If they do, we'll sue," Gribaldi said. He was a large,

meaty Deveel with a sloping forehead on which grew black eyebrows thick enough to lose an antelope in. "You agreed that we get to advertise our sponsorship."

"I know," I said. "Look, Pintubo, try it again. I just had a confab with the master wizard who was interfering, and he said he won't do it any more. Give it a try."

The tiny lizards swarmed up the cliff face and moved into position. At a signal from Pintubo, they started racing around in their designated circuits. I had to admit that the effect was pretty darned impressive. The hot orange dots seemed to blur into lines. The mountainside above us began to blink on and off. *The Geek. The Geek. The Geek.*

I put my arms around the shoulders of the Geek and Gribaldi.

"Pretty darned impressive, huh? No more accidents."

"All right," the Geek said, grudgingly. "As long as it doesn't happen again."

"It won't," I promised him. "We're all going to be one big, happy family from now on."

Chapter 29

One problem solved. Too bad there was no easy solution to the cranky crowd that now surged around us. I had thought at first there were only a few dozen, but hundreds, even thousands of Swamp Foxes had made the hike up the steep path to make their displeasure known.

I had to hand it to Matfany. He never flinched. He hopped up on a handy rock, stuck his thumb in the lapel of his coat, and addressed them:

"Good people of Foxe-Swampburg, I am happy to see you all. I want to talk to you today about our nation's prosperity. We have had some difficult times in the past. In that light, some hard decisions had to be made by me so that our nation could survive. Our resources were few, so I enlisted the help of some kindly folks to help us get back on our feet." He opened a hand toward us. When the baleful eyes of the Swamp Foxes turned our way, I wished he hadn't. Nothing like an angry mob to make you start looking for the exit.

"What are you going to do about that eyesore behind you?" a passionate female voice demanded.

"This fine exhibition is part of our recovery," Matfany said. "We have to welcome new partners into our midst for at least a time. I hope you will embrace them as I have. It is all for the benefit of our fine country. I hope to lead you into a prosperous future in which we can hold our heads high and stand proudly beside our neighbors. It is my contention that Foxe-Swampburg will return to being a kind and welcoming place for visitors . . . "

SPLAT! Streamers of stinking goo sprayed all over me and Guido. Someone in the crowd had thoughtfully brought along a basket of decayed vegetables. I backed up until I could feel the cliff face at my back.

"Mention Hermalaya," I hissed.

"Ah, yes." Matfany said, straightening his glasses. "It may take you some time to get used to the new form of government here in our nation, but it is for the best. My cabinet and I have your interests in mind. You are welcome to send queries and concerns to my office. I am especially interested in hearing where problems need to be addressed."

"What about the princess?" I hissed.

"Some of you have voiced your displeasure at the absence of Princess Hermalaya. I am afraid her actions did not fit in with the survival of our nation."

"But she's our princess!" a lone voice cried out.

"That is beside the point," Matfany said sternly. "I am your prime minister! I have been running this country throughout the crisis of the pinchbugs and the specter of bankruptcy that has followed in its wake. I am the one pulling you back from the brink of disaster." He loomed over them. His shadow seemed to cast outward over most of the crowd. "Are you questioning *my judgment*?"

They cowered back, filled with fear, until someone raised a copy of *The Princess's Diary*.

"Yes! Yes, we are! Hermalaya loved us! We want her back!"

That broke the logjam.

"Yes! Yes!" they began to chant. "Bring back our princess. Down with Matfany! Down with Matfany!" My worst nightmare loomed as the crowd started to surge toward us.

Suddenly, Salamanders began to fall off the sign above our heads. The bright orange lizards landed on the Swamp Foxes, who howled and leaped around, bellowing with pain. The Salamanders, trying to scramble to safety, accidentally set fur and signs on fire. The protesters forgot all about us in their rush to put out the blazes. I pulled back under an overhang. Pervects have tough skin, but fire is one thing that can destroy us. My companions crowded in after me. Outside, the Deveels ran in circles, howling about their precious advertising. For the moment, no one was thinking about us.

"That saved our bacon," I said. "I gotta hand it to Skeeve for timing."

"Skeeve's not doing that," Tananda said. "He would never hurt Salamanders."

"Then who?" Guido asked. "Show me the magician causing the cascade. If they are not in a concealed place, I am sure I can pick them off from here."

She looked up at the sky. I knew she was reading force lines. Since I had lost my powers, I could no longer see them. "No one is pulling magik out of there. This is a natural phenomenon of some kind."

We heard a gentle cough behind us.

"It's the Old Folks," Matfany said, squeezed into the rear

of the niche. "I told you they don't like people messing up their mountains and things."

The force of Salamanders gathered their injured members and assembled in a group at the base of the Geek's sign.

"That's it!" Pintubo squeaked indignantly at me. "We quit! This dimension is too dangerous for us to work! You'll be hearing from our legal representative! He'll burn you up!"

They flashed out of existence.

"Hey, Aahz, I warned you!" Gribaldi said, coming over to shake his fist at me. "We've had enough. You had better give us our money back."

"No!" I exclaimed. "Put up something else, anything! Your choice. I always thought Salamanders were a bad idea. How about Shutterbug photos? You could have your picture up here, too."

"No more," Matfany said. He poked a finger at the Deveel's collarbone. "We are not having Deveels leering down at us from here. You can put your names up in a more genteel fashion. Some of my folks have been out of work for a while. They'd be pleased to have the jobs. I don't want to have to make it a law to use local labor, but I will if I have to."

The assembled Swamp Foxes were outraged. "We won't work for them. And we don't want you! We want our princess back!"

They started to chant again:

"Bring back our princess! Bring back our princess!"

Something whizzed past me and impacted on the stone

face at my side. It was a rock. They had run out of vegetables, but they weren't out of missiles.

"We'd better beat a retreat," I said. I reached into my pocket for my D-hopper.

An unlucky stone smashed into my wrist. It caught the tip of the magical device and sent it spiraling out of my reach. I dashed out and made a flying leap to catch it.

Guido jumped out after me, brandishing his crossbow in an attempt to cover me, but you might as well have held up an umbrella under a waterfall. The Swamp Foxes piled onto us. I got a foot in the eye and grabbed for the nearest tail. I closed my teeth on it.

"Yow!" the owner bellowed. He must have retaliated against whoever was near his mouth, because another cry erupted from the pile of beings on my back. In a moment, it turned into a writhing, scratching, punching mass. I got off a few more bites as I scrabbled on my hands and knees toward daylight. A Swamp Fox, also on all fours, met me face to face and bared his teeth. I snarled back. He recoiled slightly, but a dozen others shouldered up beside him. I faced a ring of glowing, yellow eyes. Well, if I couldn't ignore a fight, the best thing I could do was win it. I bunched up my thigh muscles and jumped backwards, out of their way. The only real way to win a fight is not to get in it.

The Swamp Foxes were stunned for a moment, then came after me, barking and howling. I dashed around the rock Matfany was still standing on, trying to find my D-hopper or a way down off the mountain. I dodged my pursuers three times. Then, they got smart and split up. I found myself with my back to the giant rock, facing dozens of sets of teeth. Above my head, Tananda had been treed by another crowd of Swamp Foxes. Guido wrestled with one of the largest specimens I had ever seen, the two of them straining to toss the other one over.

"Stop this!" Matfany bellowed over all the noise. "Stop all this at once!"

The gang facing me straightened like chastised schoolboys and looked up at him. The prime minister stood on top of his rock with his fists on his hips. He glared at everyone over his glasses.

"Ladies and gentlemen—I hope that you all are ladies and gentlemen! How dare you show such disrespect to these people who are our guests and visitors? You were all brought up with much better manners than that! You are Swamp Foxes! Honest, courteous, sensible people. Now, I am sure that you would like to apologize to our guests. Go on! Apologize! Right this very minute!"

The leader of the pack put out a paw.

"I certainly am sorry, sir. I hope you didn't take offense from us?"

"Not at all," I said, clasping the hand and letting it go hastily. "No problem."

All around me, the locals, some of them with torn or burned fur and blackened eyes, were offering their heartfelt regrets to the Deveels and other merchants. I had to hand it to Matfany. I had never met anyone else who had such natural authority that he could call a mob to order with one bellow.

"That's better," Matfany said. He bounded lightly down from the boulder. "That's more of the civilized people that I have always known you to be. Now, may I wish you a sincere good night. Come along, Mister Aahz."

He started walking down the hill. He was so smooth that it even took *me* a moment to realize he was talking to me. I hurried after him. The mob parted to let him go by. I stepped over a sign. Guido shook hands with his wrestling partner and followed. Tananda caught up with me and tilted an incredulous glance over her shoulder at the immobile gang of protesters. I stumped beside Matfany.

"That was incredible," I whispered to him.

"Ten years of teaching high school history, sir," Matfany confided.

"How long's the lull going to hold?"

"About five more seconds. I suggest we start running, as of now . . . three, two, one . . . "

"Kill him! He exiled our princess!"

"Kill him!"

"Retreat is in order, gentlemen and madame," Matfany said. He took to his heels. Tananda dashed after him. Guido and I looked at each other and headed off in their wake.

The mob tore after us.

Chapter 30

We made it back to town fifteen times faster than we had left it. The soles of my feet were bruised and torn from running over rocks, and I had enough stitches in my side to make a quilt, but we didn't have a choice. The mob was only yards behind us. Matfany turned as we went crossed the main square and headed up the road leading to the castle.

"Bar the doors!" I bellowed as we passed the guards.

They sprang to grab hold of the enormous portals, but they were too late. The throng of angry Swamp Foxes burst in behind them, flinging the gates open until they smacked against the inner walls. Adrenaline gave me a kick in the rear. I kept running, almost into the arms of another gang of protesters who were still marching up and down on the steps of the castle itself.

Guido took point. At the sight of the sign-bearing Foxes ahead, he put his shoulder down and plowed into them like a linebacker. They went flying. Matfany trotted up the stairs in Guido's wake. I followed the white tip of Matfany's tail into the blackness of the castle hall.

I had to hand it to the guards on duty. They were on the ball. The doors opened at our rear as the prime minister reached them, and boomed shut as Tananda nipped through. The guards threw down the bar, a piece of bronze-bound wood as large as an I-beam.

"Where can we go?" Tanda asked.

Boom! Boom! Boom! The mob started pounding on the doors. The guards looked alarmed, but they mustered in a line facing the portals.

"Those can't hold forever. What's the most defensible room in this place?" I asked Matfany.

"The throne room is the most protected place," Matfany said. "Stands to reason, as that is the seat of government . . . "

"Let's go there!" I said. "Which way?"

"We can't go into the throne room, Mister Aahz," he said.

"What? Never mind!" I said, as he started to give me another one of his pedantic replies. "Don't be so squeamish about the privileges of royalty. Which way is it?"

He pointed. I ran down the hall to the inlaid double doors that towered over my head.

The guards flanking them saluted Matfany as we got closer. I ignored them and grabbed for the bronze handles. I tugged. I pulled. I twisted. I put one foot on the frame and hauled.

"Unlock them!" I bellowed.

"They're not locked, Mister Aahz," Matfany said. "I tried to tell you. The Old Folks won't let me in. They don't like me."

"What the hell, you're in charge!"

Matfany shook his head. "You just don't cross the Old Folks. They've been against me taking over the government pretty much from day one."

Boom! Boom! Boom!

"We can't stay here," Guido said. "Dose doors will not withstand forever against a thousand people. What's the next safest place you got?"

"The dungeon's safe. So is the treasury."

"Does either of them have a second way out?" I asked.

"Well, of course not, sir," Matfany said. "That wouldn't make any sense."

"We'd be trapped there?"

"I'd say so."

"Will converting the Old Folks to your government stop those people out there from protesting against you?" I asked.

"Well, possibly . . . " Matfany said.

I interrupted him. "Then the only thing we can do to stop all the chaos is to talk to the Old Folks. We have to convince them that we're doing the right thing for the kingdom."

"I don't think that's a good idea, Mister Aahz," Matfany said. "They're a little tetchy."

"So am I!" I roared. "They can't keep blocking you out of the showpiece of your castle. They have got to stop interfering with my—your ability to make money for the country. And I have no interest in being torn apart by an angry mob."

CRASH!

The castle doors slammed inward.

"Down with Matfany!" the crowd bellowed.

"We gotta move," Guido said.

"End of discussion," I said. "Where can we go?"

"Out the back way," Matfany said. "If you're so fixed on speaking to the Old Folks, that's the best suggestion I can make."

The guards formed a line across the hallway, spears pointing toward the advancing mob. Matfany led us around a corner. He pulled open a humble-looking door and ushered us into a narrow, damp-smelling spiral stairwell. Guido jammed the door closed behind us. There were no lights, but Tananda took care of that with a little spell she probably used for burglary or one of her many other sidelines. The pale golden glow surrounded us as we wound downward into the servants' quarters.

The white-clad staff in the kitchen jumped in surprise as their prime minister went tearing through with a Pervect, a Trollop, and a huge, crossbow-bearing Klahd at his heels.

"Flying inspection," he told them as he passed. "You all are doing very well. Mmm, that smells delicious," he added to a gray-haired old male stirring a pot.

"Thanks, prime minister," they all chorused.

"Forget the soap," I snarled. "We need to get out of here."

"Courtesy is never misplaced, Mister Aahz," Matfany told me reproachfully. "Down here, now. We'll go out through the gardens."

We hurried through the rear door of the kitchens, out past a stinking heap of garbage, through the herb garden and into a wide green expanse lined with tall hedges. I hurtled down the broad stone steps, heading for the gate at the rear of the extensive grounds, and immediately sank up to my ankles.

"What is this?" I bellowed. The green lawn swirled around my calves.

"Why, it's swamp, sir," Matfany said. "We are Swamp Foxes. This is our heritage."

"You can't run in this . . . muck! You can't even walk!"

"If you want to run, you need to stick to the hummocks."

"Why would royalty live like this?" I asked, outraged. "You could fill all that in and have great, rolling meadows! This isn't a garden, it's a compost heap. You've got nice dry streets in town!"

"Dry land is for tourists, sir," Matfany said. He trotted ahead of me as lightly as a feather. Grumbling, I picked myself up and followed in his footsteps. Contrary to what I thought when I first sloshed out into the yard, there were solid lumps in it. His stride was a lot longer than mine was, so I missed my footing more than once. My dapper clothes were soaked and striped with green goo by the time we got to the rear of the property. Guido didn't say anything, but I could see by the look on his face what he thought of having his beautiful, pin-striped suit redecorated by Swamps R Us. Tananda, the only one of us with magikal talent, tripped lightly over the meadow like a soap bubble. I wished I could go back in time and shoot Garkin again for taking away my powers.

The sun was going down. Thanks to Tananda's light spell, we were able to see where we were going. I almost wished we couldn't. Matfany led us under low-hanging tree branches and over ridges of stone, but all of the land underfoot was wet, wet, wet. Stinging insects took advantage of the fact I had to pay more attention to my footing than swatting them and wriggled under my scales. Guido and Tananda, whose soft skins were more vulnerable than mine, scratched and slapped at their own insect hordes.

"How much more of the World of Mildew do we have to cover before we get there?" I asked, heaving each leg laboriously out of stinking muck. I slapped at a cloud of gnats trying to gnaw on my neck.

Matfany negotiated a foot-wide bridge over a gurgling stream. "Their domain is deep in the marshlands."

"So, when you die you don't go to the gates of heaven, you go to the fens?" I grinned, hoping someone would get the pun.

Matfany regarded me solemnly. "To our ancestors, this is our bit of heaven."

The next branch he let go of hit me in the face. Some people just don't appreciate good humor.

"Aahz, we're bein' followed," Guido muttered in my ear.

"Who's back there?" I asked. I didn't ask how he knew. Guido had survival training from a number of special organizations including the Mob, and well-honed instincts.

"Can't say yet." He touched his breast pocket. "I saw a shadow as we went over the last hill. Somethin' low-slung with lots of legs. Kinda looks familiar, but I can't place it yet. I'll tell Tananda we oughta be ready to rumble."

Once Guido mentioned it, I started to get that being-watched feeling on the back of my neck. In the undergrowth, I thought I saw glowing eyes following our every move.

Pervects don't believe in ghosts. If we have an afterlife, I guess we think it's none of anyone else's business. As far as I know, none of my ancestors has bothered to come back and tell any of its descendants what it's like. And, if heaven's not a place of unlimited comfort, wealth, food, booze, sex, and entertainment, I'm not sure I care. Outside of Perv, things are different. I know Klahds believe in disembodied spirits, evidence notwithstanding. This was the first place I had visited where the nonliving existed side by side with the living as if there was little difference between the two states.

The trees opened out a little, revealing more extensive stretches of green sludge. Now there seemed to be signs of habitation. In the twilight, I saw silhouettes of houses, some grand and stately, others no more than shacks. They all shimmered in a haze of blue I put down to the gigantic moon rising just above the line of trees.

"Who lives there?" I asked, pointing to one of the elaborate mansions.

"No one," Matfany replied.

"Okay," I said, caught in my own linguistic trap. "Who *occupies* it?"

"That'd be the third Lord Protector of the Marshes," Matfany said. "He lived about fifteen hundred and twenty years ago. Most of his family is there, too."

"How about that one?" I pointed at a falling-down shanty with smoke curling out of the spindly chimney.

"Last king but two. Cornelius the Fifth never had much use for fancy things. Fishing's good, that's all he cares about."

"And who are we going to see?" Tananda asked.

"Whoever will talk to us," Matfany said. "Keep an eye out for the foxfire. That's where they'll be."

"What's foxfire?"

We stepped through an arching avenue of mangrove trees that blotted out the moon. I kept close to Tananda's light. The footing was tricky. It looked like there was only one path that didn't dump pedestrians into the soup.

Matfany jumped from hummock to tussock to slippery, moss-covered rock. I heard a curse and a splash behind me which meant Guido had missed at least one of them. All of us except the prime minister had gotten soaked numerous times.

We emerged on the other side. I had to squint at the blinding blaze of blue light that filled the clearing ahead.

"That's foxfire," Matfany said.

Glimmering figures began to rise out of the ground until I felt like the only unlit candle on top of a birthday cake. In outline they were Swamp Foxes, but when I stuck a hand through one, all I felt was the dank, cold air.

"And those are the Old Folks."

Chapter 31

Their insubstantiality only cut one way. The Old Folks grabbed us and hauled us into the middle of the brilliant blue light, which just happened to correspond exactly with the soggiest and stinkiest part of the marshland. At least they found us a relatively solid piece of turf to stand on, but it was so small that Tananda, Guido, and I were practically doing a group hug to keep from toppling into the mire. Bubbling black mud opened up belching bubbles of swamp gas. It smelled like a bar at the end of a nine-day drunk. My eyes watered, but I kept my tone friendly and diplomatic.

"Nice place you've got here," I told the towering flames who guarded me. "Great weather we're having, huh?"

They didn't answer.

Matfany stood a few yards away, surrounded by a halo of blue-light specials. These were more defined in shape than the majority of Old Folks. Between their triangular ears they had crowns on their heads, and the streams of ectoplasm that trailed behind them were embroidered, fur-trimmed cloaks. Even with my sharp ears, I had to strain to hear what they were saying to him.

"You have violated the sanctity of our wilderlands, and for what?" one long-nosed queen demanded. "For ordinary cash money?"

"I had little choice, your highness," Matfany said with a bow. "Our resources are depleted."

"Our resources are endless," a broad-faced king boomed in a surprisingly low voice. "You just needed to be patient. Instead, you have interfered with the line of succession."

"I'm very sorry you see it that way," Matfany said. "I don't need to tell you that there has been three different lines of royal house here in Foxe-Swampburg."

"But she isn't dead! My daughter doesn't have to be the last of her line!" insisted a tenor. He retained more of his shape than even his fellow royals. Matfany looked startled, then bowed deeply.

"King Tinian . . . I'm honored."

"Well, you shouldn't be," he said. "Prime ministers serve. They don't rule. If I had realized you would depose my daughter, I would never have promoted you out of the accounting office!"

"What were you thinking, letting those rude Deveels do that to the Mountains Above Town?" the deep-voiced ghost asked. "What a mess they made. And where do they go calling The Tallest Peak after a Geek?"

"Let me explain," I said, pushing forward. I felt my leg go halfway into the mud before Guido hauled me back onto the squashed marshmallow we occupied. "Don't blame Matfany. You know Deveels. You give them an inch, they take a mile. I can fix the problem. Just give us a chance. All we need is a little time for them to feel they've gotten their money's worth, then I'll make them take down all the signs and the rest of the junk."

The Old Folks turned away from Matfany and stared at me. The glowing sapphire eyes were hard to maintain contact with for long. I kept an affable smile on my face.

"I am not sure," the deep-voiced king said, "that we will do any better to depend on a Pervert than on Deveels."

"That's Per-*vect*," I said, holding my temper. "And it's not just me that Matfany hired to haul your cojones out of the cooker. There are also my associates."

Tananda leaned out from behind me to give them a little wave.

"Klahds and Trollops," Tinian said in disgust.

"Now, wait just a minute," I said. "We're M.Y.T.H., Inc. Maybe you're too far back in ancient history to have heard of us, but we have a reputation for helping people. Effectively."

"For money."

"Only a fool works for nothing, pal," I snarled. "Yeah, maybe your boy here made some stupid decisions, but he did what he had to with the best intentions. You want to keep your descendants on the throne without problem-solvers on your staff, then make sure they go to business school before they take the crown. They'll have to learn that what goes *out* has to come *in* first."

Fingernails dug into my wrist.

"Aahz, maybe the firm approach isn't the best one here?" Tananda whispered to me. I noticed that the shimmering gas flames had moved just a little closer.

"So you think that being ignorant is worthy of being condemned to death?" the long-nosed female asked me.

"Stupidity is the only capital crime in the universe, honey,"

I said. "It's always punishable by death. Commutation comes by way of mercy or pure dumb luck. Matfany here needs to learn to control his temper, but he was smart enough to know he needed help."

"And you think that letting other people take over our landscape is the way out of the problem?"

"If we didn't have a creative solution, other people would have taken over the landscape, and not in name only. I've seen your books. I haven't seen so much red ink since I read a copy-edited manuscript of the last tell-all celebrity autobiography. You're not happy about it, but isn't it up to the living to find their way out of their own jams? You had your shot. It's up to them now."

Matfany cleared his throat. "Your highnesses, I have given my word to these out-of-towners that they are allowed to commit some temporary depredations on our fair country. But only for a time. I will hold to my word. That is the only honorable thing to do. I ask that you hold back from causing trouble for them for the period of the contracts."

The flames went into a huddle.

"His word? What if he did give his word? What's that got to do with us?"

"Well, if we have no honor, then we have nothing," Tinian said. "I did trust this fellah enough to give him the top post. That means that his word is my word."

"But what about his temper? I don't like it that he can boil over like that and cause such a constitutional crisis all at once. The royal house is the royal house. While a scion of it is living, she is the rightful monarch and should be back here at home where she belongs, not hiding out in some Klahdish manor house that calls itself a castle."

Possiltum, I thought with a smirk, filing away the fact for future use. *Maybe I should arrange for a mob of adoring fans to descend on her there. Hemlock hates crowds. She'll throw Hermalaya out faster than that week's trash. That'll show Skeeve.*

"It's a pretty smart thing to do, getting people to pay for nothing."

"I don't like anybody messing up our mountains and piers like that."

"Well, you see how it backfired."

"That boy couldn't have known it would," King Tinian said. "The mistake he made was over my daughter."

"That's true. Lucky for him that's the easiest thing to remedy."

The huddle broke, and the ghostly figures drifted toward us.

"So, what's the good news?" I asked. "Let us finish up clearing your books, and in no time Foxe-Swampburg will be back to its good, old tourist-trap self. How about it?"

The deep-voiced ghost came to look me straight in the eye.

"Well, Mister Per-*vect*, we can't undo what has been done, but we can prevent any further mistakes being made by the same people, namely you all. When you don't come back, another generation of problem-solvers will arise in Foxe-Swampburg. We will guide them, but as you say, it's up to them. I hope they will be able to restore the pride that our kingdom has had in itself all these generations."

"Wait a minute," I said. "What do you mean, when we don't come back? We're not staying here. This was a courtesy call. I don't need your cooperation. You can keep throwing Salamanders off walls if you want to, but I will find a way to get Foxe-Swampburg's finances back in order, with or without your help!"

"I think you can say it's without our help," King Tinian said.

The long-nosed female smiled at us fetchingly. "You all should make yourselves just as comfortable as you can. You're going to be here for a while."

Cold water rolled up onto my insteps. I felt the semi-solid mass under our feet start to dissolve. I tried shifting to another part of the hummock, but it slid away. Hastily, I felt around for anything solid I could stand on. Guido, already up to his knees, held Tananda in his arms, keeping her out up of the mud. Matfany, out of my reach, was also starting to sink.

"Get us out of here, Tananda," I said. "I lost my D-hopper on the hill."

"I'll try. There's some weird interference here." She clapped her hands together. Nothing happened. She looked dismayed. "Something is sapping my magik. There's plenty of power here, but I can't get to it."

"It's no use fighting," said the deep-voiced ghost. "Your time in the material plane is ended."

"Hey!" I yelled at the royal spirits. "What about all that we've done for your people! Doesn't that count for anything?"

"No, sir," the voices said. "We believe you have done enough for Foxe-Swampburg. Now, this won't hurt a bit. It may feel kind of odd, but after a while you won't even remember it."

The glimmer dissipated, leaving us alone in the dark.

I'd been in mud and quicksand before. It was better to go horizontal, as disgusting as that was, and spread out your weight, than to remain vertical and let it drag me under. I flattened out with my arms spread.

"Try and lie on the surface," I said. "We can swim to the edge."

"Ugh!" Tananda exclaimed, bobbing next to me. "I'll never take mud baths at the spa again."

"Somethin's got my foot!" Guido said.

"Mine, too," Matfany said.

"What lives in these swamps?" I asked.

"Crocogators, but what you really have to look out for are the marsh squids. They'll wrap you up like a holiday bundle and eat you a piece at a time."

"*That's* what I saw back there," Guido said.

As soon as he said it, a huge tentacle broke the surface and threw itself over Matfany.

"Swim for it, friends," he said, as it wrapped itself around his shoulders. "I'm doomed."

"No, you're not," Guido said. "We don't let clients get eaten by invertebrates." He splashed toward the Reynardan. Tananda kicked after him, drawing a dagger out of who knew where in her clothing. I groaned and followed, but I didn't get far. The next tentacle wound itself around my leg. It dropped back into the mud, and started to pull me down.

"Tananda, get out of here," I said, struggling to stay on the surface.

"I can't go and leave you!"

"You're the only one with enough magik to escape. Beat it! Get help! Hurry up!"

The last sound I heard before my ears filled with mud was BAMF!

Chapter 32

———

"Money isn't everything."

—King Midas

I felt pretty miserable after Aahz confronted me in the office. I could put up with his bombast and his ridicule, but not his false accusations. He wasn't playing fair! It really hurt that the others seemed to believe him more than they did me. I wasn't used to that.

Maybe I really should go back to the inn in Klah when Hermalaya was back on her throne. It was lonely, but I wouldn't have to worry about being lied to by anybody but merchants. I could trust Gleep and Buttercup to be my true friends while I figured out exactly what I was going to do with the rest of my life. Bunny could stay in Deva, or go wherever she wanted to. She was a much more social person than I was. She didn't need to share my exile. I was grateful for all the time she had devoted to keeping me sane.

In the meantime, Hermalaya's requirements needed far outstripped my need to lick my wounds. As soon as I could, I started making the rounds again of the people who had turned me down for an interview when the Aahz-inspired Cake knockoffs started coming out.

I was getting used to doors being slammed in my face, so much so that when Elliora, a Leprechaun financier from

Ayer, said yes, I almost walked out anyhow. She dropped a loop of magik around me and hauled me back to her desk. She was a plumpish female about half my height with an upturned nose, tilted, green eyes, and shining silver hair pulled back in a long braid. Freckles were scattered across her nose. The gold that the Leprechauns were so famous for was evident in her parlor. Bureau knobs, inkwells, even picture frames were made of solid gold.

"Are you talking about Hermalaya of Foxe-Swampburg, then?" she asked me.

"Yes," I said.

"They're nice people," she said. "I've done a lot of business with them over the years. I'd love to hear what has been happening to her. Go ahead and let me see her diary. Sit down. Would you like a whisky?"

Ayerish whisky was the best in the dimensions. I accepted a 'wee, small' portion that filled a glass large enough to drown in and opened up my scroll.

By the end of the tale, Elliora was weeping into her own whisky. I waited until she had dried her tears with a beautifully embroidered handkerchief.

"Well, if there is a thing in this world that I can do for her, you have but to ask me. Go on, then, ask!"

I launched into my speech about helping her to restore the kingdom to its former prosperity, and how although her people loved her she had no real means of pulling the place out of debt or advertising to the rest of the dimensions that Foxe-Swampburg was once again open for business.

"And you want to force this nasty, rotten prime minister

out of the picture by overwhelming him with debt that can only be satisfied by restoring the rightful princess to the throne?" Her green eyes twinkled. "You're a wicked, awful boy. What else?"

I pressed on, encouraged that when I mentioned further loans or grants she nodded enthusiastically. When I got to the part about offering a Cake ceremony in exchange for Elliora's consideration, she bounded out of her chair and danced around the room.

"What a wonderful idea!" she declared. "That's a fine exchange for my time."

"Great!" I said. "So can I tell Hermalaya you want to meet her?"

"Oh, yes, and do all the fancy bibs and bobs that she does with her Cake. I've heard a lot about that in the past weeks—as you know." The eyes twinkled again. I had to shake myself not to fall into the Leprechaun's spell. "There's only one thing I would ask you in return, my lovely lad. I want to have my Cake ceremony done in the castle. In the throne room, if you don't mind. I've lent a lot of money to the royal house of Foxe-Swampburg over the last few years, but I've never been there. I want to see the place. I've heard it's a fine old building. It would please my sense of humor if the throne itself could be included in the ritual of Musical Chairs, but I'll live without that if the princess balks, of course."

I gulped. "Uh, did you hear the part where she was condemned to death, and going back would mean her life is forfeit?"

Elliora frowned at me. I could see the steel that had allowed her to become a powerhouse even among other financial advisors in Ayer. "And did I hear the part from you that with my help you can get the vile usurper out of the castle and her back in her rightful place?" She stood up. "When you can do what I want, then we'll do what you want. How about that for an idea?"

I couldn't argue with that. "We would have to sneak in, but I bet I can figure out some way," I said. "Let me check with Hermalaya."

"Good lad," she said, clapping her hands. "I'll wait to hear from you."

I hopped back to Possiltum, elated and worried at the same time. Elliora and I had discussed how much paper she held on Foxe-Swampburg. Some of it had been incurred since Matfany had taken over. I had a list of the sums involved, and they were astronomical.

"We really have him now," I finished gleefully.

"Attaboy, Skeeve," Massha cheered. "I knew Aahz couldn't keep us down forever. That Matfany is as good as exiled."

"Hear, hear," Chumley added, holding his cup of tea on high.

"Likewise," said Nunzio.

Hermalaya sighed.

"It's okay," I said to her. "Once we get the visitors coming back, you won't need him any more. You can find a better prime minister."

"I guess so," Hermalaya said, but she looked unhappy with the prospect. I was puzzled.

I looked at her. The Swamp Vixen princess kept her gaze down, playing with her Cake server.

"What's the matter?"

She lifted large, woeful eyes to me.

"Well, Mister Skeeve, I appreciate everything you have been doing. It just seems as if, in order to make me sound more vulnerable to our kindly patrons, you are well and truly blackening Matfany's name. You make him sound like a terrible man, and he's not! I really do like him."

"You do?" I asked. "After all that he did to you?"

"I do," she replied.

"How much?" Massha asked.

"Well, you know, he's honest, and hardworking, and even a little funny, and he's generous when he isn't being so worried. He's . . . well, he's the kind of guy I might have wanted to marry one day." She gave a fetching little sigh.

"He's the kind of guy, or he *is* the guy?" Massha asked, bobbing over to her on the air. Hermalaya dropped her eyes modestly.

"He is."

"Well, well, well," Massha said, beaming. "Can commoners marry royalty in your country, honey?"

"There's some precedence. About three generations back, my great-grandfather married a seamstress who beguiled him. He became the best-dressed monarch in all Foxe-Swampburg history. And there was a great-aunt about nine generations ago, too."

"Sounds like you've been looking into it."

Hermalaya's little white nose turned pink. "Just out of curiosity, Miss Massha, nothing else."

"It's good to know, though, just in case?"

I was shocked. "How can you even *think* of fraternizing with the enemy!"

"Matfany's not the enemy . . . " Hermalaya began. "Well, I guess maybe he is, but he isn't really."

"Matfany is the one who threw you off the throne, Miss Hermalaya," Nunzio said.

"I know," she said with a sigh. "But he's not a bad guy, honest. But he doesn't know any of what I just told you, so don't you go telling him!"

"You have *my* promise," I said.

"Us, too," Massha said. She squeezed Hermalaya's hand. The two of them giggled.

I was disgusted. It was completely illogical for her to feel that way.

"But that isn't our problem right now," I said. "At the moment, we have to work out how to have a Cake ceremony in your castle without getting caught."

Chapter 33

_____

"Who let these people in?"

—King Vortigern

"I'm so excited," Elliora said, as I escorted her from her office directly into the throne room of the Foxe-Swampburg castle. We arrived in an outrush of air. Hermalaya, in her headcloth and apron, knelt quietly beside the low table where the Cake sat.

I'd seen the chamber only once before, when I had delivered Hermalaya there to get everything set up. In the space of only two hours, the princess had mustered my friends to decorate the vast room. The change was astounding. Colored bunting lined the stone walls. Pride of place was given to the Dragon tapestry, which hung on the wall opposite the main doors. The thrones had been taken off the dais and were arranged back to back in a circle with several lesser seats. The war banners and suits of armor that hung from the rafters over our heads had been festooned with colored ribbons, making them look like the last battle they had waged was in a toy store. Massha must have been responsible for the aerial bombardment of glitter and streamers. She wore a lei made of braided crepe paper over her orange harem costume. Chumley's purple fur was well sprinkled with glitter. Only Nunzio had escaped any festive ornamentation. Hermalaya wore only her plain white silk apron and headcloth. Elliora was so taken by the décor that she danced around in a circle.

"Oh, it's marvelous," she exclaimed. "Is that it?" She homed in on the Cake. It was frosted in purple, but in Elliora's honor, was also adorned with gold and green. Hermalaya headed her off, but the Leprechaun peered around her waist at the table. "What a gorgeous Cake that is! I have never seen anything so beautiful in all my days."

"Shhh!" I hissed.

"Ah, that's right, then," the Leprechaun said. "I'll be quiet. I know the problem you're facing. But isn't everything marvelous!"

"Thank you, ma'am," Hermalaya said politely.

"And was the Cake made in these very kitchens?"

"We couldn't do that," I told her. "We couldn't risk tipping off anyone else that we're here. But Hermalaya baked it in the royal kitchens of Possiltum, in Klah."

Elliora wasn't disappointed. "That's right, you're a Klahd, aren't you? I won't hold that against you, lovely boy."

"Then let us begin," Hermalaya said, taking a box of candles out of the drawer in the low table. "How old are you?"

A certain amount of noise was obligatory in the ceremony, so I couldn't use a blanketing spell as I had when I helped Marmel search for his family heirloom. Instead, I modified a silence charm that should deaden the sounds we made and prevent them from escaping. I pictured the spell as a big balloon that enveloped the throne room. The trouble was, it created only a thin barrier. A really big bang would be audible on the other side of the door. I hoped none of the real balloons that Hermalaya had used to decorate would explode—at least, not until we were finished and ready to jump out. The princess crooned her weird little song and let Elliora blow out the candles stuck in the top of the Cake.

Normally, the smoke rising from the wicks just dissipated into the air. Instead, they curled around and over, spiraling around Hermalaya's hands as she cut the Cake deftly into slices and slid them onto the plates.

"That's marvelous," Elliora said. "Just a little bit of magik."

Massha and I exchanged glances of professional approval. There was something special about this particular ceremony that had been lacking in the others. Either Hermalaya had gotten so much practice lately, or performing it in her own country added an element that had been missing elsewhere. She really connected somehow with the sacred elements she always talked about. I was beginning to pick up nuances I had never previously noticed. In any case, it was hypnotically fascinating. I enjoyed it as never before.

Nevertheless, I had to keep a mental watch upon my noise-deadening spell. I'd been upset to learn the big fancy doors had no lock on them. That, too, was symbolic for the royal house of Foxe-Swampburg, telling their people that their rulers were always available. The penalty for violating Matfany's order was death. That meant anyone could walk in at any time, burst our bubble, and take the princess and the rest of us away for execution. I kept a transference charm half-brewed the whole time. If anyone interrupted us, I would grab her and get her out of there. Both Guido and Massha were armed to the teeth with their own particular forms of defense. Chumley didn't need any weapons, but I was more afraid of someone getting hurt.

My preoccupation meant that I wasn't paying as much attention as I should have to the rituals. The four of us obeyed Hermalaya's instructions to race around the chairs in the middle of the room. Her chanting stopped. I raced for a spindle-backed seat. I plopped myself down on it. Alarmed, I jumped up again.

"Yiii!"

"What's the matter, boss?" Nunzio asked.

"There's no one there!" I exclaimed. "I just sat down on someone's lap."

Hermalaya looked at the empty chair. "Oh, that's just Uncle Cyrus," she said. "We are blessed."

"Who is Uncle Cyrus?" I demanded.

Hermalaya put a pretty finger to her chin to puzzle it out. "He was king about, oh, three hundred years ago? I am so delighted. The Old Folks have come to show us that they approve of our endeavors. They just love Cake."

"Are they always here?"

"They protect us," Hermalaya said, as though I must be feeble-minded not to know that. "That's why no one was killed in the pinchbug epidemic. Those pesky little creatures drilled right through solid rock. You think they couldn't have gone through plain flesh and bone?"

"I never thought about it," I said honestly.

"Well, that's why. They didn't think about clothes, though? That's why people came to me for help."

"The family ghosts?" asked Elliora, curiously.

"Does that upset you?" I was afraid she wanted to leave.

The Leprechaun laughed. "Ach, no, not at all. We've got plenty of ghosts of our own in Ayer! Let's keep on, shall we? I've never had such a good time in my life."

Hermalaya's eyes shone with delight. "Well, you are out, Skeeve, because Uncle Cyrus beat you to the chair? One fewer seat, please!"

Nunzio courteously went to move a chair, but the family ghosts beat him to it. The gold, hoop-backed Windsor with ball-and-claw feet slid toward the wall before he could touch it. The remaining chairs moved by themselves to fill the gap.

I moved away from the ritual area, worrying whether I was going to run into another one of Hermalaya's deceased relatives. The Old Folks seemed to be having as much fun as the living. Chumley really got into the spirit of the games, letting out a refined hoot of pleasure when he successfully pinned the tail on the Dragon's rump. Five more tails attached themselves in the same vicinity.

"Cheating!" Chumley declared. The Old Folks didn't say anything. I never saw or heard any of them.

"And this is for you, my dear," Elliora said, when the festivities were finished. She handed Hermalaya a little, round, green ceramic pot sealed at the top with parchment. "Tradition begs for tradition, you see. It's how we like to keep our money." She had tears in her eyes. "I had no idea how it was here, dear princess. It's not my intention to impoverish a whole kingdom. I'll inform Matfany that we'll only keep the line of credit open only if he lets you come back. You will have to keep up on the payments, you know. We're not in the kingdom-running business, but we *are* in business."

"I understand," Hermalaya said. "I will do better in the future? I know I just have so much to learn. Thank you so much for coming."

"Thank you for inviting me," Elliora said. She winked at me. "Don't show me out. I know the way."

BAMF!

I waited nervously as Hermalaya undid the ribbon on Elliora's pot of gold. The princess poured the coins out into her palm. They overspilled her hand and bounced to the floor. Guido and Chumley bent to gather them up, but they just kept coming.

"How many are in there?" Massha asked, her eyes wide. The pool of gold scattered around the princess's feet.

"I don't know!"

"Oh, isn't she generous!" Hermalaya said. "This is going to help my people so much?"

I shoveled coins into my belt pouch, into Massha's handbag, into anything that would hold them. I was elated.

"We did it," I said. "Elliora's gift really is the tipping point. Between this and the loans she can call in on him, we have enough leverage to force Matfany out of business and get the kingdom back on its feet. We've won. No matter how much Aahz can raise, we can drain it. He'll be in negative equity."

"Hooray!" Massha yodeled, then clapped a hand over her mouth. "Oops! Sorry."

I ran to the door and planted my ear against it. I heard running footsteps. Someone had heard us.

"What's that?" Hermalaya asked. She looked at me in concern. "Auntie Xantippe says that there are guards on the way. We have to get out of here?"

Gold kept pouring out of the little pot.

"How do we make it stop?" Massha asked.

"If I may suggest," Chumley said, "a modicum of common sense dictates that if changing the orientation to horizontal precipitates the flow, then restoring it to vertical should stem it."

"Oh!" Hermalaya said. She tipped the pot upright. The jingling avalanche halted at once. "Is that what you mean, Mister Chumley?"

He smiled at her. "Just so, your highness."

"Whew," I said.

"We still have to get all those coins," Nunzio said, filling his pockets from the heap on the floor. They caused the pockets of his beautiful suit to bulge out of shape. I promised myself I would pay his cleaning bill when we got back. "Bunny won't give you credit for money she can't see."

"You're right," I said.

I let go of my escape spell. Instead, I channeled the energy into a mass of magik like a ball of sticky clay. I sent it rolling all over the room, picking up coins.

"Get ready," I said, holding out my hands like a catcher. The ball rolled toward me, a little sluggishly now that it was heavy with gold. "We're going to get out of here as soon as I have . . . "

The doors slammed open. A troop of guards in leather mail, headed by a silver-furred fox holding a wand, charged into the room. The wizard glared at us sternly. Magik crackled around him like a cloud.

"I'd advise none of you to make a single move."

I stood up very slowly with my hands over my head.

Chapter 34

———

"Just when you think you've won,
they move the finish line."

—N. Bonaparte

"Take it easy, fellahs," I said. "We were just leaving, if you don't mind. Uh, you can keep the rest of the gold on the floor here. We don't need all of it. If you would just let us get out of here . . . ?"

The captain of the guard, a russet-colored Fox, raised an eyebrow. "Attempting to bribe royal officers? Is that what you are trying to do?"

"Only if it will work," I said winningly. "I'd rather not cause any trouble. My friends and I just want to get out of here."

"Who are your friends?" the captain asked, suspiciously.

"No one," I said, trying to get a disguise spell going on my companions, but I wasn't fast enough. The wizard countered me with a blast from his wand. "No one at all," I added lamely.

"Why, that's Princess Hermalaya," a brown-furred Swamp Fox declared, gazing at the white-pelted maiden in our midst.

"It is her!" said the wizard.

"Seize them!" the captain bellowed. The guards surged forward and surrounded us.

"What?" Massha asked. "Are you people out of your minds? This is your *princess*."

"That's right, ma'am," the captain said. "And she is under a writ of exile, as signed by our current ruler, Prime Minister Matfany."

Massha went over to tickle him under the chin with a thick forefinger. "You're not going to listen to that old meanie, are you?"

The captain recoiled. "Ma'am, you are our prisoner, too. Take them away!"

"Look, here, guys," I said. "Let's be reasonable. You are going to take us down and lock us up in the dungeon. And then what? You all know what's in that writ. You're going to have to take that sweet young lady, whom you have all known since she was a little girl sitting on her father's knee, and put her to death." I flipped a hand toward Hermalaya, who, wrapped up in her oversized white apron, was looking as demure and helpless a damsel in distress as I could ever have wished. "You don't look like the kind of heartless types who can drag their very own princess down the dark steps to the *cold, dank, stone cells* and listen to her cries for mercy while you prepare for an execution which every one of you knows is completely unjust?"

I had hit my stride now. The guards, even the grizzled veterans, had tears in their eyes. The younger ones broke into open sobs.

The captain turned to the wizard. "I just can't do it."

The wizard looked just as distressed. "Neither can I."

"Gentlemen," Hermalaya said, coming over to lay a gentle

hand on each of their wrists. "You must do what you all have to do. I don't want you to get in trouble? I took my chances coming back here, and it just didn't work out. That's the way life is. My daddy would want me to march down there with my head held high and take what I've got coming to me."

"No, princess," the captain said. He pulled a handkerchief out of his sleeve and put his long nose into it. "We just won't do it. We love you. We're not gonna listen to that old Matfany."

"But you have to," Hermalaya said. "He is the law."

"No, ma'am," the wizard said with a little smile. "We are the law. He is the administrator. Most of the guard works for Matfany because they like getting paid. This particular squad here is the lawful opposition. Most of the others don't talk to us much because we won't openly renounce you. You are downright lucky that it was us on duty today. Everybody else is out there running around after those out-of-towners."

"What out-of-towners?" I asked.

"Strange looking types." He eyed Chumley up and down. "No offense, sir."

"Okay," Chumley replied, reduced to playing Big Crunch in front of strangers.

"Go on out of here, honey," the captain said with tears in his eyes. "We'll keep it quiet this time, but don't come back again. Remember the good old days and think about us some time."

Hermalaya gave him and the wizard a big hug. "Oh, I will! You all are so kind? My daddy would be so proud of you. I know I am."

"There are good new days to come," I promised, "once we get rid of Matfany."

The guards looked at each other. "We're with you, sir," they whispered.

I didn't dare wait another moment for them to change their minds. I gathered up a big ball of magik.

BAMF!

"We've won!" I announced jubilantly to Bunny. I shook my belt pouch at her. The jingle was loud enough to attract hordes of Deveels from all over the Bazaar. Massha set down her handbag. Nunzio and Chumley turned out handful after handful of coins until her desk was a glittering mass of shiny yellow. "And there's plenty more where that came from," I concluded, as Hermalaya offered the little clay pot. Bunny ignored the pile of coins. I realized that Tananda was there, wrapped in a blanket with her hair plastered to her head. Both of them looked worried. "What's wrong? Where's Aahz?"

"Skeeve, we have a problem."

"What kind of problem? Where's Aahz?"

"He's back in Foxe-Swampburg," Tananda said. "The Old Folks have been causing a bunch of trouble for Matfany, so Aahz thought it would be a good idea to go and placate them. Well, you know, tact is not exactly his strong suit."

"No kidding," said Massha.

Tananda shrugged. "The upshot is that they left us in the swamp with a marsh squid. They've got Guido, too."

"Where's Matfany?" Hermalaya asked anxiously.

"Him, too," Tananda said. "In fact, they're angrier at him than they are at us. I was the only one who could get out. You have got to go and rescue them."

"Rescue them?" I echoed. "We just got away from a bunch of Hermalaya's own castle guards who were told to kill her if she ever came back home. Let him rot. Aahz can get out of trouble on his own. As he is always telling me, he's a lot better at it than I will ever be."

"No, Skeeve," Tananda said, opening large green eyes at me. "He's not going to get out of this one without help. Those swamps are full of weird old magik like nothing I have ever seen before. It's way out of my league. That squid could drown them all before I get back. He needs you. Hurry. You can argue with him later."

"Squid?" I asked. "What squid?"

"The Old Folks sicced it on us. They're pretty angry about the advertising the Deveels plastered around the kingdom."

I was puzzled. "The Old Folks? They're not dangerous at all. They're just a bunch of ghosts. They played Musical Chairs with us. They ate Cake."

"Skeeve, he really is in trouble. This isn't a joke."

"I am afraid this lady is right?" Hermalaya said. "The Old Folks are just as formidable as they were when they were alive. Only they can't die any more, so they can indulge fits of temper when they feel like it? They had some pretty mean things to say when Matfany tossed me out of the castle, but I thought it was best for my people to comply with his wishes? But they were never happy about it. If he walked into their midst, then it could be very bad for him. For them all."

"Don't let the contest blind you to what is really important, what?" Chumley said. "Aahz isn't your enemy."

"No, he's not." My temper was softening. I remembered all the good days. I thought back fondly to those times when he called me names and made fun of me. It was nothing personal. Most Pervects didn't even talk to Klahds. Aahz had been the best friend I ever had in my life. I owed him many favors, not just one little life-saving expedition. I had to get out there. "You're right," I said. "He would do the same for me. He wouldn't leave me in danger."

"That's it," Bunny said. "This contest isn't about your friendship."

"Can you take me back?" I asked Tananda.

"Oh, I can get you in there," Tananda said. She snapped her fingers, and all the mud fell off her hair and clothes. "The Old Folks don't mind anyone coming into their domain. They're just fussy about who they let *out* again. We have to hurry!"

I reached up into the force line that stretched over the office and filled up my reserves. "I'm ready."

"Wait a minute!" Hermalaya exclaimed. She put her arms around me and Tananda. "I'm coming with you?"

"Okay by me. It's your dry cleaning bill." Tananda clapped her hands together.

BAMF!

Chapter 35

———

"One's descendants are always a disappointment."

—Rameses II

The wave of smell hit me before anything else. It was like old cheese wrapped in burning newspapers with a touch of unwashed laundry. I gagged. Hermalaya detached herself from us.

"Aahz?" Tananda called. "Can you hear me?"

" . . . Over here . . . " came a faint little voice.

I created a globe of brilliant white light. Spooky-looking trees heavy with hanging beards of moss surrounded us. Creepers dangled overhead in swags and loops. Insects homed in on the light, diving in and out of the white globe. My feet sank into the spongy surface.

"Watch it," Tananda said. "It's pretty deep."

I levitated until I could walk on the surface of the marsh. Tananda used a little of her own magik to guide me.

The ground was an expanse of uneven masses. I glided from one semisolid lump to another.

"There they are!" Tananda exclaimed, pointing to three blobs. I hurried after her. One green blob looked scalier than the others. It was Aahz's head. All three of them were buried up to their lower lips in mud. Aahz's bat-wing ears were flat on the surface of the marsh.

"Don't make waves," Guido said, stiffly. "This stuff tastes worse than dorm food."

I knelt beside them. "Are you guys all right?"

Aahz glared at me.

"What took you so long?"

Tananda burst out, "Aahz! Don't be ungrateful! Skeeve came out just as soon as we told him you were in trouble."

"What makes you think I'm in trouble?" Aahz asked. "We're just having a mud bath while a marsh squid drowns us so it can have an off-world buffet!"

"What's a marsh squid?" I asked.

A huge splash broke the silence.

"That is," Tananda said, pointing.

My globe of light wasn't large enough to illuminate the entire expanse of the creature that surfaced.

It resembled what stomach flu felt like. It was a sickly-green mass of squirming, writhing tentacles with an ugly face that even its mother must have had a hard time loving. Two big round eyes as flat as dinner plates stared at us. One of the tentacles coiled out at me faster than whipsnap.

I was ready for it. I charged up the globe of light and threw it right into those eyes. It exploded in a blazing starburst. Without eyelids to cover them, the squid was suddenly blinded. It squealed like an injured rhinophant, and contracted its body to protect its head.

I heard a yell of protest from Aahz and Guido. The waves of the thrashing squid were swamping them. I had to get my friends free before it managed to drown them by accident. I pulled some more magik out of my reserves and threw lasso-like loops around all three. Then I hoisted them into the air.

It took a lot more effort than I expected. My eyes watered as clouds of foul-smelling gas were released. I strained to hold the spell together. When their feet cleared the water, I discovered that the tentacles of the giant squid were wound around their legs and lower bodies. I couldn't let go, or it would slither back into the swamp, taking my friends with it. Instead, I reached out to the hanging creepers, some of which were thicker than my waist. Using my fast-dwindling supply of magik, I tied loops in them and captured the ends of the tentacles. The squid struggled against me. I was gasping, but I got one limb after another tied up. Pretty soon, the monster hung from the trees like a hammock.

Now that he was in no danger of drowning, Aahz took part of the rescue into his own hands. He grabbed the nearest waving arm tentacle and sank his teeth into it.

It squealed again, taking the sound up into the highest registers of sound. It threw Aahz halfway across the swamp.

"Aaaagh!" Aahz yelled, his arms and legs windmilling.

Sploop!

Guido added his strength to the escape attempt. I couldn't see what he was doing, but the squid didn't seem to like it any more than it did being bitten. It trembled so much that Guido slipped out of its clutches.

"Anyone got a rope?" he shouted.

He hung by his fingernails from a tentacle. Tananda threw him a lifeline made of magikal force. He threw her a salute and hauled himself up again.

Matfany was the only one still tied up like a spider's lunch. I didn't have a lot of magik left available. Tananda was right: I could see some perfectly good force lines, but I felt as though a glass bubble kept me from getting at them.

With only limited magik, I had to think small—like a hotfoot. I lit a white-hot flame underneath the coiled tentacle.

The squid flinched, but with the rest of it tied to the trees, it couldn't go very far. I followed it with the little fire, keeping it against the slimy green flesh until I smelled something burning.

Somehow, a whisper made itself heard over the wailing. "Excuse me, gentlemen, but it's squeezing me pretty hard."

I ran over the surface of the swamp toward Matfany. Tananda scrambled over the body of the squid, evading the tentacles that still waved free. She beat me there. With a dagger drawn from somewhere within her clothes, she stabbed the creature. I got there just in time to catch Matfany as the squid let him go. It felt after us, but I turned up the flame. It winced and curled up against the body. Tananda dropped down lightly to the surface. We each took an arm and carried Matfany over the water to a spit of nearly dry land under an arched willow bough.

Matfany brushed himself down. His somber suit and black, curly fur were plastered with green mud. "Sir, thank you for your courtesy."

"Save it," I said with no friendliness in my voice. "The Princess was nearly captured today, and that was all your fault."

ROBERT ASPRIN & JODY LYNN NYE

The prime minister managed to look dignified in spite of his condition. "I only did what I had to do, sir."

"Seems to me you could have figured something else out, a smart guy like you?"

Aahz waded through the slime towards us. He stumped up on the spit of land and wrung dry his sleeves. Gallons of water and a frog poured out.

"What a miserable place," he said. "I can't believe you Swamp Foxes think this is the nice part of town."

"How are you?" I asked.

"How do you think?" Aahz said. "I'm wet! Look at that. A Barclys of Gannet suit, brand new, ruined!"

"Haven't you got something you'd like to say to Skeeve?" Tananda asked.

He looked at me. "What do you think I should say to him?"

"Well, I don't know. How about 'Thanks, you saved my life?' " Tananda pressed him. "Aren't you grateful?"

Aahz made a face.

"That wasn't anything special. So he clotheslined a squid. I'd have done the same for him." He turned to me. "Thanks. You can go away now. We're fine from here."

I gawked at him.

"Thanks? That's it?"

He glared at me. "What do you want, a medal?"

"What about some, I don't know, gratitude?"

"You got it. I'm grateful. Happy?"

"No, in fact," I said. "You're acting like you're not happy to see me."

"And why should I be?" Aahz asked. "We're on opposite sides of this competition. You stepped in to help. Now we go back to our respective corners and keep slugging. See you at the finish line."

I felt forlorn, then upset. "That's it? Are you mad at me? Aren't we still friends?"

"Maybe later," Aahz said. I felt devastated. He prodded my chest with a talon. "No, I'm not mad at you, but I ought to be! Look, you are acting like I'm the one who left. You bugged out. You didn't talk to anyone except Bunny—unless you needed them for something. How do you think they liked that? *I* didn't see you at all after that one time. You want to talk about ungrateful? Because we didn't open up our arms and let you march right in and take up where you left off? Everybody gave you a pass because you're a nice guy, but you don't deserve it. You Klahd."

I was being pushed on the defense. "I told you, I had to get away and prove myself."

Aahz looked annoyed. "And solving problems in a dozen kingdoms in as many dimensions doesn't give you that kind of confidence? What took you so long? I thought you had some potential, but maybe I overestimated your brains."

"Aahz!" I must have shown how hurt I was.

"Aw, come on, I don't mean it like that," Aahz said. "What's a couple of months out of touch between friends? But this is *business,* kid. You've known me long enough to understand that, I hope. Nobody stands between a Pervect and something he wants, especially not former apprentices and partners who happen to be Klahds who want the same thing!"

"And dropping everything on my side of the competition to come and pull your fat out of the fire doesn't earn me even a little friendliness? If you can't even appreciate what people do for you, then I guess I don't need to have anything else to do with you."

"If you could only hear yourself, kid," Aahz said almost sadly.

I had heard myself, and I had to admit I didn't like what I heard. I was *whining*. No wonder nobody wanted to let me back in the group.

I turned to stalk away and found myself face to face with a virtual forest fire. Flickering shapes made of hot blue light surrounded me. These had to be the Old Folks. I went on guard and filled my hands with the remaining magik I had in store.

"There you are," said the leader. He had a deep, booming voice. He was shaped like a Swamp Fox, but one made of blue cellophane. His deepset eyes fixed on my face. "Those three boys aren't done with their punishment yet. You just can't take them away from here."

"Sorry to disagree with you," I said, sounding more calm than I felt. "They're my friends, and I am taking them with me. Or you can try and put me down there. But look what I've done to your pet." I gestured toward the squid, which struggled furiously against its bonds. It was tied to various tree limbs.

The deep voice sounded aghast. "What have you done to Baby?"

"Baby?" I asked. That gigantic thing was a baby?

"That wasn't nice of you, son."

A tenor-voiced Old Folk joined him. "I guess he wasn't big enough to handle all of them. I'd better summon Daddy. He'll wind them up good, and this one into the bargain."

"Bring him on! I can take him, too," I vowed.

"And Granddaddy," suggested another one of the hovering flames, a woman with a long, sharp nose.

Uh-oh. I had just dropped out of their league. I didn't stand a chance against *two* more of them.

"Stand back," I warned, igniting the power in my hands to a ball of red fire, "or I'll burn all of you back to life!"

"Didn't your mother ever show you any manners?" the female asked. She clapped a hand down on my palm. The fire went out. I was out of magik. I backed away. "I think we'll just have to sink you first and send your friends down after you!"

Plants began to wind themselves around my feet. I tugged at them.

"Now, Great-grandmother Clarissa, what are you doing?" Hermalaya was at my shoulder. She had her hands on her hips. The long-nosed female ghost looked at her.

"Hermalaya, honey, is that you?" The blue flames surrounded her.

"Hello, baby," said the tenor-voiced ghost.

"Daddy, what are you doing trying to drown my prime minister?"

"Well, baby girl, he overstepped his bounds by telling you to go away."

Hermalaya glanced back toward Matfany. Her eyes were bright, but she held her head high. "I left willingly. He was just doing what he thought was right. I'd appreciate it if you stopped interfering with those folks from out of town? For now, anyhow."

A female ghost with a sweet face came to hover beside the tenor. "Well, if you are all right, sweetheart, that's all that matters. And this is your little friend?"

"Yes, Mama. This is Skeeve the Magnificent."

"It's an honor, your majesty," I said, bowing low.

"Well, aren't you sweet?" the late queen said, bridling with pleasure. "You just go on taking care of my daughter. She's a good girl."

"Yes, ma'am. I'll do my best."

Matfany came up to touch my sleeve. "Sir, I don't want you to think that all of us are ungrateful wretches. You have saved our lives, and I will be forever in your debt. How can I repay you?"

"A life for a life," I said. "Repeal the death sentence on Hermalaya. And while you're at it, maybe you should get out of town for good yourself. She won't need you any more."

Matfany bowed. "Very well, sir. I am a man of my word. I will depart at once. I will go back to my quarters for my possessions, if you will allow that."

"I don't see why not," I said. I could be magnanimous. Inwardly I was jubilant. Just like that, I had gotten Hermalaya her throne back and gotten rid of her archenemy!

"Now, wait a minute!" Aahz protested, pushing in between us. "You can't do that!"

I turned to him calmly. "I just did."

"I want a ruling from the judge."

"What ruling? Matfany agreed. I saved his life, so he's leaving the country."

The prime minister nodded gravely. Aahz goggled.

"If you exile my client, I can't win."

"You can't win anyhow," I said, trying not to gloat and failing. "We beat you six ways from feastday. I just won. My client's got her job back, and yours has just lost his. Besides, we have the moral victory."

"Moral? This is purely a numbers game, pal." Aahz stuck his face in mine.

I didn't back down. I thrust my chin forward.

"Then we'll take it back to Bunny and ask her," I said. "All right?"

"All right!"

Chapter 36

———

"Okay, so maybe winning *is* everything."

—King Darius of Persia

Aahz and Tananda burst into the office not more than three seconds after I did. They had both cleaned up and put on fresh clothes, as I had.

"Aahz, are you all right?" Bunny asked. "We were so worried!"

"I'm fine," he said. "It was sticky, but not insurmountable. You know Pervects. We always come out on top."

"Huh," I said. So he wasn't going to tell her how I rescued him and the others. I was disgusted. I flopped down in a chair and put my head on my hand. Gleep came galloping over to greet me. I scratched his chin. Bunny looked from one of us to the other.

"Where are the clients?"

"I took Hermalaya someplace safe," I said. I didn't want to say any more than that. She had protested when I took her back to Massha's cottage in Possiltum, but I didn't want to take a chance with her well-being, not when we were about to return her triumphantly to Foxe-Swampburg.

Aahz growled. "Matfany is in an undisclosed location until I get a ruling from you on inappropriate behavior from my opponent over there."

Bunny's eyebrows rose sky high. "Inappropriate behavior

from Skeeve? What happened? Didn't he just pull all of you out of a swamp?"

"That's not the point," Aahz said. He leaned over the desk and aimed a finger at me. "He just exiled *my* client from his homeland. He can't do that!"

"Why not?" Bunny asked, not at all cowed. "It's fair. Yours did it to his."

Aahz threw up his hands. "But that's a matter of internal politics. Skeeve's an outsider. What about the Prime Directive?"

"What's that?" I asked.

"I'm not here to complete your education any more," Aahz said sourly. "What about it? Can he do that?"

Bunny turned to me. "How did you exile him?"

"Matfany asked me how he could repay me for saving his life. I told him he could get out of town. It's not my problem what it does to Aahz's mission, is it?"

"Would you have done it if Aahz hadn't been working for him?" Chumley asked.

"Yes! He deposed a sitting ruler! It's not like she can pull up stakes and go get a job somewhere. She's royalty. She belongs back home."

Aahz snorted. "Big deal. The descendant of someone else who moved in and decided that he was in charge. But does it stand?"

"I don't see why not," Bunny said. "Sounds like he made a fair deal."

"Then the contest's over," I said. "He can't earn any more for his client."

"You're right about that," Bunny agreed. "The contest as *we agreed to it* is over."

"Then let's see who won." I pulled the ledger around to look at my total. "Fifteen thousand, six hundred gold coins! Wow!" With a total like that I had to have won. I was going to be president of M.Y.T.H., Inc. again!

"Lemme see that." Aahz yanked the book away from me. "Fifteen thousand, six hundred . . . ? From serving a few lousy little pieces of cake?"

"That's Cake," I corrected him.

"No problem. I have you beaten on numbers."

"You couldn't."

"I could and I do." Aahz turned to the page with his name on it. His face fell. "Fifteen thousand, six hundred."

"What?" I asked.

"You're tied," Nunzio said.

Aahz gawked at the ledger. "Wait a minute! How could you do that? I put names on almost everything in the country!"

I held up the little clay pot. "We had a Leprechaun."

"So neither of you won," Tananda said. "You tied."

"We need a tie-breaker," I said.

"Sudden-death," Aahz said. I looked blank. He looked disgusted at my ignorance. "One contest, winner take all."

"Oh! Okay. I agree."

We turned to Bunny. "What can we do?" I asked.

Bunny looked from me to Aahz and back again with a look of absolute exasperation. I was surprised to see that all the others had the same expression.

"What's wrong?" I asked.

"What is the matter with you?" she demanded, her voice rising to glass-breaking tones. "Both of you are missing the point!"

"What point?" Aahz asked. "You set the conditions of the contest. The prize is the presidency of our organization. We tied. We won't both be president, so we need to break the tie."

"Aagh!" Bunny said, scraping the desk with her fingernails. "You men are so dense! The point is that putting Hermalaya back on the throne means she has to punish Matfany as a usurper, and she doesn't want to, does she?"

"Not really," I said uneasily. The look on her face when I left her in Possiltum reminded me of that shy confession Massha had wormed out of her.

" . . . And having Matfany in charge isn't tenable because the people like their ruling family, right, Aahz? They take pride in it. Besides, he just had a fit of temper when he tossed her off the throne and condemned her to death if she returned. Skeeve got him to agree to leave out of a sense of honor, so the princess can be in charge again, but she doesn't know that much more about business than she did when all this got started. *Both* of you are thinking that only one of them is important to the kingdom. It needs both of them. You aren't paying attention to what the clients really need any more. You forgot what it is that we do."

I rubbed my temples, where a headache was starting to grow inward. Aahz and I looked at each other.

"So what if he's unpopular now?" Aahz asked. "Matfany's a good administrator. The people will get used to the idea eventually. If Skeeve rescinds the exile order."

"Not the Old Folks," I said. "They will never allow him in the throne room, and everyone knows it. They just tried to drown him, unless you're forgetting. Besides," I glanced back at Massha, who gave me an encouraging look, "the princess is kind of in love with him. She wants to go back, but she wants him, too."

Guido cleared his throat. "I kind of see that sort of interaction from Mr. Matfany also. He is stuck on the doll, as who of his species wouldn't be?"

"Thought so!" Bunny crowed. "When those two passed each other in the waiting room, you could have lit a cigar off the sparks. Well?"

"Well, what?" Aahz and I asked at the same time.

"It's no longer about the money."

"It's *always* about the money," Aahz said.

"How are you going to bring the kingdom back together?" Bunny asked, patiently.

"I don't know," Aahz said. "Matfany's pretty much soiled the nest. Everybody's going to think it's fishy if he suddenly brings Hermalaya back and reinstalls her. It'll look desperate. Could throw the whole kingdom into a tailspin."

"She'll lose all credibility if she brings him in as her prime minister after he threw her out," I mused.

"So, you need something different," Bunny said. "Use your imagination. How do we get the fairy tale wedding without breaking the newly solvent bank?"

I frowned.

"Why don't you ask them?" Tananda asked, reasonably.

———

"Ma'am?" Matfany said, rising to his feet and bowing as I escorted Hermalaya in. Guido, Nunzio, and Chumley all rose. After a stern look from his client, Aahz grudgingly hoisted himself out of his chair.

For her part, the princess looked as nervous as Matfany did. After her bravery in the swamp, she had gone shy on me when I proposed a meeting. She held herself with dignity. I pulled out a chair for her. I thought that neither one of them was going to talk at first, but the princess managed to break the ice.

"I hope you are recovered from your misadventure?" she asked. "It's just like the Old Folks to resort to old-fashioned barbarian tactics when they are upset?"

Matfany bowed. "I am well, ma'am, thank you for asking. I trust I find you in health?"

"You do," Hermalaya said. "Though for the life of me I did not think of that as being uppermost in your mind these last weeks."

Matfany cleared his throat awkwardly. "Ma'am, you don't need to be difficult about it. I have regretted the harshness of the way I spoke to you on that day."

"Of the *way* you spoke to me? Isn't it *what* you said that took me aback? You have some nerve, even pretending that you are even concerned about me, when it seems that all along you must have had some designs on taking my place!"

The prime minister's brows went down. "Now, ma'am, you know that isn't so! If I might be so bold to ask you to examine your own behavior in those days leading up to, yes, my outburst, you might think that I was justified in expressing my concern with regard to the smooth running of the kingdom, and my concern at your seeming ignorance of its problems!"

"But not with such rancor!" Hermalaya said. "If you only knew how much it hurt me for you to burst out like that. I could have taken any kind of a scolding—I was brought up to assume responsibility for my actions—but to have you refuse to listen to me, and then banish me forever from my beloved country, just broke my poor heart?"

Matfany dropped his eyes. "Forgive me, ma'am. And I have since learned, in your own words, that you did have the kingdom's welfare in mind."

"I did! Only I was thinking more of the here and now? Not what came later. I should have asked your advice. That was wrong of me. I didn't let you do what you do so well."

"That makes me even more ashamed. I'm sorry. I have just got to curb my awful temper."

"I am so sorry, too," Hermalaya said. "You know I just don't have much head for business? I shouldn't have given away all the money without asking you."

"Well, you did it for the right reason," Matfany admitted. "I could've held off the bills another several months if I knew."

"If I'd explained," she said.

"If I'd listened," he said.

"Oh, no, it was my impatience . . . "

"My impetuousness . . . "

They were out of their seats and moving towards one another without even knowing they were doing it. Matfany took one of her hands gently in both of his and gazed down deeply into her eyes.

"I wonder, ma'am, if you might consent to sit with me one of these evenings and enjoy the moonlight? In a purely respectful context, of course."

"Why," Hermalaya sounded breathless, "I believe that would be a pleasure, sir."

"Awww," the women chorused. I suppressed a little sigh. Massha, Tanda, and Bunny were right. These two were in love with each other.

"All right, already! Let's get back to the point," Aahz insisted. Hermalaya and Matfany looked at him. The princess's little pink nose turned even more pink. Both of them retreated to their seats.

"So you see what we have to do," Bunny said. "We have to get both of them back where they belong."

Aahz turned to Hermalaya. "Okay. Here's the bottom line. We need to reinstate *you*, in some kind of realistic fashion. And we need to change *your* image," he said to Matfany.

"We can't," I said. Everybody turned to look at me. I shrugged. "He condemned a member of the royal house to death, so he's can't just quit and say he's sorry. Hermalaya can't marry a traitor. He can't just come back. He has to pay with his life."

Matfany looked taken aback. "I beg your pardon, sir?"

"You can't take him away again?"

I grinned. "Not exactly. We invent a savior for the

kingdom, someone who is willing to come in and put the princess back on her throne." I held up my hands dramatically and formed an illusion between them. "From the faraway land of, uh, Goodenrich, at the far south end of Reynardo, comes the handsome prince Fanmat, who will face the usurper and defeat him in a really dramatic duel to the death." The white-furred figure of Princess Hermalaya appeared on a castle parapet, threatened by a black-haired villain. A shining, golden-pelted hero came riding in on a stallion—I immediately nixed the stallion when everybody else in the room gave me a strange look—pushed the villain aside and took Hermalaya in his arms. "Then he can marry the princess, who gets her throne back, and the two of you can live happily ever after."

"Bravo," cheered Chumley. "Yes, I can see it. It would suit the situation precisely, what?"

"Looks good to me, too, boss," Guido said. Bunny gave a nod of approval.

The prime minister shook his head in concern. "There's no kingdom of Goodenrich or a Prince Fanmat that I know of," Matfany said, frowning. "And I don't like this idea of dying, sir, even though I admit I've been a fool."

Hermalaya tapped his wrist. "Silly, it's you."

I clapped my hands and the vision vanished. "I wouldn't be much of a magician if I couldn't create a good illusionary hero. Until you can change your appearance to match it, that is."

"I like him the way he is?" the princess protested.

"Can't do it," Aahz said, flatly.

"Why not?" Tananda asked. "Everybody will love it."

"It'll void all my contracts," Aahz complained. You're going to destroy my reputation in sixteen dimensions for a lousy love story. Matfany is the one who signed them."

"Not if I confirm them, Mister Aahz," Hermalaya said. "On a modest basis, your idea of sponsoring national landmarks might be a good thing. But no more big old gaudy signs. That destroys the natural beauty, and without that, what have you got?"

Matfany stared at her with dawning admiration. "That's some mighty good business sense, ma'am."

She blushed. "I've learned a thing or two from Mister Skeeve and his friends."

"Any more objections?" Bunny asked Aahz.

"Nope," Aahz said with resignation. "If I don't lose out on anything, I don't care what kind of shenanigans you have to go through to get what you want."

"We'll have to make it dramatic," Tananda said. "Chumley and I staged a fake assassination once. It was great!"

"Indeed," Chumley said. "Owing chiefly to the skill of the *dramatis personae*, myself included, I might humbly add."

"Oh, that sounds like fun?" Hermalaya said.

"It was," Tananda said. "Have you ever done any skits?"

"Sometimes my ladies and I act out scenes from books," Hermalaya admitted. "But this sounds much more interesting?"

"At least you won't have stage fright," Guido said. "That is the ailment that has caused more than one person of talent to have to forego a public career in spite of talent."

"Oh, I'm used to public speaking," the princess said.

Aahz seemed to be getting into the spirit. "Do we have to feed you lines, or can you memorize a script?"

"Sir," Hermalaya said, pretending to be indignant, "I have to make an hour-long speech every year on the anniversary of my ascension? Of course I can remember *lines*."

"In that, I am afraid I am your weak link," Matfany said. "I am a good public servant, but I am no actor. I do not dissemble."

"In other words, what you see is what you get?" Massha asked.

"What if we act around him?" Tananda asked, eyeing the prime minister with dismay.

"Don't worry," Aahz said, throwing an arm around my shoulders. "We'll take care of that. He doesn't have to do a thing. I have it all worked out."

Chapter 37

———

"One little piece of cake won't kill me."

—Marie Antoinette

"I still don't see why *I* have to be the bad guy," I grumbled. "He was *your* client."

"We're working together now," Aahz said. "This is for the common good of Foxe-Swampburg. How's the advance publicity going?"

Massha gave us a wicked grin.

"I started rumors in at least sixty bookstores that Hermalaya was going to defy the evil prime minister and turn up in Foxe-Swampburg tomorrow afternoon. If the response I got on was any indication, then thousands of people are going to show up just to see if it's true."

"Great," Aahz said. "The more the merrier. I want the place packed. I made a deal with the Geek and a few of our sponsors to sell souvenirs just outside the castle gates. It's a small way of making up for taking down all their billboards."

"Is anyone selling copies of *The Princess's Diary*?" Bunny asked. "I hate for Hermalaya to miss out on the best motivated crowd she's ever going to get."

"Special order from the printer," Aahz said. "The Paper Wasps promised they'd churn out a thousand copies by dawn tomorrow or they'd have to eat them. What about security? I don't want any trigger-happy yahoo thinking he can pick up a bounty from Matfany on the princess, or vice versa."

Guido lifted a finger. "We're set. I lined up some of our friends as on-the-ground security inside and outside the castle. Pookie's in charge of the force in the building and overhead. Gus has a day off from the Golden Crescent, so I made him group captain in the courtyard."

"Great," I said. "I was hoping to throw some work his way."

"How's our star doing?" Aahz asked, checking off one more item from his list.

"Letter perfect," Nunzio said. "She knows the script better than I do. She's started correcting me when I read something wrong. What a lady! She's no more nervous than a statue. She's ready to go."

So was I. We had spent the last few days working on this plan. Aahz had pretty much taken over, as I figured he would, leaving me with nothing much to do. I didn't know if he was doing it on purpose, or if the group was just used to working without me as it had been for months. I was losing hope that I could find a way to be relevant to the company as it had grown up. Everybody was being nice to me, but it wasn't the same as involving me.

Still, I played an important role in the event itself. My job was to maintain all the magik we needed for our subterfuge, including disguises. I was eager to prove myself once and for all that I was the person my friends wanted to work for again.

We sneaked into Foxe-Swampburg early the next morning. I couldn't have asked for better weather. According to Hermalaya, it was the beginning of spring. If there was birdsong, I couldn't hear it over the buzz of excited visitors. The courtyard was packed with people, mostly Swamp Foxes, but lots and lots of tourists of all races. I couldn't have been more delighted.

"Are you ready?" I asked the princess, as we watched the milling throng from behind a curtain in the balcony that overlooked the castle's front door.

"I had better be," Hermalaya said. She looked magnificent. She wore a plain white silk gown under a royal purple cloak edged with silver fur and jewels. On her head was a small crown with one fist-sized golden gem in the center that had made Aahz moan with greed when he saw it. "As they say, first impressions are the most important."

Massha came over to us with one of her bracelets buzzing.

"Everybody else is ready," she said.

"Then I'd better get set," I said. I closed my eyes and gathered up plenty of magik from the strong red force line that arched over the castle. Whoever had built this place knew what he or she was doing. My internal storage filled up in one breath.

I pictured Matfany's face and body, wearing an elegant black suit embroidered in silver, with a vent in the back for his bushy tail. I drew the image over me, until it took the place of my own face. I heard a gasp from Hermalaya.

"Why, you look just like him? It's amazing."

"All part of the service, your highness," I said. "All right, Massha."

She enveloped us both in a smothering, perfumed hug. "Good luck, honey! Knock 'em dead, Big Shot."

"Thanks. Go on, your highness. When you hear the fanfare, step through the curtain."

Matfany had given his personal orders to the royal trumpeters. At exactly midmorning, they appeared on the castle steps, pointed their instruments to the sky, and blew.

Ta-ran-tara! Taran-tara! Ta-ra-ra-ra-rantara!

Hermalaya took a deep breath, and pushed through the hanging swathes of silk.

The cheer that went up from the crowd was deafening. It was a long ten minutes before she could start her speech.

"My good and gentle people, I am so happy to be back with you again today. It has been a lonely exile, but what kept me going was thinking about all of you? It was through the graces of true friends that I have managed to return." She had to halt for cheers about every other line.

I crouched and waited for my cue.

"And nothing will ever part me from you again, my beloved people!"

I sprang. The crowd gasped.

"There you are!" I boomed. I had also laid on an aural illusion that gave me Matfany's *basso profundo* tones. Many in the crowd booed at me. I did my best to assume the prime minister's gimlet stare. Most of them subsided. I turned back to the princess, who cowered against the side of the arched window. "I warned you what would happen if you returned, princess! Guards! Seize her!"

The curtain parted, and in marched a full contingent of the castle guard, led by the royal wizard. One of them winked as he passed me. I had lined up the loyal opposition, who were delighted to have a part in helping their princess. They had a hard time keeping from grinning. I groaned inwardly. Everybody likes to ham it up.

"No!" the crowd burst out. "Let her alone!"

"I decreed if she broke her exile she must die! Take her away!"

The crowd booed as guards surrounded the princess, who did her best to look helpless and forlorn.

"Get your hands off that princess!"

From the entrance to the courtyard, Aahz's bellow echoed over the heads of the crowd. They all turned to see who was talking.

The reaction from the people told me I had given Aahz just the right disguise, though I couldn't see it. He appeared to be a Reynardan with sable-brown fur streaked with gold, wearing a silver silk tunic and blue breeches. He wore a silver circlet on his head.

I just didn't have the lungs of a Pervect, so I amplified my voice with magik. "And who are you to defy me, the prime minister of Foxe-Swampburg?" I shouted back.

"I am Fanmat, prince of Goodenrich. That lady is the rightful heir to the throne, and I have come to see her put back where she belongs."

"Oh, sir!" Hermalaya said. "I could surely use your help!"

"That's what I'm here for, little lady!"

A big sigh of relief and pleasure erupted from the audience. I looked down at them all sternly.

"Sir, justice must be done. I am the rightful ruler here now."

"Then you are the one who has to die!" Aahz marched toward me.

"And who is going to serve that sentence on me?" I demanded.

"I am!" He drew a fancy sword from a scabbard on his hilt and waved it around. At least, a sword is what the crowd saw in his hand. It was only a stick that I had disguised, in case anyone tried to take it away from him. We didn't have to worry about that. The onlookers burst into wild cheers and applause.

"Oh, go back, Prince Fanmat," Hermalaya cried, wringing her hands. "He is a formidable opponent."

Aahz struck a pose. "I am not afraid. I would fight an army for you." He marched toward us with purpose.

The crowd parted for him. He marched through the courtyard, scowling up at me. When he got close to the steps, I shouted down to the guards.

"Close the doors!"

Boom! The huge metal-clad portals slammed shut. The vibration nearly knocked me off my feet.

"There, intruder. Turn back! You can't get in now!"

Aahz half faced toward the crowd so they could see his noble jaw set. "You think that will keep me out?"

"No!" the mob chorused in unison.

"Damned straight."

Aahz sheathed the sword and took a leap for the arch of stone that enclosed the doorway. I grabbed him with a streamer of magik and helped him look like he was really climbing the face of the castle. The audience couldn't have been more impressed. They were screaming and cheering the higher he got.

That was my cue. I started dropping pillows and small pieces of furniture out of the window onto his head. They bounced off, but he kept coming, stopping every so often to declaim something heroic. Once in a while, he glanced up at me with fury rising in his eyes. Even though he had agreed to Chumley's idea that there should be some missiles thrown, he still looked madder than a wet Catrabbit by the time I ran out of ammunition.

He was panting as he got to the top and swung himself over the edge of the balcony.

"Okay, you coward. Now you're going to get what you deserve! With conversation!"

Aahz drew the sword. I, too, drew the weapon at my side.

"Then have at you!" I shouted.

"Usurper!"

Aahz swung at my head.

"Intruder!" I yelled.

I threw up my stick. His clacked off it.

"You're a lousy dresser!" he countered.

He drew back slightly, then thrust again. I swung at the

tip. I knocked it upward with a wild wave of my arm, then brought my stick down toward Aahz's knee.

"That's rich, coming from a fop like you! What do you know about governing?"

"What do you know about the love of the people?"

He dropped his sword on mine with such force that you could hear the echo in the courtyard. My hand tingled, but I just managed to hold on to my stick.

I was no swordsman. Aahz was deliberately moving slowly enough that I could see where his blows were coming from. I just did my best to get out of the way. But he couldn't miss the whole time, not with the thousands of people waiting for us. I let my guard drop.

"Ow!" The stick poked me hard in the chest.

"Gotcha!" Aahz said, with glee.

"Curse you!" I shouted. That really hurt. Instead of just warding off his strikes, I started swinging wildly. I managed to connect, bringing my sword down on top of his head.

"Ouch!" he bellowed. In an undertone, he hissed, "Watch it, kid, I'm the good guy!"

I was fuming. "Oh, yeah? Good guy? Then why did you try and mess up all the deals I made for Hermalaya? Why did you say all those things about me?"

"It's all in the game, kid!"

I felt my temper rise. "I'm not a kid any more!"

Aahz nodded, his face grim set. "Maybe you're not. But *this* isn't real. This *is* a game. Remember? We're play-acting. This is for her. It's not about you or me. We're not alone. Everybody in the known dimensions is watching. Right?"

"Right." I had to bring my temper under control. Remember the script! It was just a game. After all, who was I really mad at?

Myself. I had caused the breach in the friendship.

I knew in spite of the hurt it had caused that it was necessary to withdraw and learn about myself and my capabilities—but I could see how the others, especially Aahz, had taken it as rejection. I vowed it would be different from now on. I would make this job, and all the other jobs in the future work for us all.

"You will never defeat me, Fanmat!"

"I'll take you to pieces, Matfany!"

I retreated across the gallery. Aahz lunged at me. I stooped and swung my stick low. Aahz jumped over it, and made a cut for my head. I narrowly missed getting brained and leaped up on the rail. Our 'blades' clacked together. I did some fancy footwork, dancing along the narrow band of metal as Aahz peppered my feet with blows.

"Come back here, you coward!" he yelled.

"Fanmat! Fanmat! Fanmat!"

I recognized the voice who started the chanting as belonging to Gus the Gargoyle, but he wasn't chanting alone for long. The mob joined in, bellowing their approval. We had made them believe in our hero.

The guards watched our interplay with approval. A couple of them even seemed to follow our moves with their bodies. The princess, who had long ago forgotten that this was not a real fight, was pressed against the side of the balcony, looking terrified.

"All right, kid," Aahz whispered, "time for the big finish!"

I jumped down and the two of us closed, our 'swords' held above our heads. We turned around and around, him pushing me or me pushing him. The onlookers shouted and moaned or booed, depending on who looked like he was winning. Once I had gotten over my outburst, it was kind of fun.

With a seeming burst of strength, I threw 'Fanmat' sprawling backwards. I grabbed Hermalaya around the neck, dragged her to me, and put the point of my sword to her throat.

"Her life is forfeit. I will carry out sentence here and now!"

"Never, you evil prime minister!"

Aahz marched toward me, slashing the air with his sword. I cowered backwards with my prisoner. Aahz advanced. His blade came up from below and deftly knocked my stick flying end over end into the audience. He grabbed Hermalaya by the hand and swung her out of my arms. He set her on the other side of the window, away from the guards.

"Stay there, babe," he said. He raised his sword and backed me toward the edge of the balcony. "You're done for, buddy."

It was my turn to strike a pose.

"I did it all for my kingdom!" I declared.

"I'm sure that'll be a great comfort to your next of kin."

He swung at me. I took the blow full in the chest and remembered to create the illusion of gallons of blood spurting out of the wound. I clutched my chest. I wavered back and forth on the rail.

Then, I fell.

The crowd gasped.

Dropping any distance is no problem for a magician. I was never in any danger as I plummeted toward the courtyard. There were plenty of guards waiting to surround my body. I just figured I would lie there playing dead while Aahz proclaimed his love for the princess, who was being restored to her rightful place on the throne of Foxe-Swamburg. The guards would cover my face with a cloak and carry me inside, as we had arranged in our script.

But instead of the guards, a circle of faces wearing black headcloths and face masks leered down at me. The *snick!* of Cake servers being drawn was a chilling sound.

"You evil man! We are going to teach you what it means to attempt the life of a Cake Master!" Ninja hissed at me.

"No, wait!" I protested, holding up my hands. "I'm her friend!"

"Hiayah!" screamed Ninja.

"Hiayah!" yelled the other Cake Masters.

"Kid? Kid? Skeeve? Can you hear me? Open your eyes." Aahz's voice was full of concern.

I opened my eyes. The light hurt for a minute, but it receded to a single oil lamp burning on the table beside me. It lit up Aahz's worried face. I grinned weakly. He thumped me on the chest and grinned back, showing a gleaming mouthful of fangs.

"Good for you, kid," he said. "Glad to see you back among the living."

Practically everybody I knew was peering down at me. I

tried to sit up, but my chest felt like a thousand Centaurs had galloped across it. I groaned.

"What happened?" I asked.

Aahz poked a finger toward Ninja and her friends, now unmasked. The guards held them tightly. Pookie, Aahz's cousin, held a weird-looking wand on them. They looked terrified.

"You have one crazy fan club," Pookie said. "Why didn't you just tell me you had found some more people who wanted to kill you?"

"Are you all right, Mister Skeeve?" Princess Hermalaya asked. She and Matfany were wrapped in each other's arms. "I heard all that screaming? And there were all these people in black down there just slicing you into little ribbons. I sicced my guards on them, but they cut them up, too? My wizard had to lean over the rail and zap everybody good."

I felt my head. It was still attached, but there were thick bandages wrapped around it. Once I had noticed those, I saw the ones around my arms and hands, too.

"What do you want done to them?" Aahz asked, his eyes glowing fiercely. "Name it, Skeeve. Anything from a good spanking to shredding them nerve by nerve. I'll enjoy it. You name it. Your enemy's my enemy."

"They're not enemies," I said. It hurt to move. "They're friends. They're Cake Masters."

"Cake Masters?" Hermalaya exclaimed. "Why, what are they doing here?"

"Helping you, or so we thought," Ninja said, woefully. "Mister Skeeve, we are so sorry. We just wanted to avenge a sister of our craft!"

"Why, that's just so nice! I have met so few other Cake Masters?"

Ninja and the others bowed to Hermalaya. "What layer are you?" she asked.

"Well, I just made twelfth," Hermalaya said.

Kroka indicated Ninja. "She's the Topping of our order. She's nineteenth."

"I am so impressed!" Hermalaya bowed back. "But it wasn't nice of you to beat up Mister Skeeve."

"We just can't apologize enough! But how could we recognize him when he was dressed up as that villain?"

Matfany cleared his throat. "I beg your pardon, ladies!"

Ninja looked sheepish. "Are you going to be okay, Skeeve?"

"I'm all right," I said, trying to be upbeat because they seemed so worried. I looked up at Aahz. "Did it work?"

"The crowd loved it," Aahz said, gleefully. "No problem accepting Hermalaya's return or the new man in town. They were a little confused when your spells fizzled, leaving me there on the balcony with her with my bare face hanging out, but luckily by then Matfany was done with his tint job. He just stepped right in."

Matfany looked a little uneasy, but he seemed proud of his new fur color. He was now dark brown with gold highlights. The whole effect made him look noble and handsome. I noticed he was no longer wearing his glasses.

"Ears and Pelt number six," Massha said, proudly. "You'll only have to touch it up every six weeks."

Hermalaya touched the curls on the top of his head. "It

looks so nice. I don't know how to thank you for all you have done for us?"

I grinned. "Ask us to the wedding, of course."

Chapter 38

―――

"Being the boss is not as easy as it looked."

—Fletcher Christian

I combed confetti out of my hair and threw myself down in my desk chair.

"That was a great wedding," I said happily. Gleep galloped over to me for petting. "Here, boy!" I had brought him a roasted squab from the feast table.

"Skeeve, you have to make him work for it or he won't learn," Nunzio said, taking the meat from my hand. "C'mon, boy, sit up! Beg!"

Obediently, Gleep rocked back on his haunches and pawed the air. Nunzio tossed the treat to him, which he downed in one gulp. He dropped down again and gave me a wink when no one else could see it. He wasn't going to give away our little secret.

"What a terrific party," Tananda said, spinning until the dark purple skirts of her low-cut dress spread out like a bell. "I think I danced with every Fox in Foxe-Swampburg."

"They just couldn't get enough of you, Little Sister," Chumley said proudly. He removed the festoons of ribbons that had been wound around him by the enthusiastic partygoers. Gleep ate them as they hit the floor.

"Didn't the bride look wonderful?" Bunny asked, her eyes

shining. She leaned back in her chair and kicked her feet happily. Her party dress of brilliant blue silk shimmered around her magnificent figure. "And what a Cake! Ninja and the others did an incredible job."

"They wanted to make amends for nearly making layer cake out of Skeeve here," Guido said.

"That's the kind of cake I want when I get married," Pookie said. We all stared at her. "What are you all looking at?"

If she was embarrassed, she managed to cover it by swatting the next Humbee that came whizzing through the office. It fell to the ground in two pieces. Gleep loped over to eat them both.

"The best part," I said with satisfaction, "was when Hermalaya and Matfany went to the throne room together for the first time to accept the accolades of their subjects, and the doors actually opened up for him."

"About time," Nunzio said. "He was a decent guy."

Massha fanned her pink cheeks with a shocking turquoise feather fan. Her dress, yards of filmy chiffon, matched it in color. "Hermalaya had that consort chair made for him that goes with her throne. It's not as fancy, but he said he wasn't comfortable with something that had that much gold or gems."

"What a fool," Aahz said. "Go for what you can get, that's what I say." He took the D-hopper out of his pocket and tossed it end over end in the air. Among the whole group that jumped him and Matfany on the mountaintop, the one person who picked it up was honest enough to return it. I was glad. D-hoppers were rare, and it had been a present from me.[7]

"The Old Folks finally accepted Matfany," I said. "That's a good omen for the future."

"The dye job couldn't have fooled them?" Bunny asked.

"No, they know," I said. "Everything's great. They're going to live happily ever after."

"And the presents!" Bunny exclaimed. "There must have been thousands of packages!"

"I gave them a manual on marriage from Trollia," Tananda said, with a wicked smile. "It's got illustrations, just in case something gets lost in translation."

"I gave them the best gift possible," Aahz said. "My sage advice on staying married. I told him always to agree with everything she said. I told her to go easy on him. That ought to last them a lifetime."

"What did you give them, Skeeve?" Bunny asked.

"Oh, I went back and borrowed the Hoho Jug from Marmel in Siracoose," I said. "I wanted to make sure there was enough wine for everybody. No sense, as Matfany said, in wiping out the newly replenished treasury on unnecessary expenses."

"No wonder it was so tasty," Guido said. "And suitably potent to the occasion."

"And he paid our bill," Bunny said happily. "Both of them."

"That reminds me," Aahz said. "Who won the contest? Who is going to be president of M.Y.T.H., Inc.?"

---

[7]   For the whole intriguing yarn, read *Myth Alliances*.

Bunny threw back her head in exasperation. "Oh, how can you ask about that *now*?"

Aahz was adamant. "Because it isn't settled. We put the question aside until after we got the romance under way, but now I want to know."

"All right." Bunny sat up and became all business. She pointed at Aahz and me. "Both of you totally lost sight of the objectives—yours was to solve Matfany's PR problem and get the kingdom solvent, and yours was to put Hermalaya back on the throne."

"But they were mutually exclusive goals," I said.

"Right," Massha said. "The *really* important thing was to put the two of them face to face and sort out their personal problems. The kingdom would take care of itself. It took both of you to fix it so it would really work. And it did. They'll live happily ever after. It's soooo romantic."

"So who won?" Aahz pressed. "Who's the new president?"

It was Tananda who delivered the bad news. "Neither of you. You both tried to sabotage each other, which is a no-no. You focused on the money, which is never our primary goal. You tried to use the rest of us as spies, and you know better than that. We all got together and discussed it. We want the one person who really listened to the clients, who kept everyone organized, and who didn't indulge in fits of temper or ego or go off for months without explanation. We want a leader with common sense and a cool head." I could almost hear the drum roll as she turned and lifted a hand to gesture at that one person. "Bunny."

Bunny's eyes went as round as saucers. "Me?" she asked. "Really?"

Tananda gave her a big hug. "You. Really."

"Well, wow," she said. "I don't know what to say."

"Say yes," Chumley advised, giving her an all-enveloping hug.

"We were all incredibly impressed in how impartially you handled both of these big idiots and kept them from causing trouble for each other. Do you want the job? Because we really need you. We've been coasting for months, and we know it. We'd be pleased and honored if you'd be the president of M.Y.T.H., Inc." Tananda looked over her shoulder at me. "Oh, Skeeve. You can come back, too, if you want. We've really missed you."

"Why Bunny?" Aahz demanded with his fiercest scowl. "She doesn't have any experience as the head of a major magikal investigative organization."

Nunzio raised a finger.

"Neither did Skeeve. The operation grew with him at its head, and he did fine, but since we started diversifying, we need more than that. She's Don Bruce's niece. She was brought up to run a much bigger organization than this one."

Chumley cleared his throat. "She has a superb gift for subtlety, what? Without making a big deal out of it, she has kept Skeeve in contact with everybody else—almost everybody—and she gets along with all of us."

Aahz and I looked at each other.

"What the hell," he snorted, sitting back and crossing his legs casually. "I didn't really want it."

"Neither did I," I said. "I just wanted to come back. Now I can." I settled down and beckoned Gleep over. My dragon was happy to come and drop his head across my lap for an overdue ear-scratching. "Miss me, fellah?"

"What are you doing that for?" Bunny asked. I looked up, stunned. "I've got a new job for each of you! If you really want to handle business right after a party, move it!" I jumped up. So did Aahz. "I want you to get rid of these darned Humbees! If the Foxe-Swampburgians can fix their bug problem, we have to be able to solve ours. I mean, we're M.Y.T.H., Inc., already."

Aahz and I looked at each other and grinned.

"Whatever you say, Chief," I said.

"We'll get right on it," Aahz agreed.

Bunny smiled. She sat down and swung her silk shod feet up on the president's desk.

"That's better."